TRUTH OR CONSEQUENCES

Frank grabbed the crowbar on the seat next to him, got out of the car, and hurried toward the driver's side of the LTD.

Tito was a big man, at least six feet tall and topping two hundred pounds. But in one fluid motion Frank opened the door and, using the crowbar as a garrote, pulled Tito's flailing hulk from the car and dragged it across the sidewalk—across sand dunes, across the old Boardwalk, and out into the Absecon Inlet. When Frank stopped, he was standing in two feet of water.

"Where are you holding my wife?"

"Wha . . . what . . . man . . . what are you talking about . . . ?"

"You heard me, you son of a bitch, where are you holding Nancy Conti?"

Tito was getting his wind back and with it his courage. "Let go of me, motherfucker—"

Frank stepped on Tito's chest, and pressed down until he was completely submerged, keeping him there until the bubbles stopped coming. Then he lifted his foot and pulled Tito out by the hair.

"I'm not going to ask you again. Where are you holding my wife?"

"I'll kill you!" Tito screamed.

Frank looked down and saw the angry face of Allio threatening to send Nancy back in pieces.

He reached down, grabbed Tito's head with both hands, and twisted it until he heard the sound he was waiting for.

BLOCKBUSTER FICTION FROM PINNACLE BOOKS!

THE FINAL VOYAGE OF THE S.S.N. SKATE   (17-157, $3.95)
by Stephen Cassell
The "leper" of the U.S. Pacific Fleet, SSN 578 nuclear attack sub
SKATE, has one final mission to perform — an impossible act of
piracy that will pit the underwater deathtrap and its inexperienced
crew against the combined might of the Soviet Navy's finest!

QUEENS GATE RECKONING   (17-164, $3.95)
by Lewis Purdue
Only a wounded CIA operative and a defecting Soviet ballerina
stand in the way of a vast consortium of treason that speeds toward the hour of mankind's ultimate reckoning! From the best-
selling author of THE LINZ TESTAMENT.

FAREWELL TO RUSSIA   (17-165, $4.50)
by Richard Hugo
A KGB agent must race against time to infiltrate the confines of
U.S. nuclear technology after a terrifying accident threatens to
unleash unmitigated devastation!

THE NICODEMUS CODE   (17-133, $3.95)
by Graham N. Smith and Donna Smith
A two-thousand-year-old parchment has been unearthed, un-
leashing a terrifying conspiracy unlike any the world has previ-
ously known, one that threatens the life of the Pope himself, and
the ultimate destruction of Christianity!

*Available wherever paperbacks are sold, or order direct from the
Publisher. Send cover price plus 50¢ per copy for mailing and
handling to Pinnacle Books, Dept.17-373, 475 Park Avenue
South, New York, N.Y. 10016. Residents of New York, New Jer-
sey and Pennsylvania must include sales tax. DO NOT SEND
CASH.*

RICOCHET

OVID DEMARIS

PINNACLE BOOKS
WINDSOR PUBLISHING CORP.

PINNACLE BOOKS

are published by

Windsor Publishing Corp.
475 Park Avenue South
New York, NY 10016

First Pinnacle Books printing: July, 1990

Printed in the United States of America

FOR
Nikki Smith and Renni Browne,
my one-two combination

Part One
The Setup-1987

1

Frank Conti came awake with a start but kept his eyes closed a moment longer, as if to hold in a few seconds of peace before facing another day.

The night had been interminable, one of those nights he had prematurely, foolishly hoped were behind him. The last few weeks Nancy had seemed to be improving. Her sleep, at least, had been relatively peaceful. But last night the demons had struck again, in full force. She had tossed and turned, cried and cried out in her sleep, keeping him awake most of the night.

He opened one eye and quickly closed it again. The red digital numerals of his clock radio read 6:59, one minute before the alarm was set to ring. He reached out blindly and switched it off. The clock in his brain always awakened him a minute or two before the alarm. No matter what the designated hour — standard or daylight time, early or late — his brain somehow took care of the calculations, punching the proper neuron at the proper moment. And yet, after all these years of punctilious neuron performance, he continued to set the clock every night. It was just a habit, but sometimes it made him feel a little foolish — like a man wearing both a belt and suspenders.

He stretched and quickly stifled a yawn, not wanting to awaken Nancy. She lay on her back, so deep in sleep that she hardly seemed to be breathing. She looked comfortable now, peaceful; almost as young as when he married her eleven years ago, the long dark red hair still thick and luxurious, the lips soft and full, the fine lines tracing eyes and mouth barely visible. He wished he could lean over and kiss her without waking her up.

He pushed the covers back and slipped out of bed. He stretched, then bent at the waist to touch his toes and realized that his morning erection had slipped through the fly of his pajama bottoms. Sending a furtive glance in the direction of Nancy, still deep in sleep, he headed for the bathroom.

He caught a glimpse of his scarred legs in the door's full-length mirror just before he stepped into the shower and turned the cold water on full blast. Gasping and shuddering, he forgot about his legs. And his erection; not only had it vanished, it seemed to be seeking shelter in his shriveling testicles. He adjusted the spray to warm and began lathering his chest and arms. He'd worked behind a desk for a dozen years now, a banker whose only weapon was an M.B.A., but the muscles he had gained in that other existence were still impressive.

He tried not to think when he scrubbed his legs. The skin always reminded him of a crazy quilt, the kind his mother made when he was a boy. Rachel Conti's crazy quilts, highly prized, lasted a lifetime. So would his crazy-quilt legs, patched with skin sliced from his ass and back. It had taken surgeons nearly two years to finish the job, a lot longer than his mother took to finish a quilt.

It wasn't that he was ungrateful. The doctors had saved his legs, perhaps even his life; but he was the one who had paid, with pain that to this day made him tremble when he remembered it. Except for the memory, the only problem was a cosmetic one, easily solved by wearing trousers.

Not that he would blame anyone for being repulsed by the appearance of his legs. The scars were hideous.

Strange how slick the patches were, how foreign the skin felt on his fingers and his fingers on the skin. Even after all this time the legs didn't look or feel as if they belonged to him. For years, in his nightmares, doctors had amputated his legs and transplanted limbs from splotchy-skinned aliens, the kind you saw in horror movies.

He stepped out of the shower, wiped himself down with a towel, and wrapped it around his waist. He took a can of shaving foam from the medicine cabinet over the sink, lathered his face, and went to work on the night's stubble with a safety razor, going through the motions without really seeing himself in the mirror.

For a long time, long ago, he hadn't been able to look in a mirror and see his own face. Back in the burn ward of the military hospital in Guam, he'd seen the mutilated face of Major Hobson in every mirror.

But that was a secret Frank had never revealed to anyone. He had kept it from the army interrogators and the psychiatrists who had treated him for depression during his long hospitalization. Nor had he revealed how his unit had survived in denied territory for months on end. His response to a psychiatrist who tried to pump him on the disposition of prisoners had been, "They died."

"What do you mean they died?"

"We weren't in a headquarters environment. We were deep within their denied area, where there were thirty and forty thousand of them."

"How did they die?"

"We were a guerrilla force, didn't have the food or manpower — who's going to watch them at night, who's going to take care of them? We had no way to get them out, no conventional support."

"It would help if we could talk about it. How did you dispose of prisoners? Did you kill them?"

"I told you, they died."

"They didn't die by themselves. They didn't commit

harakiri."

"Well, they died."

And that was all anyone had ever got out of Frank
Conti.

*Down on one knee in the elephant grass, Sergeant Frank
Conti is grateful for the relief the tall, dense stalks offer from
a merciless sun. With his M-16 resting against his thigh
and his fingers playing nervously along the trigger guard,
he's ready for action, but all he can think about is water.
His swollen, furry tongue feels like a rat has crawled into
his mouth.*

*All four of his canteens are empty. The gooks have to
come down the trail pretty soon if he's going to make it. He
leans forward, listens for the telltale sounds of the Vietcong
platoon approaching the daisy chain of Claymore mines
that await their arrival.*

*The twelve-man A-Team and their fourteen Cambodian
guerrillas, called Hob's Bodes after their commander, Major Roy Hobson, have been in country eight weeks this trip,
maybe nine. They're deep in denied areas, Cambodia and
Laos mostly, and surviving by their wits: conducting raids
on enemy headquarters, blowing up bridges, destroying
weapon caches and ammunition dumps, mapping supply
lines, collecting intelligence from ambushed troops, and
killing in impressive numbers.*

*But this is to be the last kill-fire ambush this trip. In a
few hours the Hook will pick them up, and by nightfall
they'll be in Bien Hoa. Miller Time! Frank can almost
taste the cold beer flooding down his parched throat.*

*Then he hears them. There's a rustle in the grass as the
men near him lean forward in anticipation. His temples
pulse; his thirst is forgotten. He raises his M-16.*

*Even before he can see them, Frank is sure he can smell
them, smell that odor of dead fish and rotten garlic that
clings to them like an invisible shroud. Then the column*

12

comes into view, and a soldier next to Frank whispers, "Come on, you zipper-head motherfucking dinks, closer, closer, get in that fucking box." He screams "Yeah!" as the Claymores explode, sending dirt, trees, and bodies flying through the air.

Twenty-six men, their faces painted green and black to match camouflage fatigues, jerk to their feet in the elephant grass and empty their magazines, reload and move onto the trail. Bloodcurdling screams turn to groans, then whimpers. Then it's quiet. All that's left is smoke and dust.

The procedure now is to use knives. There are no prisoners taken in the bush, not when you have to live in enemy country for weeks at a time, and it's using the knife that bothers Frank the most. He doesn't like what it does to his insides when he slits a man's throat. But Major Hobson demands the knife — it makes his men colder, more efficient killers. Valiant warriors, in Hobson's words.

Except for a missing foot and the dozens of little holes made by the Claymore's ball bearings, the first body Frank comes to is fairly intact. Following orders, he slits the throat and then notices the remaining foot — still wearing a B.F. Goodrich sandal. Frank stares at the foot, intrigued by its yellow color and lifelessness. Only moments ago it was walking, bearing a man with thoughts probably very similar to Frank's. Now, in seconds, he's been transformed into garbage to be consumed by maggots and flies.

Major Hobson stands surveying the carnage as his men move among the corpses, swiftly and expertly snuffing out the enemy.

"Oh Christ," Hobson shouts, "fucking beautiful!"

Nancy was still sleeping when he returned to the bedroom. He dressed quickly in his banker's uniform, white shirt, a silk maroon tie with gray checks, gray pinstriped three-piece suit.

In the kitchen he heated water, dropped slices of

wheat bread into the toaster, poured orange juice from a carton and downed it in a couple of swallows. By the time the toast was ready, the water was hot enough to make instant coffee. He stared at the coffee as he stirred it, watching the oily granules rise to the surface without seeing them.

The phone rang and he snatched it out of its cradle in the middle of the first ring. He didn't want the bedroom extension awakening Nancy.

"Glad I caught you before you left," his father said.

"What's up, Pop?"

"Nothing much, just wanted to remind you of lunch."

Frank laughed, "We've been having lunch every Thursday for—how many years, would you say?"

"I know, but you're a busy man, you could forget, all the meetings you attend. Every time I call the bank you're in a goddamn meeting."

"Thursday lunch is always on my calendar, Pop."

"Good, make sure it stays there. I look forward to our get-togethers. Only goddamn time I spend with you these days."

Tom Conti's tone was jovial, but Frank got the message. "We'll have you at the house for dinner very soon now," he said.

"Come on, don't get serious on me."

"No, I mean it, Pop. Nancy's feeling a lot better these days."

"Glad to hear it, but don't you press her. She'll come around in her own time." He paused. "By the way, see the paper this morning?"

"Not yet. Another murder in South Philly?"

"Yeah, found one of your old school chums in a garbage bag last night. Petey Boffa—you know, the Clown. Remember him, you blackened both his eyes one time? The boys gave Petey special treatment, slugs in both kneecaps, ice picks in his balls, a .44 magnum slug be-

14

tween the eyes."

"That shouldn't make you lose any sleep."

"Can't complain, let 'em weed out the ranks. See you at lunch, kiddo."

Tom sat at the kitchen table, holding a mug of cold coffee in his large hand. Silly of him to have called Frank, who had never once forgotten their lunch date. The truth was, Tom had needed to feel connected to somebody this morning.

He'd dreamed about Rachel all night long, more like nightmares. Every time he awakened he tried to think of something else, but the moment he closed his eyes there was Rachel beating on him, scratching his face with clawlike nails, trying to gouge out his eyes. The third time it happened he gave up, got dressed, and walked around the block until the sun came up.

Stirring up the past wasn't good for his blood pressure. So many sad memories. But they weren't all sad, not by a long shot. So why couldn't he dream about the good times? All the wonderful years, over forty of them, when he'd felt like a man specially blessed. No man had ever had a better wife than Rachel.

He raised the mug to his lips. The cold coffee tasted bitter. He went to the sink, spat it out, then walked into the living room and carefully removed his shoes before stretching out on the mohair sofa.

His parents had brought the sofa from Palermo, and it was perfect for the house, which was even older than the sofa. The floors creaked if you breathed hard, the doors were hopelessly warped, half the windows refused to open, the wood siding was crusted with countless coats of paint, deeply wrinkled with the cracks of old age. Tom Conti wouldn't have traded it for a mansion.

In this house, he could close his eyes at any time and hear the excited voices of the kids getting ready for school. They had been such busy, happy years. How was it that they had gone by so fast?

Some nights it seemed, in the stillness of the house, almost incredible that any of what he remembered had really happened. Those were the nights he wanted to get on the phone, wanted to call his son or daughter, just to reassure himself that it wasn't all a dream. Once, when he couldn't reach Frank, he had called Eunice in Germany, but she was out and he'd ended up talking to her husband, an air force major, a career soldier short on small talk.

Always, it was Rachel he really wanted to talk to. He yearned for her, for the way she was before that terrible end. He yearned for their long evenings together in the old house. He yearned for her soft voice, her soft footsteps on the creaking boards. He yearned to touch her, gently, lovingly, and sometimes the yearning drove him from the house.

No one outside the family knew about Tom Conti's agony over the years it took Alzheimer's disease to finally claim its victim; no one suspected the immensity of his loss, nor his loneliness now. People took him as they found him: essentially imperturbable, a man unaffected by the meanness and violence endemic in his work.

Which was what his work demanded. Nearly thirty years as a detective in South Philadelphia hardened a man's exterior. You dealt with the scum of the earth. And so, over the years, you built your shell.

Rachel's death had reversed the order of his life. During all the good years, the days at work were long and tedious and the nights with her just flew by. Now the days flew by and the nights were endless. Too often he found himself staring at the TV set, watching sitcoms or a cop show so ludicrous that it was funnier than the sitcoms.

In the old days, he had read more. Quiet evenings with a good book, a glass of beer, and Rachel sitting across from him, sewing on one of her quilts. He would stop at an interesting paragraph, read it aloud to her, and she would laugh or smile or frown; then he'd return to his book, she to her quilt.

Except for the creaks, the house was so quiet once the kids were in bed that he could hear her breathing. Sometimes he was sure he could hear the beat of his own heart. Odd that those should be the things he remembered. Not the parties, the special occasions, the big cases he had solved, the decorations and promotions he had received, but evenings at home, two people sharing the quiet.

As for his having called Frank first thing in the morning, what of it? Who else of his own did he have to talk to these days? His parents had been dead for decades. His brother had bought it on Okinawa over forty years ago. And Timmy? His only grandson, the love of his late years? Dead almost before he had a chance to realize he was alive. Wiped out ten hours into his seventh birthday by a fifteen-year-old junkie in a stolen Trans-Am.

So where, Mr. Police Detective, does the chain of events begin? In some Colombian jungle, with peasant farmers harvesting killer crops? Who do you nail? Some black kid junkie at the end of the chain?

He sat up on the old couch from Palermo and stared down at his bare feet. They looked a lot younger than the rest of him. Pretty feet for a cop. There were advantages to being a lieutenant, even if you didn't know your ass from your armpit when it came to chains of events.

Frank Conti started up the Buick, then sat behind the wheel letting the engine warm up, looking at the house neatly framed in the windshield. They had bought it when Timmy was born, and, before the accident, they'd both been happy here. Colton, Pennsylvania, was the kind of place where everybody knew everybody and people seemed to care about each other. And yet, though he never told Nancy, Frank missed South Philadelphia and the old neighborhood where he'd taken her as a bride. It was home, the only home he had known. He missed the smells, the noise, the streets where he'd once been a wild, tough, crazy, smart-ass kid, a total stranger to the man reborn in the fire of Vietnam.

Craning his neck to see out the rear window, Frank slowly backed the Buick out of the driveway — the house was at the end of a cul-de-sac, but you never knew when some kid would come flying by on a bicycle — then drove slowly through the curved streets of the subdivision.

The light was red at the Maple Street intersection. The moment Frank stopped, his eyes went to the spot where Timmy's head had rested in a pool of blood that Sunday. It looked ordinary now, no signs that a boy had died there on the morning of his seventh birthday. Frank glanced away, impatient for the light to change.

In eight days Timmy would have been nine, and the memory of that other birthday was as fresh as the day it happened. It seemed only yesterday that he had given his son the bicycle, only the day before yesterday that Nancy had tried to argue him out of the gift and Frank had accused her of being overly protective.

"Jesus, you chauffeur him to school every day. You won't let him play outdoors unless the kids come to our yard." While he talked, Frank was removing the bicycle from its carton. "When I was his age, I'd have killed for a bike like this." He paused, a wistful look on his face. "I can still remember how I felt whenever I saw a boy on a bike. When I was Timmy's age, I remember walking to school one day in a drizzle and this kid whizzed by me on his bike so quietly that I didn't even hear him coming, and to this day I can still see the bike's tire treads on

18

that wet sidewalk."

She touched his hand. "Frank, I understand, but Timmy's not you. He's not having the same dream."

"Yes, he is," Frank said, lifting the shiny red bicycle with the thin racing tires out of the carton. "He's been after me for months."

"Can't you see it's too big? His feet won't reach the pedals."

"Sure they will, just have to lower the seat a little. Timmy's got long legs. Now, come on, be a good sport and tie a big yellow bow on the handlebars for the birthday boy. Wait till you see his eyes bug out, you'll know I'm right."

Timmy's eyes had bugged out, all right. He'd jumped up and down, showering kisses on his father and mother, then on the bike.

"See?" Frank said. "The kid's gone bananas. What'd I tell you?"

Nancy was smiling, amused by her son's antics, but Frank could tell from the expression in her eyes that she was still worried. She'd get over it once she saw that Timmy had already learned how to ride on his best friend's bike.

The news was not a hit. "I suppose the morning he's sixteen I'll find out you've taught him how to drive," she said.

But by now Timmy was straddling the bike, one foot on a pedal and the other on the pavement to maintain his balance.

"See you later, Mom, Dad."

"Where do you think you're going, young man?" Nancy called after him.

"Just want to show Arnie my new bike."

"You stay on the sidewalk with that thing, you hear me?"

"Yeah, Mom," and he started down the sidewalk.

19

"You show Arnie the bike and come right back. Fifteen minutes . . ."

By then he was already out of earshot.

Ten minutes later, while Nancy was in the bedroom dressing, the doorbell rang. Before Frank could set down the carton of eggs he'd just taken from the refrigerator, he heard a neighbor calling his name.

"Hold your horses, Ernie!" Frank called. But when he opened the front door and saw Stover's face, his heart started pounding.

"It's Timmy. Hit and run — he's real bad."

"Where?" Frank asked in a voice he couldn't recognize.

"Corner of Maple and Elm."

Frank started running. It wasn't that far if he cut across the park, which was probably what Timmy had done — but what was he doing that far from home? And what did "real bad" mean from someone like Ernie Stover? God, he hoped Stover was the excitable type.

Frank put his head down and sprinted across the baseball diamond where he had started Timmy on the fundamentals of grounders, fly balls, and hitting. Timmy was a natural athlete. He'd go far in that direction, whatever the sport.

As Frank came out of the park, he ran blindly across Elm Street, narrowly missed being hit by a truck and two passenger cars. He never saw them, never heard the screeching brakes, the horn blasts. All he could see was the knot of people, their heads lowered, staring at something on the ground. All he could hear was the blood pounding in his head.

He threw himself into the crowd, hurling bodies aside until he was standing over the broken bike and crumpled form of his son. Timmy's head lay against the curb in a pool of blood.

While a woman behind him kept screaming, "Get an

ambulance," Frank scooped his son up in his arms and ran into the middle of the intersection. It was then that he heard the horn and saw Nancy tearing down Elm Street in the Buick, braking to a screeching stop beside him. Someone opened the passenger door, and Frank climbed into the front seat next to Nancy.

The hospital was only three miles away, and Nancy, with one hand pressed against the horn, was flooring the Buick. But for Frank it was the longest ride of his life. Blood, warm and sticky, oozing from the back of Timmy's head, ran through Frank's fingers and onto his lap as he supported his son's small neck. Timmy's opened eyes were already glazed.

He heard Nancy's hysterical sobbing, saw her frantic glances at Timmy, but neither of them said a word. It was a scene cast in hell, worse than anything that had happened to him in Vietnam.

By the time they reached the hospital, he'd lost any sense of reality. He was an actor going through the motions but without any realization that the tragedy was his. He saw himself running through the emergency entrance with Timmy in his arms; saw Nancy running at his side; saw white-coated men coming toward him, taking Timmy out of his arms, placing him on a gurney; saw himself trotting after them, then watching as they worked on the broken body of this small boy. He saw them shake their heads, look toward him and Nancy, saw Nancy's mouth opening, knew she was screaming but couldn't hear the sound of it. He could feel it, though, feel her screams reverberating around the white walls in the small room.

Late that night, after Nancy finally succumbed to the sleeping pills the doctor prescribed, Frank took a bucket of warm water, detergent, a brush, and towels, and went back to the intersection. It was there — scrubbing Timmy's blood from the street — that the reality struck him.

21

On his knees, he howled his anguish into the night, cursing himself for the death of his son.

In the nearly two years since that night, Nancy had never once reproached him. She kept her anger and guilt and resentment bottled up inside her in a place Frank couldn't reach. With each day she was shrinking before his eyes, diminishing at the hands of a depression that would not lift. At first her self-medication was Valium, then it was gin mixed with the Valium, a combination that had nearly killed her on more than one occasion. Frank would come home and find her passed out across the bed, on the living-room sofa, the kitchen floor. She wouldn't listen to him when he suggested that she seek professional help, so Frank saw a psychiatrist on his own.

"She needs psychotherapy," the doctor said. "It works for many people. Antidepressant medicines are sometimes effective in severe depressions, and there's electroshock to relieve the most intractable. Without professional help, most people don't function very well—they simply wait it out."

Frank tried to wait it out, and Nancy tried gambling. By the time Frank found out, she had emptied their savings account, refinanced her Datsun, borrowed on their furniture, and pawned all the valuables pawnbrokers would accept.

Frank never reproached her, even when her gambling debts forced him to take a second mortgage on the house. How could he? If anyone was to blame for what was happening, he was. And now they lived in the same house, slept in twin beds in the same room, ate dinner at the same table, but space was all they shared. She kept her silence; he kept his distance.

The light turned green. Frank stepped on the gas and passed through the intersection one more time.

2

Nancy Conti turned on her side, drawing her legs up to her chest, her hands clasped tightly under her chin. She was a little girl, and outside it was snowing. Her mother was baking brownies, and the smell from the oven made her mouth water. Her father was swinging her in the air, and in the reflection of the kitchen window, she could see her long red pigtails flipping against her shoulders.

"Oh, Daddy, I love you," she said, and kissed his cheek.

"I love you too," her father said.

"I won't ever get married," she said. "I'm gonna live here with you and Mommy forever and ever. And I'll help you on the farm, but I can't milk cows. Mommy says it'll make my hands ugly."

"Well, now, we can't have that," he said, smiling.

"You think I've got pretty hands, Daddy?" She held up her right hand for inspection.

Nancy twisted on the bed, groaning in her sleep, knowing what was going to happen in her dream but unable to stop it.

He took her hand and was admiring it when it began to grow. His expression scared her more than the swelling of her hand.

"Hold it," she cried. "Please, Daddy, hold it tight."

He tightened his grip, but the hand grew larger and larger until finally it was too big to hold. It floated up in front of her eyes, so huge that it blocked out her father's face.

"Where are you, Daddy? Please, don't hide."

The hand was almost touching her face when she first saw the oozing blood. She screamed and fell, the hand on top of her. There was blood all over her dress, and she could feel it seeping through the thin cotton material, warm and sticky on her chest. When the hand touched her face, covering it completely, she gasped for breath.

She came awake screaming, her left hand clutching her right wrist. A moment later she sat up, relief flooding over her. She was back in her bedroom; no blood, no hand.

She couldn't count the number of times she'd had that dream in the past two years. And each time it had stayed with her all day, trapping her between dream and memory. For she could actually remember that precise morning in the kitchen, her mother baking brownies, the snow outside the window. Everything was the same, except for the hand.

The hand, she knew, was Timmy's; he was accusing her, blaming her for his death, and in a secret compartment of her brain she knew that some day the hand would suffocate her in her sleep, fit punishment for having failed her son.

She stared vaguely across the room, then pulled on a robe and wandered into the kitchen. While the water boiled, she stood in front of the stove, wondering what to do next, how to fill the day. When the kettle whistled, she poured the boiling water into a mug of instant coffee, took it to the kitchen table, and glanced through the newspaper.

In the entertainment section she saw the full-page ad for the Boardwalk Palace casino in Atlantic City. She stared at it, the coffee forgotten, her pulse quickening as she turned to face the telephone on the wall by the kitchen counter. Small beads of perspiration had formed on her upper lip by the time she finally stood up and reached for the receiver.

She swiped at her lip with a finger and dialed a number from memory.

Joey Bucci was cradled in Joyce's arms, his mouth pressed against the nipple of her right breast, when the telephone rang.

"Oh, shit," Joyce murmured, reaching over Joey's head. "Yeah?" she said.

"Get Joey on the horn."

She pushed Joey away from her breast. "Come on, for Chrissake."

Joey's long black eyelashes fluttered.

"It's Nick."

He reached for the phone. "Hey, Nick, what's happening?"

"Nancy Conti just called. Should be at the Palace around noon. Have Joyce take her upstairs to high-roller heaven."

"Jesus, the Penthouse Club? She's coming up in the world."

"Make sure Joyce's there when she gets in. The sky's the limit."

"Okay, Nick, but what's the bottom line on this broad?"

"You don't hear so good this morning. That fucking Joyce put come in your ears?"

"Nick, come on, I hear you, but you gotta give me some limit besides the sky. Don't forget, this one can run through markers like shit through a tin horn."

"Let her," Nick said. "Get her comped, nice suite, the works—whatever she wants, long as she keeps losing."

"Don't worry about that, man, she mostly loses. Want me to call if it gets too steep?"

"Hey, asshole, how high's the fucking sky?"

"Okay, okay."

"Better get your head straight, buddy, Tony wants to see you at the place. Twelve sharp."

"Okay, I'll—"

Nick Bartoli hung up. Joey glared at the dead receiver in his hand. "Some day," he growled, slamming the phone down.

Joyce laughed. "Some day what, lover?"

"Never mind," Joey said. "Nancy Conti's on her way over. Nick wants you to be there when she gets in, take her to the Club. The sky's the limit."

"What do you mean?"

"I mean, how high's the fucking sky?" Joey fell back into bed. "Hey, roll over, babe. We got time, give me some head."

Five minutes later Joyce Kresse was in the bathroom gargling with a mouthwash so astringent that her mouth felt scalded. With a stud like Joey, you never knew who or what he had been sticking it into—and who needed to take chances with AIDS?

Joyce hated the light over the bathroom vanity. For four years now she'd been thirty-six, and for more than four years she'd hated what the fluorescent light said about the face in the mirror. Every morning, before applying makeup, she gave it a minute inspection, exploring with her fingertips the faint lines—seemed like she discovered new ones every day. The skin was slightly bloated around the chin; the corners of the mouth were starting to curve downward. She almost hated to smile. Her cheeks, once so firm and rounded, were beginning to sag.

The truth was, goddamn gravity was winning. Even her tits, once her greatest asset, were beginning to sag. So was her ass. She needed a few tucks in the right places. At least her belly was still flat—thank God for little favors, and her eating habits for keeping it that way.

Well, not all was lost. Not yet. Young guys were still coming on to her. She could still walk the street with the best of them, if she had to. High rollers didn't complain when the house sent her to entertain them.

The more she studied her face in the mirror, the more convinced she became that it wasn't symmetrical, that one side sagged more than the other. What was happening? Where had she gone wrong? For the last seven years she had been religious about two things: diet and exercise. She had gotten her beauty sleep, jumped around in aerobic classes, forsaken hard booze and drugs, french fries and burgers, salt and sugar, even regular coffee.

What would she look like in ten years? She shuddered at the thought and reached for the arsenal of natural cosmetics, her weapons against time.

Nancy liked the limousine's black windows. They made her feel safe from prying eyes as the car sped along the Atlantic City Expressway. The car was black, the upholstery was black, even the driver was black. On the inside, the car was her black cocoon; on the outside, a black phantom, making her invisible to an inquisitive world.

Here she could hide for the precious moments she needed to prepare herself for what lay ahead. She closed her eyes, leaning back against the soft cushions. She would start right out with hundred-dollar chips. Blackjack was quiet and fast, yet it gave you time to think, to make decisions whose results were instantaneous. You won or you lost. It was that simple. Not like life, with all the ifs and buts and intangibles that could set treacherous, unforeseen consequences in motion.

For months after Timmy's death she had felt paralyzed. Every morning she lay in bed debating the pros and cons of getting up, unable to concentrate on anything long enough to make sense out of it. Terrible fears and agonies battled their way through her reeling brain. Making the smallest decision became all but impossible.

Then she discovered gambling.

Her first trip to Atlantic City was on a junket bus that had picked her up on a street corner. She played the slot machines, hit a quarter jackpot, returned home $51 ahead. She was pleased with her winnings, but the next time she lost $196 and found she wasn't the least disturbed by the loss.

It wasn't long before she was taking the bus two and three times a week. The trips seemed to give her life focus. On the days she didn't take the bus, she worked at raising money. That became increasingly difficult as her losses mounted—along with her feelings of guilt and shame. These, she could see clearly, were only what she deserved. She was being punished for lying and cheating and the other crime too monstrous to think about. Then she met Joyce at the Boardwalk Palace.

Joyce was nice enough to arrange for Nancy's credit line at the casino. All Nancy had to do was sign the markers pushed in front of her by pit bosses. When she won, she repaid the markers; when she lost, she was always welcomed back anyway, provided with a room, vouchers for meals in their best restaurants, free passes to their shows, free transportation in their limousine. The suite she used only when the excitement made her ill and she rushed to her room to vomit. She had no interest in food or shows. They cut into her time at the tables.

It was at the blackjack table that Nancy first experienced the feeling of being totally in command and the conviction that she could predict the value of cards milliseconds before they were dealt to her and to the dealer. The sense of omnipotence created sensations that started at the back of her head and suddenly surged to the front, a rush of excitement so intense that she had to struggle to stop herself from squirming on the chair as if

28

she'd been caught in a frenzy of orgasmic release.

She gambled to win, she told herself, but it wasn't the occasional win that kept her riveted to the table. It was the prospect of losing, of going over the edge, of forfeiting money she couldn't afford, of reaching rock bottom, of jumping off into the unknown — the nausea and sweat that came in waves brought a dark, desperate delight.

She loved the casino, the huge, low-ceilinged room; loved the mesmerizing cacophony of sounds, the madness at the crap tables clashing with the whir of a thousand slot machines; loved the smoke and smells, the intensity of players as anxious as she — the rich mixture of sensations creating the feeling of a cloister that she had once experienced in church.

And she loved the round plastic chips, the feel of them on her fingers; so smooth to the touch, so comforting when cradled in the palm of the hand. She loved the sound they made as she stacked them in neat columns in front of her; red, white, blue, black, denominations that were meaningless in any real sense, and so easily expendable.

Once she learned blackjack, win or lose, it didn't matter. What mattered was increasing the limit, to balance on that edge.

She closed her eyes, trying to calm her nerves, the restlessness she had felt all morning growing more intense the closer they came to Atlantic City. They were on the outskirts now. They had just passed the Route 9 junction, its road signs announcing Pleasantville, Northfield, Linwood, Somers Point, all familiar names of places she had never seen. They were still about ten miles away, and traffic was already slowing. Soon, she knew, they would be crawling through the snarl of cars and junket buses spewing their gasoline and diesel fumes into the air.

Sometimes it took a half hour to go six blocks. By the

time the limousine reached Pacific Avenue, she would be ready to jump out and run the blocks to the Palace. She wouldn't, of course. The city terrified her. The street people looked mean and hungry — hookers, pimps, drug pushers, muggers, parasites crawling out of the ruins. And the city itself seemed a garbage-littered, crumbling, burned-out, blighted slum. A bombed-out war zone, for all the new casinos shining in the rubble.

When the limousine pulled up at the VIP entrance, Joyce gave Nancy a warm smile and squeezed both of her hands.

"It's wonderful to see you again," she said. "We've really missed you around here." She let Nancy's hand drop, then leaned closer. "Feel lucky today?"

Nancy smiled. "I do. I really do."

Joyce led her to a private elevator attended by a strapping young man in uniform. All smiles, he pressed the button for the fifty-seventh floor.

Nancy could feel the dampness under her arms. By the time the elevator doors opened and she stepped into the Penthouse Club foyer, she was in a dream world, all reality suspended, all normal sounds and activity screened out by the euphoria surging through her body and her brain.

3

Seated behind his desk, Frank Conti had a clear view of the Colton Savings Bank lobby and the seven people in the loans and new accounts division that was his domain. Three men, four women, each looking forward to the day they succeeded him.

The bank's president, John Fuller, had indicated on several occasions that Frank was slated to move up when the present manager retired. The way Frank saw it, Fuller was cagey, a man who liked to keep his options open and the hired help in a state of happy anticipation.

All seven loans and new accounts people were busy this morning; the three sofas arranged around a large table near the coffee machine were filling with customers waiting their turn to see an officer. Staring across the lobby, Frank looked as if he were watching the entrances and exits, but in fact he was thinking about Petey Boffa. Petey the Clown, the comedian with the sense of humor of a seven-year-old, eighteen and still a freshman when Frank had been a junior, was a hulking punk who took out the frustration created by his mental limitations on kids half his size.

At six feet, Frank was three inches taller than the Clown but maybe half his weight. Watch out for Boffa, his father had warned. Control your temper, stay out of his way. He's part of Tony Allio's gang, they'll clean your clock real good if you mess around with him.

Frank obeyed his father until the day his patience ran out while he was walking home from school with a new girlfriend. Boffa grabbed her by the hair, pulled her against him, mauled her buttocks and breasts with his huge hands.

Frank jumped Boffa like a buzz saw, raining blows from every conceivable direction. The Clown went down and stayed down.

Witness to the fight was Tony Allio, a senior. At nineteen he had already reached his maximum height of five seven, but carried an equalizer, a six-inch switchblade he enjoyed using. Everybody knew Tony's father was boss of the Philadelphia Mafia family, but Tony Allio didn't need to trade on his father's reputation — his ready knife and violent temper were all he needed.

Whipping out his knife, he tapped Frank on the chest with the flat side of the blade.

"Pretty fast with the dukes there, kid," he said, tilting his head to one side as he looked up at Frank. He rolled the blade against Frank's chest and slowly pulled the sunglasses down far enough to peer over them. A cigarette dangled from a corner of a sneer. "Hey, Clown's my guy, nobody whacks my guy without my okay."

"Get that knife off my chest," Frank said.

"How'd you like to eat this fucking blade, asshole?"

"How long're we gonna stand around like this?" Frank said. "Either use it or stow it."

Allio increased the pressure on the knife until Frank could feel the point of the blade pricking through his shirt and into his skin.

"Screw it," Frank said, suddenly stepping back, spinning around, and heading off. "I've got better things to do, see you around."

Frank saw Allio signal his gang. Before he could decide whether to run or fight, they were on him with chains, brass knuckles, lead pipes, even a baseball bat. Frank realized he had never felt real pain before. There was nothing he could do to stop them, but he kept swinging and kicking anyway. If they were going to kill, he'd at least get in some licks of his own. In seconds his eyes were swelling shut, he could barely see, and he was all but choking on his own blood. Then he felt his left arm break just below the elbow, and he did something he had been promising himself he wouldn't do—he screamed. When the guy with the bat slammed it into his chest, he passed out.

No one in the crowd raised a hand to help Frank. Even the teachers who witnessed the attack waited until Allio left before calling for an ambulance.

Frank was conscious but still being worked on in the emergency room when his father reached the hospital.

"You can't come in here," he heard a nurse say.

"Says who? That's my boy on the table."

Some minutes later, Tom Conti was still in the emergency room, practically interviewing the doctor.

"For starters we know he's got at least a half-dozen broken ribs," the doctor was saying. "Could be some liver, kidney damage, other internal injuries, we need to take some pictures."

As it turned out, besides the broken arm, seven broken ribs, broken nose, two black eyes, mouth puffed up like a giant mushroom, and internal injuries, Frank's whole body was covered with bruises and contusions. It was weeks before he could move in bed without pain, long weeks during which he made two resolutions: to prepare himself for future attacks by studying the martial arts, and to catch Tony Allio alone.

Frank was still in the hospital when Tom started talking about prosecuting. Frank shook his head.

"What kind of macho bullshit is this, for Chrissake?" Tom said. "I'm telling you, we can get them heavy time on this, and they deserve every minute of it."

"Pop, I've got another year and a half at that school. I'm not going back as a squealer."

"Squealer? That's gang-mentality bullshit! Listen, they nearly killed you. What do you think cops are for? What have I spent my life doing, for Chrissake? You think we live in a jungle? No laws, survival of the fittest? Where do you get such ideas? On the street?"

Frank tried to smile, but his mouth still felt like swollen mush. "I don't know," he said. "Maybe at the movies."

"Wiseguy besides," Tom said. "Well, listen, Mr. Wise Guy, maybe you're afraid to testify against those punks. That's how they get away with this shit. They scare guys like you out of—"

"I'm not scared of them. I'll take care of Allio my way."

"Ah, so now it comes clear. The old Sicilian blood is secretly boiling, can't hardly wait to get out of here to take your revenge. I'll tell you what, Mr. Sicilian Hotblood, that's the fastest way of getting yourself killed I know. Not beaten to a pulp, I'm talking killed. Unless, of course, you plan on killing everybody—if you do, make goddamn sure you don't forget anyone. Remember, those bastards have Sicilian blood too—in fact, it's a hundred proof, which makes it twice as hot as yours."

Frank had himself back under control. "Look at me, Pop," he said softly. "Would *you* take a beating like this lying down?"

Tom turned away for a moment; when he looked back at his son, his gaze had softened.

"I don't know, Frank, I really don't. From where I'm sitting, the smartest move would be to forget the whole thing, act like it never happened, but I know that's not the way either one of us is made. Next smartest thing, get the law to take care of them. That's what we're here for. I hope that's what you'll do."

"I just can't, Pop."

Tom shook his head. "It's not that I don't understand, believe me. If I was in your shoes—if this had happened to me when I was your age—I'd probably get a gun and

34

take them all out. But when you get my age, you know better."

"No gun, Pop." Frank raised his right fist. "This is what I'm going to use. No gun, no chain, no club, no bat, no knife. Just this."

Tom leaned over and gently kissed Frank's forehead. "How'd you get so foolish and so brave this fast?"

The ringing of the phone on his desk pulled Frank back.

"Frank, Ernie Stover here. Got a minute?"

"Sure, Ernie, what can I do for you?"

Ernie cleared his throat. Frank felt his stomach muscles tense at the thought of this small, shy man looking down at his shoes, embarrassed by what he was about to say.

"Well, Frank, I hate having to do this . . . but I think you ought to know — well, let's say, I think you'd be better off knowing what's going on."

Another long pause. "It's okay," Frank said. "I appreciate your concern. Is it about Nancy? About what we discussed a while back?"

Ernie and his wife, Arline, had talked to Frank after they saw Nancy gambling at the Boardwalk Palace in Atlantic City. In the fifteen minutes they watched her she'd lost at least a thousand dollars playing blackjack with an intensity so ferocious that they finally decided it was their duty to tell Frank.

"You're right," Ernie said. "Arline just called me, and it seems Nancy was picked up by a limousine this morning and . . . well, that's about it. Thought you might want to know, in case you want to do something, you know, something for her own good."

"How long ago was she picked up?"

"Around ten, Arline says."

"Thanks, Ernie. Talk to you later."

He looked at his watch: ten minutes to twelve. His father would already be on his way to their luncheon date. Frank called Mario's, left a message. His father would be disappointed, but that couldn't be helped. A limousine picking Nancy up at the house! He'd thought she was starting to pull out of it, and all the while she'd been upgraded to high-roller status.

"Hey, you guys, strip me a couple of them femurs!" First Sergeant Mike Niles is calling to a small group of soldiers who are furiously stripping human flesh from legs not damaged by the explosions. Later, they'll attach a plaque with the outfit's insignia, use the femurs as swagger sticks.

To Frank Conti these are acts of madness, more proof—as if more were needed—that some of these guys are genuine wackos. They love killing so much they let the enemy see them first so they can enjoy the shock on their faces as they squeeze the trigger.

Major Hobson has his own weird dimension of madness. He and his two demolition technicians are booby-trapping a body now. They'll take it up in a helicopter, strap it in a sitting position until rigor mortis sets in, then find a place along a supply trail and seat the dead soldier in a chair in front of a field table with maybe a radio blaring away and a can of beer in his hand, and the area booby-trapped with artillery shells. Hobson's tar baby, his men call it. Frank calls it the way Special Forces fight a guerrilla war in enemy territory—by the dirty trick.

4

The restaurant where Joey Bucci was to meet Tony Allio at noon was eight blocks away from the casino. At five past twelve Joey was running up Florida Avenue. Going on foot was faster than driving in this traffic-choked town. He glanced at his watch, dodged across Baltic Avenue and down an alley to the restaurant's back door.

"Get you ass in here," Sal Sabato said. "You're late."

Sal shut the door, locked it, and led Joey down a short hallway to a private dining room. He frisked him, knocked, then gave Joey a swat on the ass that propelled him into the room.

Tony Allio was seated at the head of a long rectangular table. He was flanked by Nick Bartoli and by Funzi Cocchiaro, the family's underboss. Seated next to Bartoli was Allio's uncle, Rocco Iezzi, the family's *consigliere*.

"Sorry I'm late," Joey said. "The Conti broad was late getting in, the lousy traffic, you know. I got Joyce to take her upstairs, like Nick wanted me to, then I ran right over here." He took out a handkerchief to mop his wet face.

Allio nodded. "No problem, Joey. Sit down next to Nick here. Got something to discuss with you."

"Thanks, Tony."

"Know everybody here?"

"Yeah, well, everybody on a first-name basis except Mr. Iezzi. I've seen him a few times—here, there, you know—but we ain't never been formally introduced."

"So Rocco, this's Joey Bucci, a young up-and-comer we got our eye on a while. Doing some work for us at the Palace. Works with Larry, our connection in audit. You know, the guy handling credit lines for our people? Knows how to write them fuckers off with nobody the wiser."

The door leading to the kitchen opened, and the owner came in, followed by two waiters carrying trays loaded with the lunch Allio had ordered: antipasto, soup, a special veal and pasta casserole, an assortment of fruits and cheeses, jugs of red wine in wicker baskets, bottles of mineral water.

The waiters worked quickly, silently, their faces expressionless as they arranged the dishes around the table. The owner dismissed them, poured the wine, and waited.

Allio took a sip of wine, swishing it around in his mouth before swallowing it. "Not bad," he said, his eyes on Joey. The owner made a small bow and left.

"Spread okay, Joey?"

"Terrific, Tony."

"So tell me, Joey, what's with this nickname of yours?" Joey looked blank. Allio leered.

"Adonis," Allio said.

"Oh, that. I got it in high school. Just a joke — nobody calls me that anymore."

Allio looked around the table, still leering. "I hear you're hot stuff with the broads."

Joey shrugged. "I do okay."

Allio nodded and bent to his food.

Short and stocky, with a heavy shock of gray-streaked black hair combed straight back nearly covering his small ears, he was sometimes described in the local press as handsome. Certainly his dark intense eyes gave him a commanding presence — as, in Joey's opinion, did his custom-tailored suits and shirts, his silk ties, and his shoes of soft Italian leather, always highly polished. The man knew how to carry himself.

"Tell me something about your family," he was saying. "Where're they from?"

"Agrigento."

"Oh, yeah, mine too. We're good people, you and me. The same blood, good Sicilian blood. Everybody in this room's Sicilian. Italian people are okay, but Sicilian people are better. Sicily's the mother country of our thing."

Joey nodded, not knowing what to say.

"Nick here tells me you're interested in our thing. That right?"

"Yes, sir," Joey said. He'd been aching to be a member ever since he was a boy in South Philadelphia. He had seen how they lived, seen the big cars, flashy broads, sharp clothes, gold money clips jammed with C-notes. They walked down the street like kings. Nobody dared touch them, not even cops. If they wanted to kill you, they did it right there in the street or in a restaurant, any place, in front of anybody, and nobody squealed. That was power.

"Well, you know, like I said, we sort of been looking you over." As he downed half his wine, Allio's dark eyes watched Joey over the rim of the glass. Slowly, still staring Joey straight in the eye, he wiped his mouth with the large napkin he had tucked under his chin. "So far we like what we see. Right, Nick?"

"Right," Nick said. "He's okay."

Nick's endorsement surprised Joey. "Thanks," he said. "Whatever I can do, you know, you only gotta ask."

"Okay, Joey," Allio said. "But, see, we got to be careful about guys we take into the family. We got strict rules. You fuck up, you're dead." Allio pointed a forefinger and cocked his thumb. "You a stand-up guy, Joey?"

"Yes, absolutely," Joey said.

"Ever kill anybody?"

"Well . . . not really, but I know I could do it, no problem."

"Yeah? You think you could do it with a knife? You know, stick it right into somebody's gut?"

Joey shrugged. He didn't know what to say. He felt like he was being given a test and the wrong answer could ruin everything. After all, Allio's nickname was "Tony the Blade." Joey decided to tell the truth. "I never thought about doing it with a knife. I know I can ice somebody with a gun, but a knife, that takes real guts."

Allio grinned. "I was just a kid, sixteen, the first time. I took a knife and stuck it into a Jewish motherfucker that tried to fuck around with my girl at a dance. I gave him a warning, told him to get lost or I'd fucking kill him. The dumb jerk came back. I stuck the knife in his fat gut and twisted it real good."

Allio's thin voice rose to a high pitch. He laughed and slapped the table. "Guess what, I copped a plea, did three lousy months in juvie."

Joey didn't know whether to laugh or not. He'd heard stories about Allio's hair-trigger temper, how the smallest thing could set him off. In high school he had nearly killed a boy who'd called him "Stumpy."

"You own a gun, Joey?"

Joey nodded. "A small .25 automatic."

"Oh, yeah, Saturday night special, one of them little toys. How about a shotgun?"

"No," Joey said.

"Ever fire a shotgun?"

"No."

Allio leaned forward in his chair. "Listen, Joey, if we ask you to do something, anything at all, will you be okay?"

Joey felt all the eyes around the table glued on him. "I'll be okay," he said.

"You sure you can stand up?"

Joey swallowed hard. "Like I said. Absolutely."

"Good. Now I want you to go with Sal and Funzi. They'll explain the job to you on the way to Philly."

The word "job" made the short hairs on Joey's neck stand on end. "Sure, okay, Tony, like I said, anything I can do, just ask."

Allio, who was still leaning forward in his chair, pointed a finger at Joey. "Now, whatever happens this afternoon; whatever's said here is between us. This," he said, indicating moving lips with his fingers, "is bad. You do this," again he moved his fingers next to his mouth, "and you get this." He simulated the firing of a gun. "Here," tapping his head, "and here," tapping his heart.

The warning was unnecessary. Joey Bucci was already convinced he knew more than was good for him. For better or worse, and he wasn't sure which it was anymore, his lifelong dream was about to be realized.

Frank Conti was in a hurry. The rain didn't bother him. It was a light drizzle, the kind that often lingers for a while. The wind had come up fast, and the sun, which had peeked a couple of times, seemed to have vanished for good into a dark gray sky.

Except for the dull hum of the Buick's engine, the only sound was the light thumping of the windshield wipers. It was a comforting sound, reminding him of the metronome his mother had used when she gave piano lessons to neighborhood children.

Rachel Conti had possessed a kind of beauty that was rare in their Italian ghetto—long red hair, blue-green eyes, peaches-and-cream complexion. As a boy, Frank had known she was the most beautiful woman in the world. When he first met Nancy, he didn't pick up on the resemblance. "Jesus, Son," Tom said the weekend Frank brought Nancy down from Syracuse University to meet his parents, "give her another inch of height and a little more red in the hair, and you've got the spitting image of your mother twenty years back."

Ahead of him now, just visible in the rain, was the jagged skyline of the Boardwalk, with its towering casino buildings and their giant beckoning neon signs.

Frank hated the place, an ugly mixture of glitz and sleaze. Never mind the dozen casinos, never mind the two or three billion they had cost, the town still looked more like the South Bronx than a seaside resort. While thousands lived in condemned buildings or slept under the Boardwalk, scrounging for something to eat, others stole or robbed or assaulted or pushed dope. For pickings, thirty million potential victims crowding the Boardwalk every year.

Frank remembered a childhood trip to the old Atlantic City, spending the day on the beach with a picnic lunch his mother had packed. He and his father swam out beyond the breakers, floated out there for what seemed like hours. Most of the grand hotels were at a stage of terminal decline by then. Still, there was a look of grandeur about them, like dowager queens, aging but regal.

He remembered the Boardwalk, too, shooting galleries and penny arcades and carnival rides, the sideshows with the barkers hawking freaks with two heads, snakeskins, Siamese twins, fetuses in glass jars. Concession stands offered everything a boy liked to eat, from hot dogs to frozen custard and sea-foam fudge.

The outfit's second in command, Lieutenant Joe Freach, directs the men in clearing a landing zone of about thirty yards in diameter for the giant chopper that's going to pick them up.

After they've blown up trees, macheted low brush, and

42

stamped down tall grass, the men sit under a green canopy of foliage, smoke, and talk excitedly about showers, real food, booze, pot, and whores, not necessarily in that order.

Frank Conti sits on his rucksack, watching the radioman guiding what for now is just a speck on the horizon. As the chopper grows larger, the men stand up and begin to move around. Charlie could be in the bush, waiting for the bird to land before attacking.

The radioman tosses a smoke grenade into the middle of the LZ and moves back as the helicopter veers sharply, coming straight down toward the smoke. The dull *Dhup Dhup Dhup* is deafening as it hovers over the LZ, and the prop wash stirs up a whirlwind of dust, loose brush, smoke. With its tail lowered first, the giant bird squats down. The men, bent low against the blasting wind and holding their helmets against their heads, run for the opened tailgate. In a matter of seconds they are airborne. They laugh and yell, but no sound can be heard above the steady roar of the blades and buffeting wind that rushes in through the large open portholes.

It's grin-and-bear-it for the hundred miles they have to travel that day in the open chopper. Frank smokes a cigarette, cupping it with both hands. He tries to remember how long he has been with the Recondo unit. He's been in 'Nam twenty-one months, but it was only seven months ago — forever, it seems — that he stood in a bunker in Dong Xoai, waiting with the others for his first briefing by Major Hobson, one of the war's most decorated soldiers. Hunched over his cigarette, he replays that first encounter. . . .

Somebody barks "Ah-tench-hut!," and Hobson strides in. He's tall, broad-shouldered, and his heavily muscled chest and arms strain at the material of his short-sleeved shirt. "As you were," he orders, waiting for the men to sit down before going on.

He removes his green beret and holds it out. "A green beret," he says, carefully enunciating each word, "is an ar-

43

ticle of headgear that members of Special Forces, by law, are permitted to wear."

His piercing blue eyes survey the men, all of them. "Special Task Force B-32 is forming a Recondo group as part of a guerrilla unit. You'll be trained in various Special Forces techniques. We infiltrate deep within denied areas by parachute, by helicopter repel, by water, and, if need be, by foot."

A marine sergeant holds up his hand. "Excuse me, sir. You mentioned that we'd have to go in by parachute."

"That's true, Sergeant."

"Sir, I'm not parachute-qualified."

"Sergeant, I don't care about that. I'm parachute-qualified. If we go in, you'll just have to go along."

Another soldier stands up. "Sir, this sounds like a suicide outfit to me. I was told this was a volunteer unit."

"That's true," Hobson says. "B-32 has always been volunteer, but as of now it's volunteer no longer. There are four ways you can get out of this unit. One is in a body bag — if you die, there's nothing I can do about it, you're home. In view of this, I'll have my logistics officer order lightweight body bags with your number stenciled on it. There will be a zipper on the inside and a zipper on the outside, and at night you can sleep in it to keep the rain off you. If you get shot, zip yourself up if you can. The second way is to get wounded beyond repair. The third is to deruck, that is, complete your tour. The fourth is to find me a suitable replacement."

Hobson pauses to let the words sink in. "Now, have I answered all your questions?"

There's dead silence in the room. Hobson stands there, hands on his hips, meeting the gaze of each soldier willing to look directly at him. "For the first time in my life," he says, "I'm disillusioned with the army." With those words still ringing in the room, he spins on his heels and strides out.

Frank Conti is impressed. A splendid performance, heavy stuff. Hobson seems to be everything he's cracked up to

44

*be. In the weeks and months to come, all of them will be-
come devoted followers of the major. By walking on the rag-
ged edge, with death always lurking over their left shoulder,
the men discover the very sweetness of life.*

Now, as Frank Conti neared the city limits, the first
billboards loomed at the side of the road:

HARRAH'S HOT TO SLOT
OUR SLOTS ARE HOT — BALLY PARK PLACE
OUR SLOTS ARE BUSTING — CAESARS
SLOT CITY, GET A WINNING STREAK — TROPICANA
HEY, BUDDY, DON'T COME TO ATLANTIC CITY WITHOUT IT —
CLARIDGE
OVER $5 BILLION IN JACKPOTS PAID — RESORTS

He came down Mississippi Avenue, took a right on
Atlantic. Having decided to begin his search at the casino where the Stovers had seen Nancy gambling, he left
the Buick in a lot on Pacific Avenue and entered the
Boardwalk Palace.

The room Frank stepped into was as large as a football
field. The motif was Greco-Roman: there were giant al-
abaster copies of classical statues everywhere, including
the restrooms; bare-legged cocktail waitresses in skimpy
togas dashed through the crowds in the aisles, carrying
trays of drinks in one hand. Gilded mirrors on the pil-
lars, gilded mirrors on the walls; two-way mirrors overhead, concealing the television cameras that monitored
the endless action on the casino floor.

Every seat at every one of the hundred $5 and $10
blackjack tables was taken, people were three-deep at the
crap tables, lines were forming at the slots. Some of the
slot players had obviously been there for hours — robot
gamblers who dropped money and stared blankly at the
spinning drums. He knew the house took anywhere

from eighteen percent up, giving an average player five pulls every thirty seconds for his dollar, or whatever the amount he played.

Most of the day-trippers were slot players who usually ran out of money their first hour in town. On nice days they sat out on the Boardwalk, waiting for their free lunch and the bus ride back home in the late afternoon. On bad days, which would be about eighty percent of them, they wandered from casino to casino.

Walking slowly through the jam-packed casino, Frank found the noise, the smoke, the whole ambience suffocating. Like a stage set for a movie about the decline of the Roman Empire, phony and flimsy, bearing no resemblance or relation to the world outside. He pushed his way to the blackjack area, but Nancy wasn't there nor was she at any of the crap or baccarat tables. He checked the restaurants. Nothing.

Back out on the Boardwalk, he walked to the railing and looked out at the ocean, gray now in the light mist. It was low tide, and the seagulls were busy complaining, dashing back and forth on their spindle legs in their eternal search for food.

The wind coming off the ocean was cold now, but still the Boardwalk teemed with aging and busted gamblers, plenty of time on their hands and no easy way of killing it.

He had eleven more casinos to search. It was going to be a long day.

5

Joey Bucci sat in the backseat of Sal Sabato's Lincoln Continental, his eyes fixed on a long package wrapped in brown paper sticking out from under the passenger's front seat. It held, he decided, the sawed-off shotgun he'd be asked to use this afternoon to kill somebody in Philadelphia. His legs felt so weak he wasn't sure he could stand up by himself if they stopped the car and he was asked to step out. It was possible they were going to use the shotgun on him. Maybe, when they talked things over by themselves after lunch, they'd decided he couldn't be trusted.

He caught Sabato's eye in the rearview mirror and tried to smile, but he knew his face was a stiff mask.

"Hey, take it easy," Sabato said. "Sit back, relax while Funzi lays it out for you."

Seated in the front passenger seat, Funzi Cocchiaro turned to face Joey. "It's like this," he said. "There's this dirty motherfucker we gotta hit, Bobby Scolieri. Know him?"

Joey nodded. "Met him once or twice."

"Friend of yours?"

"No way."

"Well, he whacked the Clown yesterday," Funzi said. "Now we're gonna whack him. Tony wants you to do the job. Every day at four Scolieri leaves his pizza joint on Snyder, walks to this parking lot a block away, with his mother—thinks nobody's gonna touch him cause he's with mama, the dumb fuck."

47

The two men laughed, but Joey didn't even try. His mouth and throat were so dry, who knew what weird sound would come out. Funzi was looking straight at him, those dull black eyes boring into him.

"You up to it?" Funzi said.

"No problem," Joey said. "Only, I was just thinking—you know, if it's a shotgun—I never fired one before." He forced a smile. "Guess I'm pretty new at this."

Funzi looked at Sal, and they both laughed. "Today, kid," Sal said, "we get your cherry."

"Don't worry," Funzi said, "it's no big deal. Hand me the package there under my seat."

Joey gingerly lifted the package over the seat. "Is it loaded?"

"I sure fucking hope so," Funzi said. "You ain't gonna clip nobody with an empty gun." He tore the paper away from the sawed-off, double-barreled shotgun. "See, double trigger—pull them hammers back, you're in business. Give him both barrels in the fucking head."

"Front or back?"

"Front, back, side, makes no difference," Sal said.

"Right," Funzi said. "He won't have no head left anyway after them buckshots hit him. Here, take it, get used to the feel, but don't pull them hammers back until you're ready to use it."

Joey gently lowered the gun to his lap. It felt surprisingly light for something so awesome. How many sons of bitches had this gun taken out already? The stories he'd read about people getting whacked with sawed-off, double-barreled shotguns made it sound so exciting. Which it was, if you could call nearly shitting your pants exciting. He saw his wet fingerprints on the stock and barrels and reached for his handkerchief to wipe them off.

"What about gloves?" he asked.

"You're learning fast, kid." Funzi handed him a pair

of clear plastic gloves.

Joey put them on, then leaned back in the seat and closed his eyes. He needed to calm his nerves. There was no getting out of it now. The smart move was to compose himself, show them he was a stand-up guy. Gradually, he could feel his heartbeat slowing down. His hands felt dry. He could hear Funzi and Sal talking in low voices, but he didn't try to distinguish the words. It was just a sound, comforting in a way. He tried to visualize how things would go in Philadelphia. How would Bobby Scolieri react when he saw him coming with the gun? What did Bobby look like, anyway? It was ridiculous, but Joey couldn't remember. Was he tall, short, fat, skinny? What had they talked about the last time they were together? Was it at the Palace? It was weird the way his fear had erased Scolieri from his memory.

He heard his name but kept his eyes shut, trying to make his breathing perfectly even.

"Jesus," Funzi said, "talk about cool. This kid's sleeping."

"You're shitting me," Sal said.

"Hell I am." Funzi reached back to squeeze Joey's knee. "Wake up, kid. Time to go to work."

Joey reached under his sunglasses and rubbed his eyes before looking at Funzi. "We there already?"

"Just about," Sal said. "Had a good nap?"

"Yeah, guess I dozed off. Up late last night."

"How's that Joyce?" Funzi said. "Wouldn't mind a little piece of that myself."

"She's okay."

"We're here," Sal said, stopping across the street from Scolieri's pizzeria. "We're in luck. The rain's letting up."

"There's Sam pulling out," Funzi said. "Good thing he saved our spot. There ain't a parking space down this whole block."

49

Sal pulled into the space and killed the engine. Joey's gloved hands tightened on the gun.

"See the dry cleaners?" Funzi said. "See the little alley between it and the barbershop? Just stand in there and watch Sal. When he hangs his arm out the window, it means Bobby's coming down the street; when he pulls his arm back in, that means Bobby's just a couple steps from the alley. Wait till he walks by, then step out behind him, blow him away. Don't say nothing. Just give him both fucking barrels in the head. Sal makes the U-turn, you drop the gun, jump in, we're gone. Fucking piece of cake."

"Why drop the gun? Can they run ballistics on a shotgun?"

"No, but if something happens, we get stopped by cops, we don't want no gun in the car."

"What if somebody sees me? There's guys in the barbershop."

"Forget them," Sal said.

"Yeah, don't you worry about none of that shit," Funzi said. "Now get going, hide the piece under your coat."

"How long do I wait?" Joey asked as he stepped out of the Lincoln.

"Ten minutes, tops," Sal said. "Just get it done, kid, don't worry about nothing else. Funzi and me can handle any shit that comes down."

Joey jaywalked across Snyder Avenue, deftly dodging the oncoming traffic. The butt of the shotgun was jammed tightly into his armpit. A moment later he ducked into the alley.

Turning his body so that no one walking by could see what he was doing, Joey took the gun from under his coat and pulled both hammers, his finger already touching the first of the two triggers. He tried not to think of anything except the job at hand and found that he was holding his breath. "Come on, motherfucker," he whispered. "Bring me your head so I can blow it off."

He saw Sal's arm and took a deep breath. By the time the arm disappeared back into the car, the sweat was running into Joey's eyes. He heard voices, slowly let air out of his lungs, then took another deep breath just as Bobby and a gray-haired woman appeared in his blurry vision.

He waited until they walked past him before stepping out of the alley. Three quick steps brought him up close behind Bobby. He was still holding his breath when he raised the shotgun and squeezed both triggers so quickly that it sounded like one explosion. Bobby's head seem to explode into a huge bubble of red mist. Joey jumped back, afraid he'd get blood on his new suit, and turned away. He wasn't about to look at what he'd done.

Bobby's mother screamed. Joey, using the shotgun like a club, instinctively lashed out, striking her on the side of the head. Her arms shot up, her body twisted sideways, and she collapsed headlong on top of her son's body. Joey heard the squeal of tires, and when he looked up the Lincoln was waiting for him with its back door open. He dropped the shotgun in the gutter and jumped in; Sal gunned the engine before he could even close the door. The whole job had taken less than a minute. Fucking piece of cake.

For a man who had spent most of his adult life as a cop, Tom Conti had a delicate stomach when it came to mutilated corpses. Heads chopped into raw hamburger by double loads of 12-gauge double-aught bucks had a way of getting to him. He either lost his appetite if he hadn't eaten or, if he had, lost any food still in his digestive tract.

Tom had a feeling that he wasn't going to bother with

dinner tonight. Bobby Scolieri's body was still on the sidewalk, and the white towel the barber had thrown over Bobby's head was now drenched with blood.

"What a mess," Sergeant Johnny Brecato said, removing the towel.

"Oh, Christ," Tom said, turning away. "The poor bastard."

"Didn't feel a thing, Tom." Brecato dropped the towel back over what was left of Scolieri's head. "Now, his mother's another story. She's gonna have a class-A headache when she wakes up at St. Agnes—that is, if she ever wakes up. Didn't look too healthy when they hauled her out of here."

"Get a detail to the hospital," Tom said. "She probably saw the killer. Let's not take any chances. You notified homicide?"

Even as he asked the question, Tom knew that the homicide bureau, which worked out of the Round House downtown, was already on the way. Brecato didn't bother answering. They'd worked together so many years they could read each other's minds. Much of their conversation was a matter of grunts, nods, and shrugs.

Gawkers were gathering behind the barricade. The street was so full of police cars that they were blocking access to the meat-wagon boys, who would get as close to what they had to carry as humanly possible. A television crew was on the scene; Tom could see that the cameraman had his powerful lens focused on the body. Had probably gotten a good shot of it when Brecato lifted the towel. The hell with it. Let somebody else heave their cookies at dinner tonight.

"Get me the beat cop," Tom said, turning his back to the television camera. Later, he would follow procedure, send teams to question local merchants and the people living in apartments above the shops—an exercise in futility. When it came to the police, nobody ever saw anything; in reality, nothing happened on the street that wasn't closely observed by countless people. The smallest change in the day's routine, like an unfamiliar person or car coming into the neighborhood, came immediately under close scrutiny. Police didn't even bother sending undercover cops to these ghetto neighborhoods. They were instantly spotted. A new cop on the beat was kept under close observation until everybody had his routine down pat.

Brecato returned with Albert Ricupa, a patrolman who had worked the neighborhood for several years.

"How're you doing, Albert?" Tom asked him.

"Not bad, Lieutenant. Yourself?"

"Can't complain. Where were you when it happened?"

"Couple blocks away."

"Close enough to hear it?"

"Oh, I heard it, all right. Sounded like a howitzer going off. Came right over—too late, of course."

"See anything unusual?"

"What do you mean, Lieutenant?"

"See any mob guys around before the hit?"

"Well, yeah, now you mention it, earlier I saw Sal Sabato's white Continental coming up Broad."

"By any chance, did you see him turn on Snyder?"

Ricupa shook his head. "No, sorry, Lieutenant."

"Who was with him?"

"Had Funzi Cocchiaro with him and some Young Punk in the back. Don't recall ever seeing him before."

"What'd he look like?"

"They caught the light, so I got a pretty good squint at him. Late twenties, I'd say, medium size, definitely Italian, wearing fancy sunglasses with gold frames, real sharp dresser."

"That's seeing a hell of a lot in a few seconds."

Albert Ricupa grinned. "It was a long light, Lieutenant. Besides, you know, he reminded me of the actor that plays Remington Steele on TV."

"How long after you saw them at the light did you hear the shots?" Tom said.

Ricupa scratched his head. "Jesus, I don't know. Maybe fifteen, twenty minutes."

Tom looked at Brecato. "How about that for a coincidence?"

Brecato smiled. "Yeah, one in a million."

Ricupa shrugged. "I don't know, Lieutenant, them guys are in and out of here all the time."

"I know, Albert," Tom said. "Put the whole schmear on white paper, will you. Nothing official."

After Ricupa walked away, Brecato said, "Well, if they had anything to do with it, which they probably did, you can bet they hauled ass back to Atlantic City. We have zilch for extradition."

"Put a pickup on them anyway."

As they talked, Scolieri was zipped into a body bag, flung on a gurney, and wheeled up the street at a dead run.

"Must be late for dinner," Brecato said.

"I'm going to St. Agnes," Tom said, heading for his car with Brecato in tow. "Before you take off, get some of our guys to start working the neighborhood. Maybe we can find somebody else who saw Sal's Lincoln."

Before Brecato could respond, Tom drove away. It was another mob murder, the homicide boys at the Round House would handle it. Or try to, anyway. What number was this one—thirty-seven? He'd lost count. Ever since old man Vince Allio got knocked off and his son Tony claimed the godfather title, the family had been split into warring factions.

Rumors and theories abounded. One of the most persistent was that Tony Allio had put the hit on his own

54

father, giving the contract to Funzi and Sal. Tom liked that one because it made a lot of sense. Vince Allio had grown not only old but cautious — just at the moment when New Jersey legalized casino gambling in Atlantic City.

Long before the first bucket of concrete was poured for the first casino, mobsters controlling some of the unions were already buying up land along the Boardwalk to lease to prospective casino operators; others were buying, bribing, or extorting their way into businesses that would supply the casinos with everything from cigarettes, liquor, meat, and groceries to furniture, fixtures, carpeting, drapery, appliances. Then, of course, there were the standard mob operations: prostitution, drugs, bookmaking, loan-sharking, blackmail, extortion, burglary rings, hijacking, kickbacks, bribery of public officials, and other lucrative rackets that would appeal to the millions of visitors expected to visit the resort every year.

Instead of taking advantage of this new opportunity, Vince Allio had made the fatal mistake of preaching moderation. Now he was dead. War was raging, and Tom Conti, even with a weak stomach, was secretly enjoying the carnage.

6

Joey Bucci stood under a scalding shower in his Ocean Towers apartment, shampooing his hair. Earlier, following Funzi's orders, he had stuffed his suit and everything else he'd worn that afternoon, even his shoes, into a plastic trash bag. He was only too happy to oblige. The thought of Scolieri's blood put his teeth on edge.

Funzi had told him to remove all the labels from his clothing, including dry-cleaner markings, and to wait until late at night to stash the trash bag in a certain supermarket dumpster. It was the first one to be picked up in the morning, and Joey's garbage bag would be gone before the local army of scavengers began its daily forage through the town's garbage bins.

Satisfied that his hair and body were clean, he toweled off vigorously, studying himself in the door's full-length mirror. As always, Joey liked what he saw. Unlike Funzi's mottled skin, Joey's was flawless, a smooth light brown that gave him the appearance of having a perpetual suntan — the perennial beachboy.

Leaning close to the mirror, he looked straight into his dark eyes — widening them, then reaching with his fingers to pull the lower eyelids down to check the purity of the white circling the iris. He winked at himself, then stepped back to examine his body. Taking a deep breath, he expanded his chest, flexed his biceps, and assumed a bodybuilder's pose, turning sideways to examine his muscular legs and rock-hard buttocks.

Now it was time to select an outfit. Tonight his mood

was more toward a black suit, somber but not sober—the lining was a dazzling red silk. The suit, a Giorgio Armani, had cost twelve hundred dollars; Joey had several Armani suits, all tailored to perfection, with the Italianate flair that gave them that extra touch of class. A white tab-collar shirt in pinpoint cotton, black snake belt, light gray silk Armani tie with thin, scriggly black lines, full-carat diamond tie tack, half-carat-diamond-studded solid-gold cuff links, high-heeled Italian boots made to his specifications in Palermo (he needed that extra two inches to top six feet), a Rolex watch.

By the time he left the apartment, he felt like a million. Ocean Towers, the latest condominium apartment complex to grace the Boardwalk, was next door to the Palace. Although the light drizzle had started up again, Joey didn't bother with a raincoat, his hurried passage to the Palace being protected by a solid cover of canopies.

Walking through the casino, he went right to the Penthouse Club's private elevator. Compared to the main casino, highroller heaven occupied a relatively small space. Still, it was large enough to accommodate two crap, one roulette, one baccarat, and eight blackjack tables. No slot machines. No wheel of fortune. No bingo or keno. Strictly a class operation.

There was a bar, several sectionals arranged around coffee tables, plush leather chairs, and a small stage with a piano, bass, and guitar combo playing cool jazz. The carpeting was plush, the walls lined in a heavy brocade, the ceiling, like the one downstairs, mirrored to permit management's eye-in-the-sky surveillance that discouraged players and dealers from taking unfair advantage of the house.

The Penthouse Club was Joey's kind of place. A quick glance around the room revealed several movie and television stars, many of whom were headlining in various Boardwalk showrooms; a rock star awaiting trial for drug abuse; an assortment of big-time whales. Nothing unusual to see wealthy businessmen from China, Japan, Europe, Africa, the Middle East, South America; their faces were familiar to Joey, who in recent months had spent considerable time in high-roller heaven.

Tonight, however, he was interested in only two faces. He spotted them at a blackjack table and started in their direction, but Joyce moved quickly to intercept him.

"Boy, have I got a story for you," she said.

"What's happening?"

Grabbing his arm, she pulled him toward the bar. "She must be a hundred grand in the hole."

"Are you nuts? A hundred Gs?"

"That's what I said. If she hasn't reached the sky yet—remember what you said?—she's at least gone through the roof."

"Double Chivas," Joey said without looking at the bartender. "Hey, babe, don't laugh. It ain't funny. How can anybody lose a hundred grand playing fucking blackjack in a few hours? I don't get it."

"Spritzer," Joyce said to the bartender, then turned back to Joey. "It's easy, lover, when you're playing with purples."

"She's playing with thousand-dollar chips?"

"You've got it. You should see her. Five purples a hand, doubling up after wins. Hasn't taken a leak all day."

Joey gulped down half his drink. "Doesn't she ever win?"

"Depends what you call win. One time this afternoon, I kid you not, she had three chip boxes full of purples. She had to be at least a quarter million ahead, then she went completely bonkers. Started playing the whole table, all the slots. Never saw anything like it. She's trying to hit sixteens and seventeens—I mean, unbelievable. The woman's a fucking masochist!"

Nancy felt outside herself, as if she were standing to one side and watching this strange woman pushing pieces of plastic across a table. The high she had experienced earlier in the day was gone. Her stomach was queasy, her forehead feverish. She had to get away from the table, rest a moment, quiet her nerves, evaluate her situation. That exquisite feeling of possessing a special power, that certainty that she could predict the cards before they were dealt, had departed along with her winning streak.

Before it went, the feeling had been the strongest ever, and it had paid off in a deluge of purple chips, stacks and boxes of them. At no time had she had any awareness of their value in real money—until now. She had to get away.

With trembling fingers she picked up the few remaining chips and slipped off the stool. Her legs felt wobbly as she crossed the room, her heels sinking into the deep carpeting, making her feet rock. Then Joyce and Joey were at her side.

"You all right?" Joyce took Nancy's arm. "You must be exhausted. And you can't have had a thing to eat or drink all day."

"I'd like to go to my room," Nancy said, "and rest a little. Maybe an hour or so, then I'll come back."

"Why not take it easy tonight?" Joey said. "The place'll still be here tomorrow."

"What time is it?" Nancy asked.

"Ten-fifteen."

"That late? I have to get home."

"Come with me," Joyce said. "Let's go up to your nice suite, freshen up a bit. Get you something from room service. You look absolutely beat."

"Good idea," Joey said. "You two go to the suite, and I'll catch you a little later."

The moment the elevator doors closed behind them, Joey crossed to the casino cage.

"What's the damage with Nancy Conti?" he asked Dawn, a former dancer who handled the markers.

Dawn gave him a smile. "Kind of thought you'd be around."

"That bad?"

"It ain't good."

"Go ahead, hit me."

"I'll tell you one thing, she sure as hell rang all the alarm bells around here for a while. Let's see, one hundred twenty three thousand, plus a little unpaid tab of nineteen five, for a grand total of . . . one forty-two five."

Joey shook his head. "Is Max using his office right now?"

"No, he's downstairs."

"Okay, I've gotta use his phone." Joey moved toward the cage's door.

"Joey, you can't come through the cage. Use the other door."

"Oh, shit, you're right. Gimme the key, it's probably locked."

"I don't know, Joey . . ."

Joey leaned forward. "Come on, baby, you know I love you."

"Sure you do."

His dark eyes were locked on hers. "Only be a minute."

Seconds later Joey was on Max's phone, waiting for Nick Bartoli to get on the line. Sweat was running into his collar and under his arms. Switching the phone from hand to hand, he loosened his tie and slipped out of his suit jacket.

"Yeah?" Nick barked into the phone.

"I just got a report on the Conti broad. It ain't good."

"The bottom line, Joey."

"Listen, you remember telling me the sky's the limit? Well, you got it."

"How much, goddamnit?"

Joey cleared his throat. "Total, counting her previous tab, one forty-two five. I told you, this one's wild. She—"

"Perfect."

"It is?"

"You bet your sweet ass, buddy. And speaking of ass, drag yours over to the *spiaggia*."

Spiaggia, Italian for beach, was the code word for Tony Allio's home in Longport.

"Be here in thirty minutes."

Joyce opened the door to Nancy's suite. "Come on, just a few more steps," she said, steering a mildly resisting Nancy to a large sofa. "Sit right here, rest a minute while I call room service. A little something hot, maybe some soup, would really hit the spot."

"Where's the bathroom?" Nancy asked, lurching to her feet. "Here, let me help you," Joyce said. "Must be about ready to bust. I swear I don't know how you gamblers do it. They say Nick the Greek used to stand at a crap table for twenty-four hours without once going to the john."

A moment later, the bathroom door locked behind her, Nancy was on her hands and knees, her head hanging over the toilet bowl, a cold film of sweat covering her body. Chills made her tremble so violently that she had to hold onto the bowl to keep from rolling on the floor. Then it came, the bile and mucus, followed by the wrenching dry heaves that went on until she thought she would die there on her knees, with her head in the toilet.

A fitting end, her brain screamed at her as she twisted in agony, unable to stop the spasms. Tears streaked her face, her nose ran, and she heard herself groaning like a wounded animal.

Allio's Longport estate occupied nearly four acres at the end of Seagull Lane, which dead-ended in Great Egg Harbor Inlet. Hidden behind an eight-foot brick wall, the estate had its own private beach and a main house built during the Roaring Twenties by a New York City millionaire. In the 1930s the estate had been owned by Abner "Longy" Zwillman, a millionaire bootlegger. During World War II the army had used the estate as a training camp for Signal Corps officers. Over the next thirty years it slipped into disrepair until Tony Allio acquired it, spending an undisclosed amount to restore it to its earlier splendor. Besides the large main house, there were three good-size residences occupied by his uncles — brothers of his mother, Chiara — and their large families. Nobody knew how many people lived behind the walls of Allio's compound.

The limousine pulled up in front of a black iron gate; the driver, a member of Allio's crime family, whispered into his walkie-talkie and the gates swung open. Joey could see armed men standing on each side of the gate as they glided through.

The limousine moved along a winding tree-lined drive, pulling up in front of wide stone steps leading up to the mansion. A guard opened the door, ushered Joey through a huge living room, down a long hallway, and into a room that had once been the millionaire's library. Except for the rosewood paneling, the room looked more like a rumpus room: a bar and stools, a large card table with six leather chairs, dart board, bumper pool table, and sofas and easy chairs along the walls. There wasn't a book or magazine in sight.

Sal Sabato and Funzi Cocchiaro were seated on a sofa with a man Joey had never seen before; Tony Allio and Nick Bartoli were at the card table. Allio was reaching into a dish of mixed nuts; his hand stopped over the dish when he saw Joey. He looked up, smiled, and rose to his feet.

"Come here," Allio said, grabbing Joey by the arms, pulling him up close. "Good work today," he said, looking him straight in the eye.

"Thanks, Tony."

Allio's grip on Joey's arms tightened. "I'm going to need your good work again, in a more pleasant matter this time."

"Sure, Tony. Like I said at lunch, anything at all."

Allio smiled. "Here, sit down, Joey, next to me. Want a drink? Ugo, get him a drink. Whatever he wants."

"Scotch—Chivas, if you've got it—with a squirt."

"Oh, I think we've got it," Allio said. "Right, Ugo?"

"Wouldn't be surprised," Ugo Failla said. He was short, with shoulder-length blond hair and the delicate features of a woman, his movements catlike as he went to the bar.

"So I told Uncle about the Conti cunt's streak of bad luck," Nick said. "He thinks maybe she's run out her string."

"I wasn't even there when she lost it," Joey said, dying to take a swallow but not wanting to seem anxious. "You know where I was this afternoon. All I did was tell Joyce what you told me." He stopped, looked at Nick, then at Allio. "Christ, so much has happened today."

Allio chuckled, leaning back in his chair. "Don't worry about the money," he said, tapping Joey's arm with a clenched fist. "I think it's a good investment, which leads me back to you. To protect the investment, I want you to keep an eye on her. Think you can do that for me?"

Joey nodded. "Sure. What do I do?"

"You've seen her suite?" Tony said. "Comfortable place, plenty of space. Two or three people could set up house in there."

"She's not going to be there long," Joey said. "In fact, she's probably gone right now. She's really beat."

"No, no, she's not gone. You're not listening to me, Joey. You look like you're listening, but you're not hearing me. Why's that?"

"Sorry, Tony—I mean, maybe I missed something."

"Hey, Uncle, let me spell it out," Nick touched his forehead. "Fuckhead here's a little slow sometime."

"I'll explain it," Allio said. "And cut that fuckhead shit. Joey's one of us now—or will be soon, amounts to the same thing. We treat each other with respect. I don't want none of you to forget that. Now, Joey, I need you to keep the lady occupied for a few days. Keep her happy, but away from the tables. You're a swinger. And she ain't all that shabby-looking, right?"

Joey shrugged. "I never thought of her that way, you know. She's a degenerate gambler, got a one-track mind. I don't think she's got the slightest interest in sex. One look at her tells you that."

"Well, get her interested. An Adonis like you, you'll be in her pants like a fucking flash. Anyway, that's just the icing. The point is I want her kept in that room a couple of days, sort of your prisoner of love. Remember that old song?"

Joey smiled, for the first time. "That's what you meant by protecting your investment?"

"Bingo," Allio said. "She gives you any trouble, let her have a couple of pills—Nick has a bottle."

"What about phones, what if she wants to make a call?"

"No problem. They're all gone except one, and it's cordless. The base unit is locked in the cabinet under the TV. There's two handsets, so there's one charging while you're using the other. Just make sure you lock them both up when you leave. And to make sure she don't sneak out the door when you're gone, I had a special lock installed that opens only with a key. Nick'll give it to you."

"What about Joyce? She in on this?"

Allio shrugged. "You need help?"

"I don't know. Depends how long it takes, you know."

Allio looked around the table at the other men, reached over for a handful of nuts and chewed them slowly, his fierce eyes narrowing as they returned to study Joey.

"Seems to me a guy like you should be able to handle a little woman by himself," he said, reaching for more nuts. "Let's keep this in the family, know what I mean? Joyce don't have to know nothing about it."

"Okay, no problem."

"That's great, Joey. Knew I could count on you."

Joey nodded, then gathered his nerve. "So," he said finally. "What's the deal, anyway?"

"The deal?" Allio said. "No big deal, Joey. You just keep the broad on ice a couple days while I negotiate with her husband. Know him?"

Joey shook his head.

"Too bad," Allio said. "Great guy. Well, who knows, maybe someday soon now you'll get a chance to meet him up close. Real close."

7

In the past five hours Frank Conti had been through the casinos on the Boardwalk and the ones in the inlet three times. He'd questioned cocktail waitresses, dealers, pit bosses.

He stopped at a pay phone and called the house. There was no answer, but then Nancy seldom answered the phone. . . . She could have lost all her money and be on her way back home at that very moment. Either way, she was probably long gone from this miserable place, while he was out here chasing around like a lunatic.

He headed for the parking lot where he'd left the Buick. If she wasn't home when he got there, she would be soon. She never stayed out past midnight. When he saw her this time, he'd get help for her no matter what it took.

After the firefight, they find that three soldiers, along with an old woman and two small girls, have survived. The soldiers are promptly executed, but the woman and children become Frank Conti's problem since he's on the roster that day to take care of just a situation.

Frank decides to lay the problem in the major's lap. "Sir, I know we're deep behind enemy lines and we don't have the food or manpower to maintain prisoners, but I don't feel right about doing what I'm supposed to do here."

"What do you propose? They're your responsibility."

"I know, sir. Can I tie them up and bring them with us?"

"To our secret base, where we're going to circle our wagons for the night?"

"Yes, sir."

"You going to feed them your rations?"

"No problem, sir. We're being resupplied day after tomorrow, and they don't eat all that much anyway."

The major stares at him a long time before answering. "Okay, but you better have a solution in the morning."

In the morning, Frank says, "Well, Major, what do you want me to do with the prisoners now?"

Hobson studies him. "I don't know, Conti. What options do we have?"

"I can take care of them."

"When are you going to sleep?"

"I'm okay, I feel fine."

"What if we get in a firefight?"

"I'll handle it, no problem."

"Got any morphine?"

"Yes, sir. We can shoot them up with it, but you've got to understand that we're probably going to have to tape the kids' mouths shut."

Hobson shakes his head. "Okay, okay, Conti. Just keep their hands tied today and put them by your hammock tonight. Tomorrow we'll talk."

Frank lies awake all night. They'll be on the move twelve, fourteen hours the next day, but he can't get a wink of sleep. The woman and children are the family of an enemy unit; to let them go free could mean the signing of their outfit's death warrant.

In the morning the major says, "Well, Conti?"

"I think I have a solution, Major. Wilson has a bad foot infection. Pretty soon we'll have to carry him." They both know it takes six men to carry one. "When the fighters come with the supplies, could you call and have

67

the Hook pick up Wilson while our fly-boys are stirring up Charlie with napalm?"

Hobson nods. "And while they're at it, they might as well pick up your civilians?"

"Exactly my thought, sir."

Hobson shakes his head. "You're devious, Conti."

Frank shrugs.

"Okay, if I can find a volunteer crazy enough to fly in here, we'll do it."

Later that day, during the air strike, the Hook slips in and Frank helps load his charges on the helicopter. Once they fly away, he draws his first deep breath in three days.

Tom Conti stood at the foot of the hospital bed looking down at Anna Scolieri. She lay with a tube up each nostril, an IV in each arm, heart-monitor leads taped to her chest, a urine bag hanging from the side of the bed.

Anna was a good-looking old woman, her face softened by the years. At the end of her life she was alone in a hospital room, her last son, the third son to die in this factional war, lying on a morgue slab with a tag on his big toe.

Tom wondered if she had known that Bobby was a killer, at least suspected as much from newspaper accounts in recent years. If so, had it made a difference to her? After all, she came from a long line of career criminals. Her husband and his father, both dead many years, were relics from the old Mustache Pete era. In those days, mafiosi didn't kill sons in front of their mothers.

The more Tom looked at her, the more he could see her resemblance to Rachel. Of course, Rachel was younger when she died, but Alzheimer's had aged her far beyond her years. He remembered standing in a hospital room much like this one and looking down at

Rachel, plugged into tubes and monitors like Anna Scolieri, watching the life ebb out of her exhausted body. He had reached for her hand, so small and dry and fragile, the same hand he had slipped the gold band on so many years ago.

What a beautiful girl she had been, far too beautiful for the likes of him. From the moment he walked into her father's small pub in London's Bayswater district, Tom was a goner. Four days after he met her, on June 13, 1944, he flew his first mission as a gunner on a B-17 bomber.

A couple of bomb runs later, Tom was back at the bar, nursing a Guinness, his eyes glued to Rachel, who was washing glasses. Tom wanted to talk to her, but in front of her father he could manage only friendly smiles, for which he received only mild encouragement.

He dreamed about her that night. It was a week before he could get back to see her again. Tom drank Guinnesses until he thought his kidneys would explode. He hadn't spoken to the girl, but he'd heard her father call her Rachel. He was trying to decide what color her eyes were when he saw her coming toward him. Tom summoned his courage.

"Can you direct me to the, ah, bathroom?" he asked her. "Or whatever you call it around here?"

She smiled. "Loo."

"No, my name's Tom, Tomasso really—it's Italian. Conti's the last name. I have to tell you—really, I'm serious—I think you're the most beautiful, the most gorgeous, the prettiest girl I ever met in my whole life."

"What an extravagant mouthful," she said with a smile. Green, he decided. Her eyes were definitely green. "But as to your question, in London we call your bathroom a loo."

Tom laughed. "So where're you hiding your loo?"

"Actually, we don't have one."

"My God," Tom said. "I thought England was a civilized country."

"Silly," she said, shaking her head, her long red hair brushing gently against her shoulders. They looked brave, those shoulders. "We have one, but not for the use of our customers."

"Englishmen must have strong kidneys."

"Its the bladder that's important," she said, just as soberly. "Englishmen are known for their sturdy bladders."

Tom leaned forward. "Do you like dancing?"

"Oh, well, that's a different kettle of fish entirely, now isn't it."

"If you're saying I'm fishing, you're right. Can you jitterbug?"

She dabbed at the bar with a damp cloth. "In my own fashion, I suppose, but most English boys aren't keen on jitterbugging, so we don't get much practice at it. I suppose, like all American boys, you're an expert."

"I've got a shelf full of trophies to prove it."

"Trophies, mind you? You get trophies for jitterbugging in America?"

"Dance contests. I've won a whole slew of them back home. You happen to be talking to the jitterbug king of South Philadelphia."

She raised her eyebrows. "Royalty, no less."

"I'll tell you one thing, I'd feel like a king if you'd go dancing with me."

"You're a fast worker," she said, hands on her hips. "You don't even know me."

"I know you've knocked me for a loop."

She slapped at the bar with the damp cloth. "Do you say that to all the girls? Do any of them ever believe you?"

Tom shook his head. "I've never said that to a girl in

my whole life."

She laughed. "I'll bet you've said *that* before, too."

"Okay, don't believe me. But at least give me a chance to show you what a great jitterbugger I am. If I can get a pass Saturday night, will you come to the dance with me? You do have dances in England, don't you?"

"Yes, at Covent Garden Royal Opera House."

"Is that yes, it's a date?"

"It's yes we have dances, and it's maybe about Saturday night. If you're still of a mind, that is."

On Saturday the target was Munich. They caught it good. Tom got one burst at an Fw190, saw smoke; then a cannon shell sliced one cable, flak was puncturing the gas tanks, the PFF radio caught on fire, two engines were hit. The pilot was hit in the foot, and *Bunky,* their plane, had over a hundred holes in her when they landed by A.F.C.E.

Tom lost little time in getting back to the Johnson pub. From the motor-pool sergeant, a boy from South Philadelphia, he got a jeep for his two-day pass; from the mess hall, a picnic lunch. And from Rachel, a smile that made everything he'd gone through worth it.

"Can you get away from here?" he asked her. "I've got a jeep outside, let's go for a ride."

She directed him to a park, complete with a stream, where they feasted and flirted the afternoon away.

That night they went jitterbugging. Two months later, they were married.

A young nurse bustled into the room, leaned over Anna Scolieri's bed, fussed with the tubes and leads, checked the urine bag, took a close look at the patient—and ran from the room. Tom looked down at the old woman and realized that she was dead. For

71

how long, he had no idea; he had been lost in his loss, his war, his courtship. Now it was time to come see if he could do something about the lousy bastards who had killed this old woman.

A cop—even an old one—ought to be good for something besides pushing around a bunch of papers that nobody ever really read.

All the way back to the Palace, Joey Bucci was trying to figure how to get Joyce out of the way without arousing her suspicion. By the time he let himself into the suite, he thought he had it worked out.

Joyce was sitting on the sofa, watching television. "Where's the Conti broad?"

"Her name's Nancy."

"Jesus, gimme a break, I don't need no woman-lib shit tonight. Where the fuck is she?"

"Hey, slow down, she's taking a nap."

He headed into the bedroom. Nancy lay in the middle of the huge round bed, curled up in the fetal position, sound asleep. Joey moved up close for a better look, then backed out of the room, gently closing the door.

"She looks dead," he said. "What'd you give her?"

"A couple of sleeping pills. She needs rest. She's totally thrashed. The way she gambles would thrash anybody. You should've been here. She puked her head off."

Joey dropped down on the sofa in front of the TV. "What're you watching besides commercials?"

"The news. Did you hear about Bobby Scolieri getting hit today? Whoever did it also killed his mother."

"You mean she's dead?"

"Yeah, the guy shot Bobby in front of her, then slugged her with the shotgun. What a bastard."

The news pleased Joey. He hadn't told anyone, but before he'd hit the old woman she got a pretty good make on him. She'd seen the gun barrel coming at her head, and for all Joey knew she had still been looking straight at him when he delivered the blow.

"What the hell, her life was over anyway," Joey said. "She was just an old woman."

"What an attitude. Well, whoever did it is gonna get heat. The press's bound to jump on the story. Which means the cops will probably have to get off their fat asses and make like they're interested."

Joey laughed. "Give it a week and they'll find other things to jump on. We're not worried."

"What the hell does that mean?"

"Nothing," Joey said. "I meant nobody worries about the press. It's just bullshit."

"You're probably right," she said. "Hey, Joey, lighten up. Come here, put your head in my lap, I'll massage your temples. Nick must be giving you a hard time. You're really tense."

Joey stood up. "Later, babe. Right now what I need is a drink." He went to the bar, fixed himself a Chivas. "Listen, speaking of Nick, he wants you back down in the casino, working up a little juice action."

"What about Nancy? Don't you think I ought to wait until she wakes up, help her down to the limo? She wants to go home."

"I'll handle it," he said.

"You trying to get me out of here so you can make it with her? Forget it, she ain't interested."

"Don't be stupid," Joey said, his voice rising. "Do I look that hard up?"

"Look, Joey, just leave her alone. She's got all she can handle right now."

He smiled. "Trust me, I won't lay a finger on her."

"It's not your finger I'm thinking about. Joey, what's

73

with her, anyway? I've gotta tell you, I'm more than a little curious. She married to some rich dude? Is that it?"

"You got it," Joey said, grateful for the idea. "The broad's a fucking fruitcake. Her husband talked to Nick, wants us to hold her till he gets here himself. . . . See, he's coming over with her shrink and a couple of boys with butterfly nets."

"That sucks," Joyce said. "She's not that fucked up. Look, Joey, I want to stay with her until her husband shows up. I want to meet this jerk."

"I told you, Nick wants you downstairs. Hey, that's what the man told me—I'm just the messenger boy. But let me give you a friendly tip. He's gonna be downstairs himself later tonight. If I was you, I'd be there."

8

The doorbell rang, and Frank Conti came awake with a start. He sat up straight and looked around the room, trying to isolate the noise, then checked his watch. Six minutes past midnight. He'd fallen asleep on the living-room sofa waiting for Nancy.

The doorbell sounded again. When he opened the door, his father was standing there, looking at him with the expression his mother had called his "detective face."

"Why all the lights on?" Tom asked.

"Come in, Pop."

"Place looks like you're having an open house. Expecting late guests?"

Frank smiled, "No, Pop. Can I get you anything? A beer, maybe?"

"Yeah, a beer's fine. Thanks."

Frank went to the kitchen, came back with two beers. "To your health, Pop," he said, handing over a can. "So how's it going?"

Tom leaned back in the easy chair, closed his eyes, and pressed the cool can against his brow. "Christ, that feels good." He paused a moment and kept his eyes closed. "I was thinking about your mother tonight. God, she was a gorgeous girl — I wanted to drown in those big green eyes."

He opened his eyes, took a swig of beer. "Did you know she was a great ice skater, your mother? We used to go skating at the Sports Palace — I'm trying to remember where that was." He pinched his brow with his fingers. "Oh, yeah, Richmond, a suburb of London. The ice wasn't that good because a doodle bug — that's what they called buzz bombs, great sense of understated humor, the English — had landed near there, knocking most of the pipe connections loose. Would you believe it, the whole city bombed to hell, and they were trying to repair the ice rink? You know, you've got to hand it to people who think like that."

Frank smiled. "Those daylight raids must have been rough."

Tom shrugged. "Not a bad war on the whole. A stroll in the park compared to what you went through in Vietnam, believe me. And for a bonus, I got your mother. How lucky can a guy get?"

They sat without talking for a while. Finally, Frank said, "I suppose you're wondering what happened at noon."

"You could say it crossed my mind," Tom said. "Plus, you missed a terrific lasagna."

"Sorry I couldn't make it. Something came up."

"So tell me about it, I've got time."

Frank rubbed his eyes. "Everything's under control, Pop."

"If you say so. Remember, you've got an ear whenever you need one."

"I know. But right now you've got an ear for memories of Mom — what got you going with them, anyway?"

"This old woman who died tonight," Tom said. "I was right there in the hospital room with her, and she slipped away so quietly I didn't even know when she left. She was all alone in the world. That's a terrible thing, Frank, to be alone, especially when you get along in years. In the old country, no one's ever alone. It's all family there, kids and relatives popping out all over the place. Old people are revered, not a nuisance. Well, in her case, her son thought she was his life insurance policy. It didn't work out quite that way. So now they're both dead."

Frank had never heard his father ramble on this way before, and it made him uneasy.

"You all right, Pop?"

"Sure, Frank, sure," Tom said, sitting up straight in the chair. "Feeling a little nostalgic, I guess. Been that kind of a day. How's Nancy?"

Frank shrugged. "Well, you know, the usual. I don't know when she's going to snap out of it. At times, I must admit, it looks pretty hopeless."

"Don't lose heart, Son. One of these days she'll come around."

"That's what I keep telling myself, but my voice is getting a hollow ring."

"Well, hang in there. Losing a child is hard on a mother."

"It's hard on a father, too. I still —"

"I know, Son. And it's hard on a grandfather. But it's hardest of all for a mother. You've got to stick by her, Son."

"I am, Pop. Don't ever worry about that. It's just . . . I feel so goddamn helpless."

"I had the same feeling with your mother. All I could do was stand there and watch her disappear on me. It breaks your heart, all right. Cruel and unusual punishment."

"I know, Pop. But in your case you didn't deserve it."

Tom stood and walked to the door. "You don't deserve it either. You did what you thought was right for Timmy. Go down any block in any city, you'll find kids Timmy's age on bikes. It was just a freak accident. Same as Alzheimer's is a freak accident. It can happen to anybody anywhere, at any time. Well, time to say goodnight. Thanks for the beer—and the ear."

Frank sat dozing in the living room until three o'clock before giving up and going to bed. At seven-thirty he was still there, staring up at the ceiling. He had decided to stay home from work, to be there when Nancy returned. He would take her in his arms, not let her squirm away, somehow find the words that would convince her to go for help.

When the phone rang, he grabbed for it.

"Frank Conti?" a voice asked.

"Yes," Frank said.

"I've got a message for you."

"From my wife? From Mrs. Conti?"

"Yeah, well, not exactly from her. It's about her."

"Do you know where she is?"

"Yeah. I'm delivering a message for Mr. Tony Allio. He wants to see you at ten o'clock, meet him for breakfast at Bocchino's."

"Is my wife there? May I speak to her?"

"Hey, relax, I told you, I'm just a messenger. Be there. Ten sharp."

The line went dead.

Frank dropped the receiver back in its cradle

and sat on the edge of the bed, arms folded across his chest, hugging himself. The messenger didn't have to explain. Frank knew only too well. After all these years, Tony Allio was about to exact his pound of flesh.

9

When Tom Conti arrived at the precinct on Friday morning, two homicide detectives from the Round House were in the operations room talking with Sergeant Johnny Brecato. Irish cops close to retirement age, they'd always reminded Tom of Laurel and Hardy. Not that either one of them had ever made anyone laugh, but Phil Mooney was tall and fat and sleepy, and Jack McGeary was short and skinny and as charged up as a live wire.

Tom slid into his chair, motioning for Brecato to go on.

"I was just telling them, nobody in the neighborhood saw a thing when Scolieri got it," Brecato said.

"Nothing surprising about that," McGeary said. "The day anybody in that neighborhood sees anything—that's the day I'll be surprised."

Brecato ignored him. "Lieutenant, the guys in the barbershop had a front-row seat. The one in the barber chair, facing a plate-glass window splattered with Scolieri's brain cells, swears on a stack of Bibles he saw nothing."

"They're all scared shitless," Mooney drawled, barely able to keep his washed-out blue eyes open.

"Canvassing the neighborhood is a royal waste of time," McGeary said. "What if you did find somebody dumb enough to come forward? How long before he gets a couple of calls and decides his mouth is dangerous to his health?"

"What about Albert spotting Funzi and Sal at the traffic light before the shooting?" Mooney asked.

"Its a lead," Tom said.

"Wonder who the pretty boy in the backseat was," McGeary said. "A young button on his first hit? They need new soldiers. With the bloodbath we've had around here, a good shooter must be getting hard to come by."

"You kidding?" Mooney said. "Them fucking wops are like cockroaches. Kill one and ten new ones come crawling out of the woodwork."

The phone rang, and Tom took the call.

"This Lieutenant Tom Conti?" a man's voice asked.

"Yes."

"Listen, Conti, the guy who hit Bobby Scolieri was Joey Bucci. Lives in a condo at Ocean Towers down in Atlantic City."

Tom stood, taking the telephone with him as he moved away from the desk, his back to the room. "I need a name," he said, lowering his voice.

"No way, José."

"Tell me, did you actually see it?"

"Bet your ass."

"What was he wearing?"

"Dark suit, black or dark blue, and fancy fucking sunglasses, like a move star."

"Okay," Tom said, "now —"

"Forget it, that's all she wrote. Go get the murdering bastard, burn his ass."

Tom heard the click but kept the receiver to his ear and moved back to his desk. "Okay, Frank, see you tonight. Take care."

He hung up and leaned back in his chair. Had anyone asked him why he was keeping the phone call to himself, he wouldn't have been able to answer.

The closer Frank got to Atlantic City, the heavier was the traffic on the expressway, but for him it didn't really exist. His mind was on the past—nearly twenty years past.

It had taken him fourteen months to fulfill the two promises he'd made to himself while he recovered from the injuries Allio's gang had dealt him.

Keeping the first promise was a pleasure, for he soon fell in love with karate. He embraced its discipline and concentration as a way of life and a way of thinking, an environment that demanded his respect. Everybody he met who wore a higher-degree belt was stronger, better. It was that simple.

Karate taught its practitioners to block, punch, kick, to kill with their bare hands if necessary, but nobody acted like they were holding magnums pointed at each other. What they all learned was technique and information and respect.

Keeping the second promise was more complicated.

Once he had acquired the necessary skills, Frank began following Allio from a safe distance, learning his habits and daily routine. Having graduated from high school the spring of his attack on Frank, Allio was now working for his father, learning the business of organized crime from the street up.

His old high school gang was gone, replaced by older, more experienced family members like Sal Sabato and Funzi Cocchiaro. Flanked by killers, little Tony swaggered as he ran his father's errands in the Italian community of South Philadelphia, his violent temper earning him a new nickname, "Tony the Blade."

He'd left home and was living in a high rise with around-the-clock security. Both Sabato and Cocchiaro had apartments in the same building. He was never alone. Whether working or going to bars and nightclubs with a date, he was surrounded by members of his father's family.

Much against his father's wishes, when Frank graduated from high school he didn't even apply to college. Instead he got a job as a delivery boy at an all-night pizzeria near Allio's apartment building. Several of the tenants were steady customers, and in time Frank became friendly with the building's security people.

One of the pizzeria's steadiest customers was Sal Sabato, a six-foot-three, 260-pound eating machine who could polish off two large pizzas in the middle of the night. Frank listened carefully whenever he made a delivery to Sabato—noting his speech patterns and the sound of his voice, then practicing his impersonation until he felt he had it down pat.

After waiting five months for Allio to order a pizza late at night, he decided it was time to create the opportunity. And so, when a call came from a customer at the high rise at two o'clock one morning, Frank walked into the building's lobby and found his favorite security guard on duty.

"This's for a Mr. Allio, he's in . . . oh, what the hell, I've got it here somewhere . . ."

"Twenty-two C," the guard said.

"Right," Frank said. "By the way, Oscar, this's my last delivery tonight. I'm gonna be upstairs a little while. Mrs. . . . well, I better keep her name out of it—anyway, she called and wants me to do a couple of little jobs for her."

The guard nodded and winked. "I think I might know the lady in question. Well, don't do nothing I wouldn't do."

In the elevator, Frank took the pizza out of its cardboard box. Its spicy aroma filled the car. He took a huge bite, chewing carefully, keeping most of it in his mouth. He had learned that he could do a better imitation of Sal Sabato if his mouth was nearly full.

He rang the doorbell of apartment 22 C.

A moment later a voice said, "Yeah, what is it?"

"Tony, it's Sal, gotta talk."

"What the fuck." The door unlocked—first the dead bolt, then the night chain.

Frank's first move was to hit Allio in the face with the pizza; his second, to slam the door shut and turn the dead bolt.

Allio sputtered, blowing pizza from his mouth and nose, ripping it away from his eyes. He was naked, his broad shoulders and a long, thick, powerful torso anchored on stubby muscular legs.

Hearing a cry, Frank spun around. A black girl was kneeling on the bed, no more than seventeen, her large eyes round and ringed with white.

"You motherfucker," Allio screamed in his high-pitched voice. "You're dead."

Frank assumed the karate attack position. "Get your knife," he said, "and let's see how good you are on your own."

Allio stepped back, reached for his pants, which he had thrown across a chair. Frank was on him, pulling the pants out of his hands.

"Just making sure it's a knife, not a gun," he said. He pulled the knife out of the pocket, held it up high over his head, out of Allio's reach.

Allio watched like a cat waiting for a mouse to move. Frank dropped the knife on the floor and stepped back.

Allio snatched the knife from the floor and came up snarling, the six inch switchblade glinting in his hand. He moved toward Frank in a crouch, his eyes on Frank's hands.

Frank made lightning-fast karate moves with his hands to hold Allio's attention, then threw a side kick at his knee. Allio screamed, and Frank snapped a palm-heel strike to the jaw, following with a knife-hand blow across the nose. Blood spurted as Frank felt the bridge of Allio's nose collapse. Allio staggered back, nearly losing his balance, then suddenly lunged forward, slashing with the knife, nicking Frank's stomach, drawing blood. Frank shifted sideways, again kicked him in the knee, and knew instantly the knee was gone. He stepped in as Allio was falling, with his left hand grabbed the wrist of Allio's knife hand and levered it back. Using both thumbs on both hands to push outward, he pressed back until the wrist snapped. The knife fell, and Allio's high-pitched scream filled the room. He was holding his broken wrist when Frank delivered the coup de grace: a crane-head strike against the temple. Allio fell, unconscious before he hit the floor. Frank reached down, slipped the knife blade under his foot and snapped it off.

The girl was still kneeling on the bed, paralyzed with fear.

"Don't be afraid," Frank said. "I'm leaving. Maybe you better leave, too."

Allio, he sensed, would despise anyone who had witnessed his humiliation.

Frank never knew whether she'd gone or stayed behind, but a few days later he read in the paper that the body of a teenage black girl had been found in an alley in South Philadelphia. Two months later, Frank joined the Army Rangers and was gone from Philadelphia. The revenge he had expected never came.

The closer he got to Atlantic City, the more convinced he became that it was coming now.

"Look at yourselves, you're a fucking disgrace," Hobson says, grinning as the men slouch in what is supposed to be a straight line. Each man seems to be dressed in some makeshift uniform of his own choosing. Some wear camouflage pants with just a flak jacket, others jungle blouses or T-shirts, some all three. Most wear decorations taken from the enemy; all carry their weapons.

"You are, without a doubt, the sorriest, dirtiest, raggedest, scraggliest bunch of warriors I've ever laid eyes on."

"You betcha, Major," Frank calls out.

"Okay, but we're going to behave like gentlemen this weekend, right?"

This is greeted with yells, hoots, and whistles. *"Okay, let's roll."*

By noon the troops and their whores are in two birds heading for Vung Tao. Frank's whore, a Chinese girl from Hanoi, is sitting in his lap, drinking red wine from a half-gallon jug. This is the first time he's been with her, having met her in the bar that morning. Some of the men always come back to the same whores. Some consider them their mistresses and keep them in apartments in Cambode Alley, an off-limits area in Saigon.

"Hey, Frank," she yells in his ear, *"you horny, boy?"*

Frank laughs. *"You betcha little ass, baby."*

She giggles. "Angel got real hot pussy for you. You go crazy when you see it, I promise."

Frank keeps laughing. He's happy. The wine has relaxed him, and the girl isn't bad. A little on the skinny side but with large slanted eyes and a cute face.

"Frank, you like big tits?"

He shrugs, knowing she hasn't any.

"That's okay, Frank, you wait, you like Angel boo-coo, okay, Frank?" Her hand moves across his crotch. "Hey, Frank, you got boo-coo stiff dick. Angel make you hot, uh, Frank?"

Across from Frank and Angel, Niles and his whore are already in action. She sits in his lap, facing away from him, her red shorts pulled down to her knees, slowly grinding her hips in a circular motion.

"Hot damn," a soldier laughs. "Sarge's got it up her bunghole."

Everybody yells encouragement.

In the cockpit of the lead helicopter, Major Hobson is looking for a place to land as they fly over Vung Tao.

"Over there," he says, pointing to a large white building near the beach. It's the Grand Hotel, and the management isn't too happy about the sandstorm created by the two choppers; nor is it too happy when the men take over the bar.

By evening the party has moved to the beach, where the men and their whores sit around a fire to drink, pop pills, smoke pot, then wander off into the dark for sex.

"Hey, Frank," Angel says, reaching into her large handbag, "you want some boo-coo good shit?"

Already high on wine, Frank says, "Sure."

She giggles and hands him a very thin, tightly rolled joint. It's mild and burns very slowly. "Hey,

Angel, this's pretty weak shit."

"You want another one, Frank? Angel got plenty more."

"Hold your horses," he says, standing up. "Let's take a walk."

He hasn't walked more than a few feet before it hits him. It feels like a hand is squeezing his brain while his legs are dissolving under him. He sits down and holds his head. "Christ," he groans, "what's in that shit?"

"Boo-coo good shit. You high as kite, Frank."

He holds on to her and pulls himself up. "Let's walk, I've got to clear my head." He staggers, unable to control his gait, and heads for the water. He wades into the surf until it's up to his hips, stands there, staring off into space, waiting to regain control of his body. He's never felt this way before and wonders if the marijuana was laced with some powerful drug whose potency might destroy his brain. The thought terrifies him. He wants to ask Angel about it, but he can't seem to find words, much less actually speak them.

Suddenly, he's standing in front of the Grand Hotel. Angel is nowhere in sight. How has he gotten here? He feels something warm running down his leg and realizes that he's pissing in his pants.

Where the hell's Angel? He staggers sideways, falls to his knees, lets his face drop into the sand. His head swirls, his stomach turns over, and a moment later he's vomiting, his body wracked by agonizing convulsions. His brain has slowed down the passage of time to the point where it seems as if he'll vomit forever.

A moment later, or so it seems, he's behind the Grand Hotel, looking for a place to sleep, no idea how he got there. His brain's playing tricks with *time. Seconds seem like hours, and hours like seconds. Where's Angel? When did he smoke the pot? Yesterday? Last week? Last year? Two minutes ago? He curls up behind stacks of outdoor furniture and closes his eyes. His brain keeps whirling, and he presses his fingers into his closed eyeballs, trying to slow it down.*

Tom Conti lost little time in setting out for Atlantic City. He dismissed the idea of discussing the anonymous call with his boss, a tight-ass, ambitious cop young enough to be Tom's son.

Rolling along on the Atlantic City Expressway, he observed, as was his custom, all the cars on the road, glancing at license plates and drivers. He was almost at the Bader Field Airport exit when he spotted Frank's Buick in front of him. His first thought was to honk and wave, but the cop in him took over and he slowed down, dropping back in the line of traffic.

Moments after his son pulled to a stop at Bocchino's, Tom Conti cruised past the parking lot. He was having a hard time believing his eyes. Bocchino's was a mob hangout. And parked only a few feet away from Frank's Buick was Sal Sabato's white Continental.

10

Other than Allio's occasional use of the premises during the day, Bocchino's was a dinner-only place. Sal Sabato was the sole occupant of the dining room when Frank Conti came through the door. Sabato was sitting alone at a table, smoking a cigar, relaxing in a brown-velour jogging outfit. He looked Frank over carefully, his dark eyes vaguely amused.

"Kind of filled out since you used to bring me pizzas," he said.

Frank nodded. "Where's Allio?"

"Take it easy," Sabato said, standing and motioning for Frank to follow him. He moved slowly, puffing on the cigar, to a closed door. "Ready for the big scene?"

Frank stared at him. They were almost the same height, but Sabato was a lot wider and heavier, a destruction machine under the control of a professional destroyer.

"This'll just take a second," Sabato said as he expertly frisked Frank. He grinned, opened the door, waved him in.

It had been nearly twenty years, but Frank could have recognized Tony Allio at twenty paces. He still looked like the street punk he had been, but now he was an expensively dressed punk whose thick dark hair was streaked with gray at the temples.

"Well, if it ain't my old asshole buddy," Allio said. He turned to Nick Bartoli, seated next to him at a large round table in the middle of the room. "I've known this guy like forever, you know. We was kids together. He joined the fucking army, can you believe that, went off to Vietnam and came back a fucking hero. . . . What was that medal you got, man, for getting your ass shot off?"

"I came down here to get my wife, Allio, not to chat."

"So sit down," Allio said, waving one hand at a chair across the table from him.

"I'll stand," Frank said.

"Suit yourself." Allio turned to Bartoli. "Give hero here the bottom line."

"Well, Conti, it's like this," Nick said. "Your wife's into us for one forty-two five. And that ain't counting the juice."

Allio raised one eyebrow. "Got it on you?"

"What are you talking about?" Frank said, his voice flat.

"I'm talking markers," Bartoli said. "Your wife's a gambling junkie."

"What's that got to do with you?"

"We been bankrolling her action, picking up her markers. How do you think she got all that credit? On your fucking name?"

Frank was silent for a moment. "I don't think I understand the numbers," he said finally, wishing it were true.

Allio leaned back in his chair, folding his arms across his massive chest. "What's the matter, a big

91

banker like you don't understand numbers? That's a hundred and forty-two big ones and a nickel."

"I'd like to see my wife," Frank said. "Where is she?"

Allio shrugged. "Last I heard she was sleeping like a little baby—but, you know, not so innocent. She was a real bad girl yesterday. I'll tell you something, she's some crazy gambler, your wife. Bets like money's gone out of style or something."

Frank heard the words, but anger seemed to have paralyzed his brain. He stood staring at Allio's smug face, his fists clenched at his side.

"I don't have that kind of money," he said. "And I don't understand how you figure in this deal. My wife would never borrow money from the likes of you."

Allio banged the table with both hands. "Watch your fucking mouth," he screamed.

The noise startled Frank. The smirks on Sal's and Nick's faces suddenly disappeared.

"Hey, motherfucker, who the fuck you think you're talking to?" Allio was yelling at the top of his lungs, his face livid, his facial muscles twisting into an ugly mask, the cords in his neck swelling like ropes anchoring his head to his shoulders. "You want to see your fucking wife again, you show respect. You hear me?"

Allio must have heard about Nancy's gambling addiction and somehow seen it as his opportunity for revenge. Frank lowered his voice. "Sorry," he said. "You understand that I'm extremely concerned about my wife's welfare."

"Sure," Allio said, leaning back in the chair, the anger gone as suddenly as it had come.

"I'd like to see her."

92

"First let's see the money," Allio said. "This's strictly a cash-and-carry proposition. You bring me the cash, you carry the merchandise home."

"I told you, I don't have that kind of money. In fact, I don't have any cash or any asset that's not mortgaged, including my house."

Allio seemed amused. "Hey, I say you're good for it. What do you think of that?"

"I think you must know something I don't."

Allio grinned. "Don't sell yourself short, banker. Here you are sitting on a fucking gold mine, and you're telling me you don't know where to go when you need a little gold."

The bank. That was what this was all about. "I can't do that," Frank said.

"Sure you can. And you will, if you want to see your wife again. Listen, I ain't jerking you off. It's either come up with the dough or forget about her. You understand what I'm saying to you?"

Frank pulled a chair away from the table and sat down. "I want to see my wife, talk to her," he said. "How do I know any of this is true unless I talk to her?"

"You don't get it yet, do you?" Allio said. "Let me read you the score here. All you got to worry about is what I tell you. That's the only fucking proof you're gonna get, understand? Am I getting through to you? Am I?"

Frank looked away and nodded.

"Look at me, hero! This's a legit deal. We didn't kidnap your wife. She's just being detained—like she's in hock, you know—until you reclaim her."

This brought loud chuckles from Sal and Nick.

"And don't go to your old man," Allio said. "He can't help you this time." He stopped and stared hard at Frank. "Know what I'm talking about?"

Frank shook his head.

"I was gonna waste you after you broke into my room that night, but that shithead pig father of yours went to my old man and threatened him. Said we was even, and if I touched you he'd waste *me*. And my old man fucking bought it. Some godfather, huh? Chickenshit in his fucking veins. He shipped me here to Atlantic City when this place was like fucking Siberia. Well, I'm running the show now, and you're lucky I let you live. Yeah, that's right, you're alive because I want you alive. I wanted you dead, you'd be dead. And don't ever think I can't do it, either. Lots of guys made that mistake ain't around no more."

Frank nodded. He read the newspapers. Except for three months' time served as a juvenile for a fatal stabbing, all that ever happened to Allio was routine police questioning and prompt release. He was above the law, had held the power of life and death in his hands so long, Frank was convinced, that he'd reached a point where he believed himself to be unstoppable.

All of which meant Frank would have to find a way to get Nancy away from Allio before he could figure out what to do next.

"If I bring you the money, you'll release my wife?"

"Absolutely."

"Release her now, I'll get the money."

"Cash-and-carry," Allio reminded him.

"It's going to take time. I can't walk out of the bank with that much money."

"Sure you can, piece of cake," Allio said, turning to Bartoli. "Give him the scam."

94

Nick leaned forward in his chair and tossed a sheet of paper across the table. "You're the fucking loan officer at your bank, right? So here's the name of a couple of companies. Make loans to them."

"Who are the officers? Will they sign for the loans?"

"No, what the fuck, they're dummy outfits. You make out the loans, forge the names, cash the checks, and bring us the cash."

"It's not that simple. I can't approve a loan and pay out the money on the same day as the application."

"Fake it, stupid. Date the application three months back."

"Okay, enough bullshit," Allio said. "Have the money back here this afternoon. Four sharp. Right here, in this room. If it ain't here, I'll write it off and you can write off your fucking wife. Got it?"

Frank nodded, his mind already working on the problems he'd face at the bank.

The security guard at Ocean Towers was a retired Philadelphia patrolman in his early seventies, stooped but alert, his watery blue eyes still suspicious from the days when he had never taken anything for granted.

Tom remembered he was called Teddy but couldn't for the life of him recall his last name. No matter. Teddy seemed delighted to see him.

"Holy Jesus, Tom, what brings you to this neck of the woods?" Teddy was sitting on a high stool behind an elevated circular reception desk in a lobby of gleaming artificial marble, complete with

95

the imperfections that were supposed to make it look genuine.

"Good to see you again, Teddy. When did you retire from the force?"

"They turned me out to pasture going on six years now."

"Well, looks like you landed a pretty cushy job here. I'm gonna be looking for something myself before long. How'd you swing this?"

Teddy laughed, displaying a sparkling set of new dentures.

"Take it from me, Tom, retirement's for the birds. I sat around the house four years and drove the old lady up the wall. Now I live in this little basement room here five days a week, go home on my days off, so Millie's happy again. Like old times. How's your wife? I forget her name."

"Rachel," Tom said. "She passed away last year."

"Oh, Jesus, Tom, sorry to hear it. So what can I do you for? Here on business, are you?"

"Well, sort of on the qt, Teddy. I'm interested in one of your tenants."

"Kinda out of your bailiwick, ain't you?"

"I sure am."

"Got the okay from the boys at City Hall?"

"Haven't got around to it just yet. Later, if I need to."

"Well, Jesus, Tom, whatever you do, keep me out of it. Anything I tell you is strictly between us. I don't know you and you don't know me and this meeting never took place. Okay?"

"Got you, Teddy. I'm interested in Joey Bucci. Understand he has a condo here. What can you tell me about him."

Teddy nodded, his suspicious blue eyes worried

as he pondered his answer. "Not much, I'm afraid."

"That's okay. Tell me what you know."

"Well, he's up on the thirty-second floor." He flipped through index cards in a metal box. "Here it is, thirty-two twelve, ocean view, one of the prime condos, but I don't think he owns it."

"You mean he rents?"

Teddy shrugged. "Don't know. Lives there with this redhead, little older than him, I think, but really stacked."

"What's her name?"

"Joyce Kresse."

"She selling it?"

"Wouldn't be surprised. She's been around. Hangs out at the Boardwalk Palace, I've seen her at the baccarat table. My guess is she's strictly high-roller pussy."

"What about Bucci, what's his action?"

Teddy blinked and looked away. "Jesus, Tom, you've got to protect me on this one. This guy's connected. Dresses like a TV star, but some of his visitors look like Murder, Inc."

"Recognized any of them?"

Teddy nodded. "Nick Bartoli," he said, his voice barely above a whisper. "Don't want him after my ass. I'm too old to start worrying about that shit."

Tom Conti reached over and patted Teddy on the shoulder. "No cause to worry," he said. "Anybody in the apartment right now?"

"She probably is, but he ain't. Was out all night, in early this morning, lit out of here real fast with a suitcase and a garment bag about an hour or so later. Must have been catching a flight, but I didn't see his limo."

"Joyce didn't leave with him?"

"No, my guess is she's up there now. You never see her in the morning."

"Thanks, Teddy. Think I'll go pay my respects."

"Sure thing, long as you leave me out of it."

Tom grinned. "Leave you out of what? Don't know what you're talking about, stranger."

Joey sat on the edge of the bed, waiting for Nancy to open her eyes.

She hadn't paid too much attention to him; still, with a classy dame like her you never knew what they were thinking until they hit you with it. Then they were like sex maniacs, so hot for it they drooled all over you. Joey'd had his share of society broads. You couldn't work a place like the Palace without meeting them.

This one was definitely a class act. Probably had gone to one of those fancy colleges for women. You could tell she was class by the way she carried herself. Reserved, that debutante look, with the long legs and graceful walk—probably studied ballet.

And her face was something special. High cheekbones, green eyes with a little slant to them, a cute nose, full lower lip, the kind Joey like to nibble on.

Okay, so she had problems. Still she was a woman, and a woman couldn't live by gambling alone. Not in his book.

She was lying on her back, her arms stretched out over her head, the blanket covering her breasts.

What the fuck, if he was careful he could peel off the sheet and blanket and get a real close-up look at her works. He could feel himself getting hard. He leaned forward. Christ, she looked dead to the world, knocked almost comatose by the pills he'd given her when she'd awakened during the night still groggy from Joyce's dosage.

He took hold of the sheet and blanket, slowly peeled them back until they were in a heap at the foot of the bed. She was naked, and she was gorgeous.

He reached out to touch her, then pulled back. Shit, that wasn't his style. Joey Bucci liked his women alive and coming on to him.

As he drove back to Colton, ideas rushed through Frank's head, most of them colliding. He thought of going to his father, but once his father was in on it, he'd never be able to take money from the bank. He'd find himself committed to a course of action that could cost Nancy her life.

She was just a pawn in the game Allio had devised to punish Frank, but he'd kill her if he had to. Twenty years — a long time to wait, but the Sicilian mind, as his father had told him more than once, was incapable of forgetting or forgiving an insult. Mafiosi had been known to wait thirty, forty years, a lifetime.

He'd just have to beat Allio at the game. If he kept the loans under fifty thousand, if he created three or four bogus companies, arranged a repayment schedule that he could handle for a while, he might be able to figure out a way of repaying the loans without the bank's ever finding him out. It wasn't that great a plan, but it was the best he could come up with between the restaurant in Atlantic City and the parking lot of the Colton Sav-

Frank leans back against a fence. On the horizon, dawn is breaking. He looks toward the beach, and it's empty. The guys and their whores have gone. But where? His legs buckle under his weight, and he falls to his knees. Where have they gone all of a sudden? He forces himself to his feet.

Someone is calling his name. He turns, struggles to keep his balance. Top Kick Mike Niles is hurrying toward him.

"There you are," Niles barks. "What the fuck you doing here, man?"

Frank tries to smile. Niles is his buddy—but he isn't sure what kind of message his facial muscles are giving out. "Man, I'm wasted," he says. "Where's everybody?"

"We're shipping out. Get your gear."

Frank reaches down for his M-16 and nearly falls on his face. Niles grabs him by the arm, straightens him up. "You're wasted, all right. Come on, man, I'll help you."

"Thanks," Frank says. "Man, I smoked some bad shit. Feels like I'm losing my fucking mind."

"Don't sweat it, you'll be okay. Let's go."

With Niles's help, Frank makes it to the truck in the parking lot. He stands there, staring at the high tailgate, until hands reach out to pull him in. He lands on his knees and rolls over on his back. His head is whirling again, his vision blurred as he tries to make out the faces of the men in the truck.

He ignores the good-natured ribbing, covers his face with his hands. The words and laughter seem to come from far away. He wants to scream that he needs a doctor, but he can't open his mouth.

One moment the truck is bouncing over a rough road and the next thing he knows there's the Whap Whap Whap of the helicopter's blades and the wind is tearing at his clothing and skin. He's sitting next to Niles on the steel floor of the stripped-down chopper. He looks wildly around him, wondering how the hell he got here.

He tries to get up, but Niles clamps a beefy hand on his shoulder and pushes him back down again. Then he sees Major Hobson squatting near the tailgate. They're getting ready to land. God, he can't go into action in this condition.

He shakes his head, trying to clear it. He knows the minute the tailgate drops, he has to move out fast. The bird hovers only seconds over an LZ. Thank God they don't have to parachute or repel. But you never know about an LZ. There's always the chance it could be hot. More than one chopper has landed in the middle of a gook regiment.

The tailgate opens, and he feels the skids hit the ground. Hands lift him and propel him toward the opening. Men are rushing out, hitting the tailgate at a run, heading for the nearest cover.

"Move your ass!" Niles yells in Frank's ear as he shoves him down the tailgate. Then all hell breaks loose. Somewhere in his befuddled brain, Frank recognizes the heavy popping sound of the gook AK-47. Someone's yelling, "Get down! Hot LZ!"

Frank's first reaction is bewilderment. He tries to run and falls to his knees. A strong hand grips his arm, pulling him to his feet. "Conti, pick up your weapon, move out. Come on, follow me."

Frank recognizes the major's voice and manages to mumble, "Yes, sir."

They head across the clearing toward the heavy fo-

101

liage of the jungle woods some twenty yards away. BNOWP— BNOWP— BNOWP— BNOWP go the AK-47s. WHUUMPZT— WHUUMPZT— WHUUMPZT go the mortars. The earth shakes and shudders; men scream in pain and terror.

A great thudding blast showers him with dirt, knocking him to his knees. He scrambles to his feet, raises his M-16, and begins firing as he runs for the cover of the jungle. As Hobson turns to wave him on, a burst from Frank's rifle smashes into his face just above the bridge of the nose, taking out both eyes and the top of the skull. Frank sees the blood spurt out, completely covering what is left of the major's face, sees him topple over backward, his Swedish K submachine gun flying in the air as he crashes to the ground, his legs folding under him like the legs of a puppet.

11

The doorbell finally penetrated Joyce's sleep, "Oh, shit," she moaned, rolling over on her side. She opened one eye, peered at the alarm clock on the nightstand next to her bed. The red digital numerals read 10:47 A.M. She had taken a couple of sleeping pills in the middle of the night, and her mouth was so dry she could barely swallow.

She reached over for the glass of water next to the alarm clock. Except for the soft glow of the clock, the room was pitch black. She touched a button and the heavy drapes parted a crack, letting in a sliver of gray light from an overcast sky.

The chimes played their tune again. Whoever was pushing that button was persistent. She sat up, yawned, stretched, scratched under both breasts.

She slept naked, and for a moment she wondered if she should put something on. Her clothes were on the floor, scattered where she'd left them the night before. That was one advantage of not having Joey around, couldn't bitch about her being a slob. His closets and chest of drawers looked like they had been arranged by a gay haberdasher. His shoes in trees, his suits in garment bags, his ties on special hangers, his shirts stacked in drawers. Pretty damn strange for someone brought up in a South Philly pigsty.

It was either answer the door or go insane with that cheerful sound. She stumbled to the door, opened it a crack, and peered into a face that looked like it had been chiseled out of granite.

"Joyce Kresse?"

She nodded.

"I'm Tom."

"Yeah? Tom who?"

"Tom Conti. Is Joey here? Nick sent me."

The two names collided in Joyce's head, like puzzle pieces that didn't fit.

"Nick sent you?"

"That's right."

"I don't get it."

"What don't you get?"

"I don't get what you're doing here. You sure Nick didn't say the Palace?"

"Is Joey there?"

"Wait a minute, you got some ID?"

The man produced a policeman's badge. "Will this do for openers?"

"And for closers."

She slammed the door shut and leaned against it. What the hell was going on here? This guy couldn't be Nancy Conti's rich dude husband. Some real screwy shit was going down, and she had nearly put her foot in it. Now the question was: should she or should she not call Nick and tell him about Tom Conti with the granite face and policeman's badge?

Tom always got a kick out of the brass plaque in the lobby of City Hall in Atlantic City. It honored

104

the five city commissioners responsible for the new building erected in 1968. Four of the five commissioners, two of them former mayors, had ended up in prison for extortion and bribery. The dedication was signed "Frank 'Hap' Farley," the city's political boss for thirty years and the only boss in the last hundred years who hadn't ended up in the slammer—not because he was honest, but because he was smarter.

Some town, Tom Conti thought as he made his way to the wing that housed the police department. Tom knew several of the cops on a first-name basis, including Lieutenant Jim Ferris, head of the organized crime squad. What he didn't know was how far he could trust any of them.

Tall and skinny, Jim Ferris had always impressed Tom as a high-strung man struggling to appear low-key. Tom tapped lightly on the open door of a glass cubicle; Ferris looked up from a batch of papers and waved him in.

"Come on in, Tom, sit down, be with you in a minute." Tom took a chair facing the desk and waited while Ferris stapled papers together, tossed them into the top drawer of his desk, then leaned back in his chair. "What's up?"

"Not much. Was in town, thought I'd drop in, pick your brain a little."

Ferris nodded. "And I've got a few questions for you on the Bobby Scolieri hit. You investigating that?"

Tom shrugged. "The Round House has taken over, but naturally I'm curious. My guess is Allio's behind it."

"I wouldn't bet against it. Got any suspects?"

"No, but I was wondering about Nick Bartoli."

105

"The Bat? That fucking animal. That whole bunch living up there in Longport, like rats in a nest. You got the background on him?"

"Well, I know he's been involved in a lot of heavy stuff, at least seven hits, no convictions."

"Let me tell you about this particular animal. His mother's Allio's sister. Her husband was Eddie Bartoli, very close to the old man, Vince Allio. When Tony Allio had his old man hit, he had Eddie taken out too, didn't want him coming back at him.

"Nick was a teenager then, but he knew the score. In fact, I hear he helped set up the hit on his own father. As for Nick's mother, I also hear she knows that baby brother Tony killed their daddy and that her own fucking son killed her husband." He swung back in his chair. "Now that's some weird family, wouldn't you say?"

Tom shrugged. "I've heard about Tony putting the hit on his own father, but never saw any real evidence to support it."

Ferris grinned. "Close the door, Tom, and I'll play you a little tape you might find interesting."

He opened a drawer filled with cassette tapes, found the one he was looking for, then took a small recorder from another drawer. "Its a conversation between Sal Sabato and Funzi Cocchiaro, a nice little friendly chat between two killers."

Ferris punched a button on the recorder. Silence, and then Tom recognized Funzi Cocchiaro's voice.

"And that was your first hit?"

Sal Sabato burst out laughing. "Man, I'll never forget that fucking day long as I live. Shit, that was maybe twenty-five, thirty years . . ."

Ferris punched the fast forward button.

". . . Talking about the old man brings up memories," Funzi was saying. "I loved that guy in the old days when I was first made. I used to look up to him, you know?"

Sal: Yeah, well, we all get old sooner or later.

Funzi: Sure, but we don't all get stupid. I remember trying to get him to see Atlantic City was our chance to get ourselves set up for life, but he wasn't buying, afraid of the fucking heat, he was. Had them old fucking ways and wasn't getting out of them, know what I mean? Them old guys, they get the fucking money for themselves, hide it in the fucking mattress like squirrels with nuts, live like fucking peasants just off the boat. Shit, the old man lived in the same row house in that shit-bucket street all his fucking life. What good's the money? I ask you. I says, "Vince, I've been poor all my fucking life. Whatever I've got, I had to steal. So I'm getting old fast, and I still ain't got no big money. I want to enjoy my fucking life, make my killing when the killing's good." See, Tony's with me, we're trying to get the old man to move in on Atlantic City before the New York families get their fucking hooks in there. But the old man won't listen to Tony either. Starts shouting, "Forget Atlantic City, don't bring it up no more." So that was that. No talking to him. He's made his fucking bundle, so he don't give a shit about us.

Sal: I know, kind of funny just the same when you think about it. My first hit was a kid whose father wanted him dead, and now, you know, all them years later, I hit the old man and it's Tony, his own fucking kid, that orders the hit. . . .

Ferris turned off the recorder and leaned back in his chair. "Evidence enough for you, Tom?"

"Christ, where'd you get that tape?"

"I have my sources," Ferris said, grinning.

"You've got one that says Tony had Nick help set up his own father?"

"No. But that's not to say it doesn't exist. You'd be surprised how much shit the Feds have on them. All illegal, can't use any of it."

Tom remembered the old man's face when Tom delivered his ultimatum: "As God is my witness, if Tony harms my son I will kill him." Vincenzo Allio's dark eyes had searched Tom's for a long time. "Don't worry about it," he said, waving his hands in dismissal. He'd kept his word, too. As Mafia dons go, Vincenzo Allio had been better than most. During the forty-odd years he'd headed the Philadelphia family, there had been fewer than a dozen gang murders. The old man had been a shrewd manipulator, getting his way through cunning rather than violence. Somehow, in his old age, he'd forgotten that the purpose for the very existence of the family was to make money for its members. And he'd forgotten his own origins, how as a young and hungry mafioso he had fought his way to the top by killing whoever stood in his way, the ancient way of succession for kings and gangsters. Worst of all, he'd forgotten to protect his back from his own son, inviting a fate not even a godfather deserved.

"What about Tony's mother?" Tom asked. "You think she knows he hit the old man?"

"Wouldn't surprise me. That old bitch's a real spider. Runs the Longport compound just the way little

Tony wants it. He put the property in her name to fuck over the IRS. The story is, Tony bought the place for a hundred thousand with only ten down. Now, you tell me, you've seen the place. Worth a couple million if a penny. Hell, he probably spent that much renovating it, but he did it with the companies he controls, and there's no record of any of those expenses. So the whole clan lives there, Tony and his wife and his two boys from a previous marriage — his first wife died suddenly, when he fell for his second wife. Then there's his mother and her three brothers with all their kids, some married with kids of their own. And don't forget the army of bodyguards. Incredible. Must cost a fortune just to keep them all in pasta."

Tom shook his head. "Must be a happy household, with all the incestuous murders going on."

"Yeah, our own Sicilian soap opera."

"How about your sources, they got any bugs in there?"

"They've tried, but there's an electronics expert living on the property, sweeps the place regularly. Important calls are made from pay phones — Tony runs around with a bag full of coins. Wish I had one of those laser devices cops have on TV shows. I'd have that baby on him twenty-four hours a day."

"Who's hanging around Bartoli these days? Any new recruits?"

"The usual assortment of young punks. Anybody in mind?"

Tom scratched his head. "Well, as a matter of fact, I saw Nick coming out of Ocean Towers this morning. He was with Sal Sabato and a good-looking kid, probably late twenties, never saw him before."

"Sharp dresser?"

"Very sharp."

"Joey Bucci. Started out with a call-girl service here, now hangs around the Boardwalk Palace. Maybe loan-sharking, maybe pushing cocaine to high rollers and entertainers."

"Anything heavy?"

"Naw, I'd say lightweight. You know, those pretty boys don't like to get their hands dirty."

"Got a mug shot?"

"No, but I've got a good surveillance shot. Make you a copy?"

"Thanks."

"Anything going down on him?"

Tom shook his head. "Just trying to keep tabs on the players."

"Goddamn animals, that's all they are. Well, at least they're knocking each other off. If we take it easy, kind of look the other way, maybe they'll blow themselves away until we're left with lightweights like Joey Bucci."

Nancy was moaning in her sleep, and Joey wondered if she was having a wet dream. Maybe she knew he had uncovered her and was dreaming about making it with him.

The telephone rang. He hurried into the living room, his erection deflating like a punctured balloon.

"Joey?" It was Joyce. "Do you know a Tom Conti?"

"Naw—unless he's this broad's husband?"

"I don't think so. He's a cop. He was just up here looking for you."

"For me, are you kidding?"

"Said Nick sent him. What's going on?"

"Have you called Nick?"

"No. Want me to?"

"Yeah. Tell him I said to call."

"Will do. How's Nancy this morning?"

"How the hell would I know, she's still out like a light. Nick gave me some pills, keep her mellow until her husband shows up."

"She's had enough sleep, Joey. What she needs is food. Get her something, maybe some soup, something light at first."

"Hey, what's with you? She's a little old for you to be playing mama."

"And lay off her. I told you last night, I mean it."

"I heard you, for Chrissake."

Joyce's voice softened. "Thanks, lover. Otherwise, how're they hanging this morning?"

He laughed. "Pretty tight, babe. Need you to loosen 'em up."

"How sweet. I can pop over and—"

"Stay where you are, babe, and keep your motor running. I'll be there soon as I can."

Nancy screamed. Frank was gone—he'd never been there, she'd been dreaming. Her head throbbed, her throat ached. She opened her eyes. Joey Bucci was standing beside the bed, looking down at her, a puzzled expression on his handsome face.

"What's wrong? You okay?"

Nancy pulled the blanket up to her chin. "What are you doing here?"

"Jesus, you scared the shit out of me, screaming like that. What's the matter with you?"

111

"I was having a nightmare. Where's Joyce?"

"She's out right now, she'll be back soon. Why don't you go back to sleep?"

"Please, leave the room, I want to get dressed."

"What for?"

"I want to go home. My God, what time is it?"

"Around noon. Listen, take my advice, go back to sleep."

Nancy sat up. "Now, you get out of here. I told you. I want to get dressed. Call the limousine, I'm going home."

"Sorry, sweetheart, but you're not going anywhere until your husband gets here and pays off your markers." He smiled. "He's gonna be unhappy to the tune of one hundred forty-two thousand five hundred smackers."

Nancy held her hands against her ears. "Stop it!"

"Don't get so upset. Everything's cool."

"You're crazy. Who ever heard of a casino holding someone prisoner until . . . they paid their losses? You're making this up."

"It ain't me, sweetheart. It's Allio. Your husband's settling accounts with him today."

"Tony Allio? The gangster?"

"Hey, don't let him hear you call him that. Tony's your own personal banker."

"What do you mean?"

"I mean he backed your action. You don't think the Palace would give you that kind of credit without the okay of someone important, do you?"

"You're crazy! I want to get out of here." There were tears in her eyes and a hysterical edge to her voice.

"You're staying, baby, until I get word your husband has settled the account. So you might as well go back to sleep. Unless you'd like to fool around a little. After all, we're alone here. Who's to know? I guarantee you, you'll enjoy it." He leaned over the bed until his face was only a few inches from hers. "Here, give us a little kiss."

"Get away from me!" She reached for the sheet to cover her body and edged off the bed. "I'm getting out of here."

Joey grabbed her by the shoulders and spun her back onto the bed. "Stay there, you dizzy cunt. And don't move."

"You'll go to jail for this," she hissed.

"You lay there and shut up about jail. Or so help me, I'll bust your fucking face wide open."

12

Chiara was waiting to talk to her son. His wife, Stella, needed some straightening out. Here at the Longport compound, Chiara ran the household operation. Only when people defied her queenly will did Antonio step in to exercise his kingly prerogatives.

Chiara enjoyed wielding power. For too many years she had been nothing more than a baby maker and a servant to her husband, the *pezzo grosso*, the big shot who treated her like dirt. She had given birth to four girls and finally a boy, Antonio, her baby, the apple of her eye.

As a girl, Chiara's skin had been so fair that her mother called her "my white rose." She had been a white rose in the thorn garden of the tiny Sicilian mountain village where Vincenzo Allio found her. She was fourteen, the most beautiful girl in all the villages of that mountain; he was nine years older, a city boy from the ancient metropolis of Agrigento.

Vincenzo was short, his head covered with tight black curls, his eyes blacker even than his hair. He was a smooth talker, a real charmer who spun fairy tales about America and how he was going to conquer this new world and lay his great fortune at

Chiara's dainty feet. His stories enthralled her, and in her rush to escape her dreary existence she soon lost her heart to his dreams.

Vincenzo took his bride to South Philadelphia, where he opened a small grocery store. For a while it looked to Chiara like the new world was going to conquer Vincenzo and not the other way around. When a Black Hand extortion ring that preyed on Italian immigrants started after him, Vincenzo went to the police. His testimony led to the ring boss's conviction. That was in 1929, at the height of the Roaring Twenties. Two years later police found a five-hundred-gallon still in the basement of his grocery store and caught Chiara's brother, Rocco, running from the store. Both men denied any knowledge of the bootlegging operation and were found not guilty.

Vincenzo was soon permitted to operate his own numbers book, which gave him the opportunity to demonstrate his organizational skill to Michele Bulgarino, his sponsor in the Philadelphia family. Five years later a police raid on one of his numbers books netted sixty thousand numbers slips as evidence. Convicted of operating an illegal lottery, he was fined five hundred dollars and placed on two years' probation. Several other arrests followed for various crimes, but Vincenzo never spent a night in jail.

Promoted to *capo regime*, he joined forces with two other capos. When Bulgarino fled to Sicily to escape prison in 1940, Vincenzo stepped into his shoes and stayed in them until his own son blew him out of them.

Chiara, who knew nothing, had her suspicions nonetheless. What she didn't have was regrets: every night, as soon as Vincenzo came home, she'd had to

115

run to the basement to fill a small pitcher from a barrel of homemade dago red—the first of many nightly trips. While he puffed on a little cigar and swilled the wine, she'd remove his shoes and socks, wash his feet, dry and massage them, do everything but kiss them.

At supper the children had sat quietly and waited for the old man to take his place at the kitchen table before anyone could eat. Chiara filled his plate, cut his meat, buttered his bread, kept quiet while he tasted the food, smacking his lips several times before saying, without fail, "Arrrgh, same old *porco* shit."

Even as a small boy, Antonio had told her he wanted to kill his father for the way he treated her. But in front of the old man he never showed his anger. He'd have been cold cocked right there on the spot. Many were the nights Antonio was awakened by a barrage of blows because he'd forgotten to perform a chore. Of the four girls, three were now in mental institutions and the fourth, Dorotea, who was Nick's mother, lived in fear of the old man even after his death.

Although Vincenzo was worth millions, they continued to live in one of the roughest sections of South Philadelphia. That was the first thing that changed after Antonio took over. Now they lived like royalty—except, of course, they couldn't have servants, and the women of the household had to perform the domestic chores along the lines laid out by the queen.

Which was why Chiara needed to talk to her son. Stella was still in bed, which meant that her duties fell upon the overworked shoulders of Chiara and Dorotea.

Chiara waited in the breakfast room, nursing a

cold espresso. Reached on the intercom in the library, Antonio had promised to be out in a few minutes. That was nearly an hour ago. Chiara had a million things to do, and here she was waiting like a patient in a doctor's office to talk to her own son about his own lazy wife.

The truth was, Chiara had never liked Stella. She had stolen Antonio from the mother of his children. Maybe she was prettier—younger, certainly—than his first wife, but she was *stupido*. She knew nothing about cooking or housecleaning. All she ever wanted to do was lie around in bed all day, watching trashy soap operas on television. The only thing that girl liked doing was to go out and spend money on clothes. She dressed up around the house like that slut on "Dynasty," shamelessly revealing herself. And when Antonio grabbed at her, she just giggled like a foolish schoolgirl. She had no *dignità*.

When Allio came into the breakfast room, Chiara smiled and held her arms out to him. He came to her, leaned over, and she planted a kiss on his forehead.

"What's up, Ma?" he said, straightening up.

"It's Stella again," the old woman said, trying to keep the anger out of her voice. "Another cold, she always got cold. I don't know how she get so many colds."

Allio shrugged. "Weak *costituzione*, Ma."

"Me and your sister have to do all the work."

"I know, Ma, but you don't want her spreading her cold around. I sure don't want you catching it."

"This is big house, Antonio."

"I know."

"And you want everything kept spotless clean, everything done *perfetto*."

"That's right."

117

"It's not fair that she lays around in bed all day while we work like dogs to make things nice for you and your friends."

"The woman is sick, Ma. What do you want from me?"

"Talk to her, Antonio. She listens to you."

"Okay, okay, I'll talk to her. All right?"

Chiara smiled. *"Grazie."*

When Allio came into the bedroom, Stella was stretched out in front of the television watching "Days of Our Lives."

"Why ain't you out there helping Ma?" Allio said as he approached the bed.

"I'm sick," she said, switching off the television with the remote control. "I've got a fever. Feel my forehead."

He reached down and felt it. "Don't seem hot to me."

"Well, I've got a sore throat," she said, opening her mouth and sticking out her tongue.

He grinned as he leaned over to peer down her throat. She was so damn cute he couldn't really get mad at her when she looked like that, so young and helpless, like a little kid. After all, she *was* just a kid, barely in her twenties, only seventeen when he married her.

"Your throat looks okay to me," he said. "Come on, get your ass out of bed. It's not fair to dump all that work on Ma and Dorotea."

Tears came into her eyes. "I want to go out, go somewhere, do something," she said, sniffling. "I feel like a prisoner, stuck behind these walls, with guards on the gate—they won't let me out unless they get your permission. And your mother and sister are after me all the time, do this, do that, I never get a moment to myself unless I tell them I'm sick and come here to my room."

"Come on, Stel, cut it out."

"Why can't we have servants? You're rich—rich people have servants."

"I told you before, I don't want no strangers in the compound."

She buried her face in the pillow and sobbed, her shoulders trembling.

He reached down and touched her head. Her hair felt like silk under his fingers. "Ah, Christ," he said, stepping back, "I don't have time for this shit. Okay, stay in bed, take the day off."

When Allio came out of the bedroom, Chiara was waiting for him down the hall. "She's got a cold, all right," he said. "I told her to take it easy today. Sorry, Ma. Gotta run. Ciao."

It was ten minutes to four when Frank Conti reached Bocchino's. In his right hand was a briefcase with $142,500 in hundred-dollar bills. Sal Sabato was waiting for him at the same table, smoking a cigar, but this time he wasn't alone. Waiters and busboys were setting up tables for the evening's dinner crowd.

Sabato stood, led the way to the banquet room, opened the door, and waved Frank in. Allio and Bartoli were in the same chairs around the table. Seated to Allio's left was Funzi Cocchiaro.

Sabato lifted the briefcase out of Frank's hand, dumped the stacks of bills on the table, then turned to Frank.

"Okay, take off your jacket, loosen your tie, open your shirt, unbuckle your belt, drop your pants."

The examination was thorough. Sabato stepped

back and nodded to Allio. "He's clean."

"Okay, hero, you can get dressed now," Allio said. "Just making sure your old man didn't wire you for sound."

"Where's my wife?"

Allio turned to Bartoli. "Count it and separate it like I told you." He pointed his index finger at Frank and cocked his thumb. "What's your old man doing down here, running all over town, asking questions about Joey Bucci?"

"How would I know?" Frank said. "Who's Joey Bucci?"

"Listen, hero, you talked to your old man, your wife's dead. You understand?"

"If I'd talked to him, I wouldn't be here with the money, would I?"

"Knowing what a hard-ass he is, you're probably right."

Bartoli had separated the bills into two piles.

"Got all of it?"

"Yeah, he's a good boy."

"Okay. Put a hundred grand back in the case."

Bartoli dropped the bills in the briefcase, closed it, pushed it across the table toward Frank.

"That's for you, hero," Allio said.

"What's that supposed to mean? All I want is my wife."

"Take the money. I've got a little job for you in Tijuana."

"Forget it! We had a deal. I'm here with the money, and I want my wife."

Allio shrugged. "So I lied."

"I didn't go through all this to play games. Where is she?"

"Never mind about your wife," Allio said. "First things first. You take this hundred grand and deliver

120

it to the address on that piece of paper on the table there. It's a garage on the main drag in Tijuana. El Vagon, it's called, one of them body shops for smugglers. Just give them your name, they're expecting you and the money. They'll have a car for you to drive back over the border."

Allio leaned forward. "Now, there'll be a few kilos of primo coke in secret compartments. They'll show you where, so when you get to San Diego you take it out, rent a car, and drive it back here. If you push it, you can make it back in four days. Bring it to Harper's Warehouse at the corner of Melrose and Maine. You got it? Funzi will fill you in on the rest. Now, you do this right, get back here safely with the coke, and we'll take real good care of your wife."

Frank stood there shaking his head.

"What's the matter, hero," Allio said, smiling. "Going too fast for you?"

"You think this is funny? What's funny was my thinking a punk like you would keep his word."

"So what do you want from me?" Allio said with a shrug. "I'm in business here. Lots of action in this town. It's not all at the crap tables, you know. A little coke here, a little coke there, it all adds up. You make a great fucking mule, man. Who'd ever suspect someone like you of moving shit? You're perfect."

"Forget it, I'm not going."

"Oh, yes, you are."

"Look, you've got the money. That was the deal, and that's as far as it goes. You've already turned me into an embezzler. You're not going to make me a dope runner. Forget it."

"Wait a fucking minute—hold it!" Allio's high-pitched voice rose. "Now let me tell you something, Mr. Tough Guy Hero. In the old days, if you stole, they chopped off your hands. Right? Those guys didn't fuck around, and I don't either. Your wife gambled with my money, and now you're trying to fuck with me. Forget it, I'll cut her fucking fingers off one at a time until they're all gone, then we go with hands, then arms, you know, until you get the whole package back in little pieces. Is that what you want, Mr. Vietnam Hero? If it is, you're gonna get it. If it ain't—if you want to get the whole package back in *one* piece—you make the trip. That's the fucking bottom line. So let's see how tough you really are."

Frank nodded. "When do I leave?"

"You're booked for tomorrow afternoon. Funzi will drive you to the airport, lay it all out for you. You guys bunk together tonight, a hotel room at the airport, no phone calls, and after he puts you on the plane, you're on your own. You want to fuck up, go ahead, but start watching your mail for packages. And if you think your old man's gonna get me, forget about it. It ain't gonna happen."

Funzi stood up and came over to Frank. "This way out, banker."

Saturday afternoon Frank Conti, wearing a safari jacket with its numerous pockets stuffed with a thousand one-hundred-dollar bills, walked through the security check at the Philadelphia airport. Funzi followed him, two passengers behind.

Frank's ticket was for first class, which had surprised him when Funzi handed it to him in the hotel room on Friday night.

"See, banker," Funzi had said, "we're not bad guys. We're businessmen like you."

Frank had ignored him, staring blindly at the tele-

122

vision, feeling as unreal as if it were he on the screen.

At the departure gate Funzi took the seat next to Frank, his dark, ugly face impassive until the doors opened and the passengers started to board. He stood then and took Frank's arm. "A guy named Gus's gonna meet you in Los Angeles, he'll be at the San Diego departure gate. You do what he tells you, understand?"

Frank nodded.

Funzi suddenly grinned. "Don't worry about it, banker," he said, giving Frank a friendly pat on the back. "You're gonna make a terrific mule."

Frank keeps running. He has to get out of there. Then he's in the jungle, tumbling through brush, tripping and falling, crawling and getting up again, until he can't go any farther. He falls headlong and crawls to a large rotting branch, pressing himself tightly against it, burrowing his face into the ground, his body into the soft earth. He has to sleep, to make everything go away, but when he closes his eyes he sees the blood spurting from the major's head. It's a bad dream, a crazy nightmare created by the pot. Probably laced with acid. That's it. He's still somewhere on the beach in Vung Tao. Pretty soon the nightmare will end — it has to — and everything will be back to normal.

Finally, he sleeps. When he wakes, he's not on the beach in Vung Tao; he hears the excited voices of gook soldiers coming from what seems only a few yards away. Slowly, ever so slowly, he turns his head and opens his eyes.

There's nobody there. He can't understand it. The voices seem so near. He begins crawling toward the voices, slowly inching his way along the jungle floor, stopping every few seconds to make sure he isn't being observed. Where's the rest of the Recondo team? Gradually, he realizes that he's moving toward the LZ and starts crawling faster.

The first thing he sees when he reaches the clearing is the naked body of Major Hobson hanging from a tree. Large sections of skin have been stripped from his chest and stomach. Frank recoils in horror, burying his face in his hands. Slowly, he opens his eyes and looks again. The major's testicles have been sliced off and jammed into his mouth.

"Barbaric bastards," Frank swears under his breath — then the full panorama hits him. Recondo men are hanging from trees circling the LZ. There's Johnson, Weitzel, Niles, Freach — the whole team, all twenty-five members, all dead.

Frank's teeth begin chattering, and then his whole body is caught in a spasm, arms and legs convulsing so violently that he's afraid the gooks assembled at the far edge of the clearing will hear the sound. They stand at attention, listening to an officer who's talking and gesticulating, most of them younger than Frank — who, at barely twenty, feels like an old man.

His brain is still befuddled, but Frank knows that his only chance of survival is to hide and wait for the chopper to return — Special Forces would never abandon twenty-six men. But the gooks know this too, which means they'll be waiting with another ambush, which, of course, is exactly what Special Forces expects them to do. So where does all this leave him?

13

Patrolman Albert Ricupa had no problem picking Joey Bucci out of the batch of photos Tom Conti handed him.

"Yeah, Lieutenant, that's the guy I saw in Sal's Lincoln."

"Positive?"

"Absolutely."

Sergeant Brecato clapped Ricupa on the back. "Good going, Al," he said, leaning over Ricupa's shoulder to take another look at the surveillance photograph Lieutenant Ferris had given Tom. "Any luck on the street?"

"I've talked to everybody and his brother, and nobody saw nothing. Same old story."

"Tell us about it," Brecato said.

Tom sat at his desk watching the two men, his eyes veiled. He was pleased with the identification of Joey Bucci and with the possibility that the anonymous phone tip about Bucci was correct, but he was worried about Frank. He'd called several times, had even driven over, but there was no one at home. He had talked to the Stovers, Frank's next-door neighbors, only to learn that they hadn't seen Nancy since a limousine picked her up on Thursday and that Frank had been gone since Friday morning.

Tom stood up. "I'm going home. Al, for the time

being, keep this under your hat. I don't know what I've got here. When I find out, I'll let you know. You've made a proper identification, picked his mug out of a stack—no hesitation, let's remember that if it becomes important later on."

"You bet, Lieutenant," Ricupa said. "No report, right?"

"Right," Tom said as he walked out of the office.

Frank had nearly three hours to kill in Los Angeles. The terminal for his connecting flight to San Diego was at the opposite end of Los Angeles International Airport, and he took his time getting there, stopping off for coffee at one of the restaurants. It was Saturday night, and the place was jammed with travelers. He thought about his father and wondered if he should call him. If he did, he'd have to keep it short.

Tom was at the kitchen table, drinking lukewarm coffee and puffing on a cigar. God, how long since he had smoked a cigar? He couldn't remember. Somebody at the office had given it to him, he couldn't remember who. Somebody must have had a baby. A boy, no doubt. Not many cops gave cigars for daughters.

Back in the old days, he had smoked a cigar after dinner. Rachel had liked the aroma of a good cigar. Gradually, he had gotten out of the habit, so why was he puffing away like a maniac on one right now?

"That goddamn phone better ring," he said aloud, "and it better be you on the line, sonny boy, if you know what's good for you. I'm getting goddamned

126

mad, being kept in the dark like some lousy stranger."

He stopped and shook his head. He was losing his marbles, talking to himself out loud like that, no question about it. "Fuck it!" he yelled. "Ring, you lousy goddamn phone!"

The phone rang. He stared at it as if it were a snake coiled to strike, then snatched up the receiver.

"Pop, I've only got a couple of minutes. I'm in L.A., catching a flight to San Diego—"

"Wait, wait just a goddamn minute," Tom yelled. "What're you doing in L.A.?"

"Bank business, Pop. Tell you about it when I get back."

"Not so fast. What bank business?"

"Banking convention in San Diego."

"Yeah, well, why didn't you tell me before you left?"

"Couldn't reach you, Pop. Had to run, I was a last-minute substitution."

"Where were you last night?"

"I'll explain when I get back."

"You'd better explain right now what you were doing at Bocchino's Friday morning if you know what's—"

"Bank business, Bocchino's applying for a loan on his restaurant. What's the problem?"

"Where's Nancy?"

"In Boston, visiting an old school chum. Sorry, Pop, got to run or I'll miss my plane. Take care."

"Just a—" The line went dead.

When Frank reached the check-in counter at the gate, all the passengers had boarded except one, a tall, gaunt man wearing light blue cotton pants and a red polo shirt.

"Hey, you Frank Conti?"

"Yes."

"Where the fuck you been, man? Let's go, want to miss the flight?"

The man pushed Frank into the tunnel leading to the plane. The stewardess smiled at Frank, looked at his boarding pass, and pointed to a window seat in first class. The man in the red polo shirt slipped into the seat next to Frank's.

"I'm Gus," he said, "I'm here to brief you on your mission."

"Mission? I already know my mission."

"Yeah, well, did you know we're sharing a room at the Holiday Inn?"

"Sounds great."

"Never mind with the sarcasm."

Gus was silent until they were airborne. "I hate fucking takeoffs and landings," he said.

Frank looked out the window at the vast array of lights outlining the Los Angeles sprawl. The wheels had barely left the ground before the stewardess was offering them champagne or cocktails. Frank accepted the champagne; Gus asked for Scotch.

"Now listen," Gus said, after their drinks came, "this is important. You pick up the shit at El Vagon on Revolution Street, that's right downtown, the main drag, at five o'clock Sunday afternoon. See, that's when the Caliente racetrack empties out. The cars are lined up for miles. The custom agents go ape, they're so fucking busy they don't have time to check everybody. A guy like you, they don't look at twice. You'll go through like shit through a tin horn."

"Excuse me," Frank said, standing up and stepping over Gus's legs.

"Where you going?"

"I'm going to walk the rest of the way."

"Okay, wise guy, suit yourself. See you when we land."

Frank walked to the rear of the plane. The last six rows were empty; he took a window seat in the last row, released the reclining lever, and stretched out. Anything was better than having to listen to Gus. As for sharing a room with him, he'd see about that when the time came. For now he didn't want to think about Gus. Or Nancy, or his father, and certainly not Allio and his hoods. He closed his eyes, hoping the drone of the engines would lull him to sleep.

14

He came awake the moment the stewardess touched his shoulder.

"Please adjust your seat and fasten your seat belt," she said. "We're coming in for a landing."

"Thanks." Frank released the seat lever and fastened his seat belt. He looked out the window and saw ground only a few feet below, but he couldn't see any runway lights. Somewhere he had heard that San Diego's Lindbergh Municipal Airport had a short runway; the pilot must be planning to use all of it. He felt a bump. The 727 shot up, too fast, maneuvered—much too fast—to the left, then the right. A horrendous shudder sent overhead luggage bounding into the aisles and seats. Frank's body lurched and flailed in all directions, as if someone had him by the throat and was shaking him like a rag doll. His teeth chattered; at any moment, he knew, his neck would snap.

A series of rapid explosions was followed by a deafening screech of tearing metal. A second later, Frank was upside down in his seat. There was a whooshing sound, a solid sheet of flames shooting up the aisle toward him—

The last thing he felt was the heat.

The last thing he thought was *I'm dead.*

* * *

He was out on the grass, lying on his side, still strapped in his seat. The tail section of the 727 lay smoldering fifty yards away. The rest of the plane, now an inferno, was sliding and spinning crazily down the runway, spewing fire and metal fragments everywhere like shrapnel. The noise was deafening, the heat unbearable.

He checked quickly to see if he was burned, if he still had all his parts. Satisfied that he was in one piece, he unbuckled his belt and ran. He had to get out of there before the gooks came back. His buddies were dead. Nobody inside that plane could have survived. Nobody except him had escaped the flames.

He felt dizzy, disoriented as he ran away from the plane and the eerie light created by the flames, ran searching for the cover of the jungle, into the cover of darkness at the far end of the field. His only thought was escape. A seven-foot wooden fence shot up suddenly in front of him, and he ran blindly into it, bouncing off, looking around him wildly. Regaining his bearings, he ran alongside the fence, looking for an opening, finally reached up with both hands and vaulted over the fence, landing on all fours.

Voices. Less than a hundred feet away, men were running to the fence and climbing over it, confirming his suspicions of an enemy attack. In the distance he heard sirens, and he crouched against the fence, trembling, his mind furiously trying to sort out the names of the men in his unit who had been in the plane with him. What about Major Hobson? Was he on board? Had he gone down with the others? He shuddered. A moment later he had slipped to the ground, unconscious.

* * *

Frank starts crawling backward. He hasn't moved more than a few feet when he notices that the gooks have dispersed and are scampering into the jungle. He looks up, sees a familiar glint of silver as a Phantom Jet rolls into a high arc and dives straight down toward the clearing. Frank watches, enthralled, as the first 250-pound bomb drops only a few feet from the spot where the gooks have been standing. The earth shakes, and the shock waves roll over him like a giant cresting ocean swell. It isn't the first time that he's felt the power of the bomb, but it's never been more welcome.

Now he knows just what is going to happen. After the bomb raid, the Hook will come in real fast. It's up to him to be ready. Which means he has to stay on the edge of the clearing and take his chances on the bombs' missing him. Holding his helmet tightly against his head with one hand, he lies flat, grasping at the ground with the other hand as bomb after bomb shakes him to the very marrow of his bones. Looking up, he sees huge balls of fire and trees flying in the air.

It seems like it'll go on forever, but in fact it's over in a matter of minutes. A moment later, he hears the Dhup Dhup Dhup of the Hook. He scrambles to his feet and begins running into the clearing, stumbling over roots and loose branches, getting up again, only to trip and land flat on his face.

He sees the Hook hit the ground with its tailgate open and screams, "Wait!" Scrambling again to his feet, he drops the M-16 and runs full tilt. When he reaches the tailgate, the chopper is already two feet off the ground. He leaps headlong inside, rolls over on his back.

Before he can move he hears the pinging sound of bullets ripping holes into the chopper's metal skin. He cries out, "Go, go, go, go — Tommy, get out of here!" The chopper has to get beyond the range of the AK-47s

*and the Soviet SKSs before they turn it — and him — into
a sieve.*

*The chopper shudders, shaking Frank's every bone as
it moves sideways at treetop level.*

Tommy screams. "Jump, we're on fire!"

Frank looks up, incredulous. "Jump?"

"Bail out, we're over water. It's only — "

*There's an ear-shattering explosion followed by a ball
of fire that whooshes through the helicopter's cockpit,
turning it into an inferno. As flames shoot into the
cargo bay, Frank scurries on all fours toward the opened
tailgate. The heat makes his blood feel like it's boiling
and his skin like it's going to melt. He feels the flames
on his legs and screams with the pain. By then he has
reached the opening, but before he can jump out there's a
brilliant flash, and he feels his body lifting and tumbling through the air. He can see his flaming legs, a
human pinwheel flipping through space, but he feels no
pain and hears no sound.*

*Frank lands on his back in three feet of water in a
rice paddy, sinks into the muddy bottom. He comes up
gasping for air. The chopper, by now a gigantic fireball, disappears into the jungle. Moments later it
crashes, sending up a final fireball.*

*Frank knows he's finished. Blood oozes from his
nose, mouth, eyes. He tries to stand up and his legs
collapse beneath him. Falling and getting up again, he
makes his way out of the rice paddy and into the jungle. He knows the gooks are looking for the chopper.
Maybe they didn't see him fall. If they think he died in
the crash, they'll leave him alone.*

*He looks down at his legs. All he can see is charred
meat and blood. He can smell the burnt flesh, though,
and for the first time he feels the terrible pain. He's not
going to make it. He's going to die here, in this miserable hellhole. A moment later he passes out.*

133

When he comes to, it's dark. Quiet, except for the usual jungle noises. They aren't looking for him. He sits up. He can barely see the outline of his legs in the darkness, but he can smell them and the smell of them scares him more than the look of them did. They feel like they're still on fire. He tries to stand up, but his legs won't support him.

One thing is in his favor. He has enough water and rice and dried fish in his rucksack to last him a week. Sweat rolls down his face, stinging his eyes, blinding him. He starts crawling through the jungle, dragging his legs against the rough terrain, the pain excruciating. He grits his teeth and keeps going. "I will not die here," he keeps repeating under his breath.

He has spent so much time in these jungles that he has a sense of the general direction other A-teams are operating in. By the third day he loses all track of time. He has seen plenty of gooks but no Americans. His burnt and bleeding legs are swollen with infection, and the foul odor of the rotting flesh nauseates him with every breath he draws.

By the fourth day delirium has set in, but he keeps crawling, stopping briefly to eat and drink only when his strength is totally spent.

On the sixth day a Special Forces sergeant watches in astonishment as Frank slithers into a clearing. "Holy shit!" he shouts. "Lieutenant, look what I've found!"

Part Two
The Search-1987

15

The first rays of sunlight felt almost warm on Frank's face when he opened his eyes. Memories of the night's events flooded into his brain. A deserted road ran alongside the fence, and in the distance he could see buildings that looked like army barracks. He shimmied up the fence and saw the charred remains of a jet aircraft and the severed tail section, some of the seats in the last two rows still intact.

It was then that it hit him. He was in San Diego. His plane had crashed, and somehow he had survived. He started walking down the road, away from the buildings, determined to get out without being seen for reasons he hadn't even formulated. To his right he saw several army vehicles in a parking lot, confirming his suspicion that he was on an army base. The road and the fence, he soon realized, circled the base. Then he saw the sign, USMC RECRUIT DEPOT, and a guard gate ahead.

The fence was lower now, about five feet, and hidden by tall shrubs. Peering over it, he saw a city street with stores and shops and light traffic. The moment there were no cars in sight, he leaped over the fence and crossed the street. At a small grocery store, he saw the headline:

137

91 KILLED IN JET CRASH,
NO SURVIVORS

The president of California Airways had a decision to make. He'd reported ninety-one passengers killed in the crash, and the remains of only ninety bodies had been found. More specifically, ninety heads. Either the loading list given to him by the gate attendant in Los Angeles was inaccurate, or someone had failed to board at the last minute. Or they were just plain missing a head. In that event, there was still a chance they'd find it somewhere in the rubble, jammed in some part of the twisted fuselage. Or it could have completely disintegrated in the fire — unlikely, but possible.

He studied the seating arrangement. Forget first class. They were gone! As for the coach passengers, the tail section and the last two rows of seats had broken off. Somebody seated there could conceivably have survived — but no passenger had been assigned a seat in the last six rows.

He had to do something, but what? He could report the discrepancy, or he could sit back and wait to see what developed. He decided to ignore the discrepancy and release the names.

When the telephone rang, Tom Conti was catnapping on the living-room sofa. He'd been up all night calling the airline, trying to find out if Frank had been a passenger on the ill-fated flight.

On the second ring, Tom was already in the kitchen. At the other end of the line was a representative of California Airways.

"Just a moment," Tom said, pulling up a chair. He knew he couldn't take this news standing up.

Frank dropped the newspaper back in its rack and started walking in the direction of the airport. The weather had turned gloomy, matching his mood. There was a muskiness in the air that reminded him of the jungle. At certain moments — usually triggered by smells, sounds, or sights — his mind had a way of swinging back to Vietnam.

During the years when his marriage was happy, he had seldom thought about the war. Now he found himself thinking about it a lot. He hated war, it was ugly and evil and wasteful. Yet he seemed to long for it, like an old man longing for his lost youth. The feeling was one he never tried to explain. War was adventure, excitement of incredible intensity — Major Hobson had called it eye fucking. A special world with no gray areas, life reduced to its basics. You knew your friends and you knew your enemies, and you were given the means to deal with both.

He increased his pace as he approached the airport's passenger entrance. Two words kept going around in his head: "No survivors." To all intents and purposes, he was dead. Which meant that Allio no longer had any reason for holding Nancy. Or any reason to watch out for Frank.

Whenever Joyce was alone in the apartment, all three television sets were tuned to CNN, the all-news channel. Not that she was all that involved in

139

what was going on in the rest of the world. On occasion a news event would pique her interest, but mostly it was the familiar voices of the newscasters that she liked.

One of the sets was on a bathroom shelf, facing the Jacuzzi. She stretched languidly and yawned. God, this was heavenly. Reaching behind her, she picked up a mirror and studied her face, running her fingers over her cheeks, spreading the beads of perspiration until her skin was a slick mask. Turning the mirror over to its magnifying side, she examined the lines and pores with the concentration of an artist working in miniature.

In a few minutes she'd start another Sunday ritual, one that took nearly an hour. It began in the shower. She'd wash her body, this time with aloe vera bath gel, stimulate it with spearmint leaf scrub, soothe it with a French massage formula, and protect it with pH-balanced body lotion. For her face, she'd use citrus cleansing cream, scrub it with sea kelp facial grains, tighten the pores with a clay and ginseng mask, tone it with lemon astringent, firm it with elastin concentrate, moisturize it with bee-pollen jojoba cream, enrich it with ginseng-collagen, and nourish it with high-potency E-cellular formula.

When Joey was home, he often joined her in the Jacuzzi for some fantastic sex. But with him or without him, she loved her bathroom. It was bigger than any of the houses she'd grown up in, usually beat-up shacks in some godforsaken Texas outpost populated by a bunch of boozing oil-field roughnecks. Her father had drilled so many dry holes, dusters, that her mother called him Dusty behind his back. And he loved his beer. When he wasn't drilling for oil, he was pouring beer down his throat. Her mother preferred the hard stuff.

The image of her father that she carried with her was one of a foul-smelling hulk who threw food if he was mad enough, constantly threatening his wife and daughter, his fists raised, his bloated face twisted in anger over grievances Joyce never understood. Whenever he started hitting her mother, Joyce would run and hide in a closet. There, in the dark, she'd shake so violently that she was afraid he might hear her, come in the closet, and kill her with one swat of his giant arm. The best day of her childhood was the day he left for good.

She remembered standing on a chair and cooking for her mother—who was stretched out on the kitchen floor—hoping the smell of hot, nourishing food would get her up to the table. When she was fifteen, she came home one day and found her mother covered with blood, dead on the kitchen floor. The woman who came to take Joyce away to a foster home said her mother had hemorrhaged—from cirrhosis, a condition Joyce felt she should have been able to prevent.

After only one night in the foster home, Joyce stuffed her belongings into two shopping bags and left for Dallas and a new life. She dyed her brown hair a flaming red, applied cosmetics with a heavy hand, and found work as a waitress in a private club. Her career advanced rapidly—from cocktail waitress to go-go dancer to featured stripper in a city where strip joints were the only nightclubs. From there it wasn't that long a stretch to selling her favors to big spenders.

At twenty-eight she migrated to Las Vegas, where she worked exclusively for a hotel-casino entertaining high rollers and, in time, hooked up with Joey Bucci. Having first sampled her wares as a customer, Joey convinced her that going to Atlantic City with him would be an important career move for both of them.

From where she sat now, watching cable television from a Jacuzzi in a palatial bathroom, she'd have to say he was right.

Mary Alice Williams, one of Joyce's favorite CNN newscasters, was describing a plane crash in San Diego. California Airways, Mary Alice was saying, had released the list of victims. There were shots of the burned 727 airliner and of workers carrying half-filled body bags. Oh, God, they must be finding just pieces of people, charred pieces at that. Sometimes, when flying, Joyce would stare at a wing and wonder how she'd react if it fell off. . . .

She shuddered, stood up, and stepped out of the tub. As she reached for the aloe gel and leaf scrub, she heard a name she recognized: Conti. She grabbed the hand remote and flipped through local Philadelphia channels until she found one that was reporting the death of Frank Conti. They had a picture of him, taken with a fat little man identified as John Fuller, the president of the Colton Savings Bank.

So this was Nancy's husband. She liked what she saw, a tall, handsome man in a three-piece suit, a faint smile barely curling the corners of a strong mouth. But why had he been on his way to San Diego when he was supposed to be coming to the Palace for his wife?

Joey Bucci was bored. He'd been trapped in the

place going on four days, baby-sitting a comatose broad, nothing better to do than watch television. He'd watched more damned television than he had in a year, more than he'd ever want to watch again.

Sitting around drove him nuts. He liked action, doing his thing, going places, meeting important people, impressing them with his talk and his clothes and his moves and his primo coke, making them feel grateful, working up scams, pulling in the bread, making out like gangbusters with the broads—being out there, in circulation.

Joey was watching the only kind of entertainment he liked on television, a gangster movie. Chuck Norris was kicking the shit out of the Chicago mob, going through it with his karate moves like a buzz saw through butter. A one-man police force. Joey couldn't help laughing. He'd like to see Norris come up against Sal or Funzi. Shit, they'd have him for breakfast and after one fart they'd be hungry again—he was about as awesome as a bowl of Wheaties.

Joey heard a buzz and reached for the cordless phone he kept at his side. It was Joyce. "Joey, are you watching the news?"

"No, what's up?"

"Frank Conti was killed in a plane crash. In San Diego. They just announced his name on local television."

"What the hell was he doing in San Diego?"

"That's what I'm asking myself."

"Are you sure it's her husband?"

"They said he worked at the Colton bank. How many Frank Contis could they have working at that bank? Something fucking weird's going down."

"Babe, let me catch the news, and then I'll call

Nick. See if I can learn something."

"Look, Joey, you've gotta tell her."

"Don't jump the gun."

"Want me to come over? Maybe I should tell her."

"I'll handle it. Give me a minute to get organized."

"Get back to me soon as you know something. That woman's gonna need a soft shoulder."

"I know, I know."

"I mean it, Joey. You get right back to me or I'm coming over there."

"Sit tight, babe. I'll call you."

16

With a couple of hours to kill before his meeting with Allio, Joey fell asleep on the sofa. Across the room, crouching behind a large chair, Nancy kept her eyes fixed on the cordless phone on the floor directly under Joey's hand, which hung limply over the side of the sofa. Awakened earlier by the television, she had slipped into the living room and had been waiting for just such a moment.

Still groggy from the pills, she listened to Joey's breathing, waited until he began to snore, then moved across the room on all fours. She paused at the sofa and slowly reached out, her hand grasping the phone. Holding her breath, she retreated to the bedroom.

She noticed that the red light on the handset was blinking, indicating that the battery was low. Still holding her breath, she pulled out the telescopic antenna, flipped the talk switch, and quickly dialed her home number. "Oh, Frank, please be home," she whispered. After ten rings, she pressed the cancel key and dialed Tom Conti.

When she heard his voice, it was all she could do to keep from screaming. "Dad, it's Nancy," she whispered.

"Who is it?"

His voice sounded as if it were coming to her on ocean waves. The batteries must be nearly exhausted.

"It's Nancy . . . I'm in trouble."

"Is that you, Nance? Speak up, louder."

"Dad, I'm being held prisoner . . . please help me!"

"What? What did you say?"

"I'm being held prisoner."

"Bad connection, speak up, can't hear you."

"I said . . . I'm a prisoner!" Her voice rose. "Please help me!"

"For God's sake, where are you?"

"I'm—"

She heard a sharp intake of breath, felt the phone being ripped out of her hand.

"You bitch!" Joey hurled the phone across the room.

She scrambled on all fours, trying to get to the phone; he kicked her in the back and knocked her down. She rolled away, her arms flailing, but he stayed right with her, slapping at her head and body, but she fought back, hitting and kicking. In a burst of anger, he smacked her above the bridge of her nose with his fist. She saw lights flashing and rolled over onto her back.

"Now, goddamnit, cool it," he yelled, kicking her in the side. "Who the fuck was on the phone?"

"My husband . . . he's coming . . . coming right now."

"Fuck he is. Your husband's dead, you crazy bitch." He reached down and got a handful of hair, pulling her to her knees.

"What . . . what'd you say—"

"He's fucking dead, you hear me?"

"I don't believe you! You're lying, you're trying to scare me."

He twisted her head. "Tell me who that was on the phone?" he shouted into her ear. "Or I'll hurt you bad."

"Where's my husband?"

He slapped her across the face. Blood spurted from her nose. Both her eyes were swollen shut. "Tell me!"

"My father . . . my father-in . . . in . . . in-law," she sobbed, blood from her nose running into her mouth.

"The goddamn cop? Well, fuck him! I heard you, you told him shit."

"He's . . . he's coming right over, he'll—"

"Bullshit!"

"—he'll put you in jail."

"Shut up." Joey shouted, shaking his fist at her. Suddenly, her eyes began to roll up into her head and she slumped against him, unconscious.

He picked her up and dumped her in the bed. Back in the living room, he retrieved the phone, switched it off, unlocked the cabinet where the second handset was being charged on the base unit, grabbed it, and dialed Joyce's number.

"Hey, babe, I'm going over to see Tony. Call you soon as I get back."

"Have you told her yet?"

"What?"

"Have you told Nancy about her husband?"

"Oh, sure, told her a while back."

"How's she handling it?"

"Not too good, what can you expect? Looks like she'll be okay, though. Gotta run, babe, stay put till I call you."

Tom Conti had never felt more helpless. He'd heard the fear in Nancy's voice when she said the word "prisoner," but something had been wrong with the connection, unless she was calling from a foreign country. Could she be in Mexico? Was that why Frank had been going to San Diego? He shook his head as he hurried to his car. Too far-fetched. She had to be in Atlantic City, and Allio had to have a hand in whatever was happening.

If only Allio were in Philadelphia, Tom could bring him in for questioning on one pretext or another. But Atlantic City was in New Jersey, and Tom's shield had no jurisdiction there.

Before leaving the house, Tom had called Jim Ferris and laid all his cards on the table. It was risky, but he needed Ferris's cooperation to pick up Joey Bucci for questioning. Maybe, with luck, Joey might lead them to Sal and Funzi, and from them up the line to Allio. And maybe, if he shook them hard enough and often enough, he might convince them that holding on to Nancy, if they were holding Nancy, wasn't worth the trouble of being rousted every time they turned around.

As he saw it, his best bet was Joey Bucci, who was probably still learning the ropes. Push him hard enough—out of the mouths of babes, and so on—and who knew what would come out in the confusion?

Whenever Tony Allio walked into Donjo's with his entourage—even on a slow Sunday evening

148

when the nude dancers were off for the day and most of the customers were men watching a sports event on the wide-screen TV—an electrical current seemed to pass through everyone in the room.

Donjo, his dark moon face beaming, led Allio to his favorite corner booth at the far end of the room. Seated with his back to the wall and his bodyguards occupying the adjoining booths, Allio was as safe as he could be in a public place.

Sal and Funzi usually shared the booth with Allio and Nick, but today they took the adjoining booths along with Ugo Failla, Rocco Iezzi, and his son, Tito.

"Ah, my *capitano, come sei bene?*" Donjo said, as he waved Allio into the booth.

"Motto bene," Allio said.

"Ah, *S'abbenedica,* my *figlio.*"

Allio laughed. "You're full of shit, you know it?"

Donjo grinned. "Makes my heart sing to have you grace these humble premises on the Lord's Sabbath, my *capitano*. What is your pleasure today?"

"Mineral water and something to chew on—no pretzels. *Capisci?*"

"Si, si, my *capitano*. Don't worry, I bring you everything you like."

"And keep your eyes peeled for Arthur."

"Si, the *avvocato, molto intelligente."*

"And Joey."

"Si, si, molto bello, this one," Donjo said, rolling his eyes. "First I take him out back, hump him *rapido,* and bring him right over with a big smile on his face."

Nick slapped the table, laughing. "That I'd like to see."

"Don't give me that bullshit," Allio said. "Your old dong's dead as a doorknob."

"*Si*, for girls," Donjo said, "but not for pretty boys. The older I get, the more they excite me."

"Get out of here, you old *depravare*."

"*Si, padrone*, be right back with your good shit."

Tony Allio had known Donjo all his life. When Tony was first banished to Atlantic City by his father, he'd worked for Donjo, who fronted the place for the father and was now fronting it for the son. For three decades before casino gambling was legalized in Atlantic City, Donjo's had been the resort's most popular nightclub, its showroom featuring some of the country's top headliners, some performing free of charge to show their respect for the godfather. Its back room had housed a plush casino that offered everything from baccarat to slot machines. Today the showroom was a parking lot but the back-room casino, which still offered craps, blackjack, and poker, was open until the wee hours. Many a hard-core gambler crossed over to Donjo's after the Boardwalk casinos closed for the night.

The tourist trade was gone, the visitors now preferring the luxury and safety of the Boardwalk hotel-casinos, which was fine with Allio. Donjo's was now the "in" place for politicians, judges, high-ranking cops, lawyers, drug dealers, local businessmen, and mafiosi. It was here one winter evening that Nick Bartoli had walked in wearing a ski mask and shot a judge who'd passed a severe sentence on a member of Allio's family.

"That Donjo," Nick said, still laughing. "I think he'd do it to Joey in a minute if he got half a chance."

"No way," Allio said. "The old *bastardo* talks a lot because he can't do a lot."

"Yeah, well, I wouldn't bet on it. I seen him back there with the dancers. Always got his hands on their asses and tits."

A waiter brought large bowls of mixed nuts, Fritos, potato chips, and bottles of mineral water and glasses to the table. A moment later, Donjo escorted a tall, skinny man with close-cropped, kinky grayish hair to the booth.

Allio reached across the table to shake hands. "Counselor, glad you could make it."

"Happy to oblige, Tony," the man said, shaking hands with Allio and leaning forward to shake hands with Nick. "Evening, Nick."

"I know you like to spend Sundays with the family," Allio said, "so thanks for coming over on such short notice."

"My pleasure, Tony," he said, scooping up a handful of mixed nuts and stuffing them in his mouth. He raised his arm, and a waiter hurried over to the booth. "Double Stolichnaya on the rocks, twist of lemon," he said, taking another handful of nuts. "I haven't had any lunch."

"Shit, order something," Allio said. "How about a nice juicy steak? Let me get Donjo over here."

"I'm okay, Tony, really. I've got to eat with the family tonight or the wife will skin me alive." He removed his John Lennon eyeglasses with the thick lenses in the gold-wire frames and rubbed his eyes. "What's up?"

His name was Arthur Goodnough. In his late forties, Goodnough was a fast-talking mob lawyer with all the answers, an accessory before and after the fact, for the members of Allio's family. He was also a heavy gambler who owed the Internal Revenue Service nearly a million dollars in income-tax deficiencies.

"Before we get into new business," Goodnough said, rubbing his long, sharp nose, "let me assure you that I've taken care of that little matter at the Colton bank. I passed the info on Conti's embezzlement to my contact at the *City Press,* who'll query Fuller at the bank on it. Should be a story in the paper in a couple of days."

"Good work," Allio said, "but try to have him run the story the day of the funeral."

"Shovel a little shit on top of his head as they plant him in the ground," Nick said. "Give his old man something to chew on for a while."

"His old man's getting to be a pain in the ass," Allio said, then paused as Donjo approached the booth with Joey Bucci. "Here you are," he said, waving Joey into the booth next to Nick. "Donjo, bring us some hot antipasto."

"Am I late?" Joey looked at his watch—two minutes past seven. "Sorry, I—"

"Forget it, you're okay. You know my counselor here?"

"Yeah, sure—hi," Joey said, shaking hands.

Goodnough smiled. "Joey takes good care of me when I visit the Penthouse Club."

"Okay, you guys," Allio said, "I wanted you here because we've got us a little problem. With Conti getting himself killed, we gotta decide what to do with the wife."

Joey glanced at Nick. "He told me to keep her on ice."

"Let me put it this way," Allio said. "Do we keep her on ice, or do we ice her?"

152

"What does she know exactly?" Goodnough asked.

"Nothing," Joey said.

Allio's eyes bored into Joey's. "You ever mention my name in front of her?"

Beads of perspiration broke out on Joey's brow. "Never."

"You one hundred percent sure?"

"Absolutely."

"I don't want no shit bouncing back on me if we let her go and she goes to the cops, which she'll probably do the minute she's out of there."

"No problem, Tony," Joey said, trying to wipe his brow with his fingertips without calling attention to what he was doing.

"What's the matter with you?"

"I'm hot," Joey said, removing his suit jacket. "I ran all the way over here."

Allio studied him in silence.

"Man, I guess I'm out of shape."

"Hell, you weren't sweating when you got here," Nick said.

"It's hot in here."

"Anybody else hot around here?" Allio asked.

"Not me," Nick said. "You worried about something, Joey?"

"No, really I'm fine."

"Okay, all right," Allio said, turning to Goodnough. "So what do we do?"

"Let me see if I understand the scenario here," Goodnough said. "Joey, hasn't she asked any questions?"

"Naw, she's been asleep most of the time."

"When you say asleep, I presume you mean drugged?"

"Right, gave her some pills, kept her real quiet. She's been no problem."

"Well, what does she think is happening? She must have said something at one time or another unless she's comatose."

"Once she said she wanted to go home, and I said your husband is coming to get you. She said okay, and went back to sleep. That was it."

"What kind of pills you giving her?"

"I don't know, got them from Nick."

"Mivan," Nick supplied.

Goodnough smiled. "Pretty potent stuff. I can see why she hasn't been too responsive."

"So what do you think?" Allio said. "Do we let her go or what?"

"I'd let her go," Goodnough said, "but I'd protect myself. She's a degenerate gambler, which we assume is a well-known fact. Get Larry at the Palace to come up with a figure, something realistic, say twenty, thirty thousand she owes the casino. Between her husband's death and the drugs—Mivan can cause memory lapses—she'll probably be glad to get this whole experience behind her. Must seem like a bad dream by now. But play it safe. Have Joey get some cocaine into her before she's released. Then, if she tries to make trouble, I'll demand she be tested."

"Great idea," Allio said, turning to Joey. "Can you handle it? Need any help?"

"No problem. I'll do it right away."

"And, Joey," Goodnough said, "if the cops ever question you about it, you can always say you two shacked up, that she was after you to ball her and you did. That's it."

Joey started sliding out of the booth.

154

"Wait a fucking minute," Allio said. "Listen, get a lot of shit into her. I want her feeling no pain when she leaves."

"Don't worry, she won't," Joey promised.

work, at weighing himself. Allio had fired.

Flic Indde the hard shooting style to stomach veen the taxies. Flic more Frank looted over the unknown, the world from a taxiee.

17

From the Philadelphia airport, Frank took a taxi to Colton and got out two blocks from his house. He walked the rest of the way, staying in the shadows, not sure what he would do if Nancy wasn't home.

On the flight back, he had tried to work out a plan for finding her without revealing his presence. The problem was, he didn't know all that much about Allio. He'd read about the estate in Longport the press called a compound, but he had never seen it. And he didn't know anything about Allio's lifestyle, the places he patronized, or the businesses he visited—except for Harper's Warehouse, the building where Frank had been told to bring the cocaine.

One thing was for sure, he needed to stay dead a while longer. Alive, he'd be sent right back to Tijuana for the cocaine. And if he complied with that demand, he had no assurance that Allio would keep his word. Chances were he'd become what Funzi had called him at the airport, a mule—an indentured mule trapped into performing whatever criminal service Allio ordered, with no guarantee that Nancy would be released. Allio held all the cards. The best Frank could do at the moment was to avoid playing into his hand.

The house was dark. Keeping close to the shrubbery surrounding the house, Frank moved to the back and pulled his key ring out of his pocket, unable to see the keys in the darkness as he fumbled for the one to the back door. The neighbor's dog to his right started barking just as Frank turned the key in the lock and quickly slipped into the house.

Joey had the air-conditioning on full blast in the limousine and still he was sweating. Why had he told that broad about Allio? And now he'd lied about it. That alone could get him killed, not to mention tortured. Which was something Joey figured he could stand for about six seconds.

He didn't want to die, but if it ever came down to that, he wanted it to be quick and clean. Which was what he had in mind for Nancy. That was his only out. Give her an injection of one hundred percent hydrochloride cocaine, enough to electrocute her brain in a matter of seconds. Then stuff more shit up her nose, make it look like she sniffed it, move her body to a motel, leave a few grams on the nightstand, make it easy for the cops.

When Allio heard about it, Joey could always say it was a hot batch; that plus all the Mivan he'd fed her had been too much for her heart. What could Allio say? He'd have to buy it. Hot shots happened all the time — to rock and movie stars, athletes, all kinds of famous people. So why couldn't it happen to a fucked-up housewife?

The big problem was getting her body from the fortieth floor of the Palace to the subterranean garage without being observed. He could hide her in a laundry cart, but no way could Joey Bucci look like a man who belonged behind one. He'd have to do it during that dead time between 4:00 and 8:00 A.M., when the casino was closed. What if he stacked a couple of suitcases on top of the cart, made it look like he was using it to carry his luggage down to the garage and his Lincoln Mark VII? Joey liked that idea. Nothing seemed impossible once he put his mind to it.

By the time the limousine dropped him off at the condo, Joey had stopped sweating. The situation was under control.

Arline Stover was a light sleeper. The moment she heard the dog barking she was up at the window, peeking through the curtains. There was a flash of light in the bedroom window of the Conti house, but it was so quick that she wasn't sure she'd seen it.

"Ernie, wake up. Something's going on next door."

Ernie sat right up. "What?"

"I think there's somebody in Nancy's house."

"Maybe she's back."

"I don't think so, the lights aren't on. And I didn't hear her drive in."

Ernie rubbed sleep from his eyes. "Well, what do you think? A burglar?"

"I don't know—oh, come here quick, I saw a flash of light again!"

Ernie jumped out of bed and rushed to the window. "I don't see anything."

"I think we should call Lieutenant Conti."

"Maybe I better go over there and see if Nancy's home. She could have come back without our hearing her."

"I don't think so. Oh, God, what if it's a burglar?"

Ernie reached for his robe. "Where's the flashlight?"

"In the kitchen. But—"

"Let me get some shoes," Ernie said, heading for the closet.

"Please, Ernie. Be careful!"

"Don't worry, I will," he said, going to the nightstand for the small automatic he kept there.

"Maybe we should wait a while," Arline said, still peeking through the curtains. "Wait a minute—the garage door is opening. Ernie, hurry, somebody's stealing Frank's Buick!"

Ernie ran through the house and out the front door just as the Buick's engine started and its lights came on.

"Stop," Ernie cried, as the Buick swung out of the driveway and backed up the street. "I'll shoot!" He ran up the street after the car, its headlights blinding him.

Holding the gun with both hands, Ernie fired until the magazine was empty and the Buick had swung around at the intersection and disappeared down the street.

Arline came running out of the house. "Are you all right, Ernie?"

Ernie lowered the gun, his face grim as he looked at his wife.

"Did you hit him?"

"I don't think so," he said, staring at the gun as if he were seeing it for the first time. "I never fired it before."

"Did you see the burglar?"

"Not too good," he said lowering the gun to his side. "A big man, more or less Frank's size."

"Poor Frank," she said, taking Ernie's arm. "Let's go in, and I'll make you something to eat."

"Sounds great," he said. "Suddenly, I'm famished."

"It's all the excitement, Ernie. I think I'll join you. And while I'm cooking, why don't you call Tom Conti."

Joey hurried across his living room toward the spare bedroom. Joyce grabbed his arm, pulling him up short.

"Wait one fucking minute, willya?"

"Later," he said, pulling his arm free. "There's something I gotta do first."

"Well, you better slow down, pal. That cop was just up here looking for you again."

That stopped him. "What's his fucking problem?"

"Maybe he knows something. His son could have told him about the money Nancy lost."

"So what? What's it got to do with me? You don't think Nick or Tony told him I was holding her, do you? Jesus, babe, wise up."

"How could I know what they told him? You never tell me anything."

"I need a drink," he said.

Joyce followed him to the bar. "Hey, Joey, look at me."

"I'm looking, I'm looking," he said, glaring at her over the rim of his glass.

"What's the score with Nancy? When's she going home?"

"Tonight."

"When tonight?"

160

"Soon as I get over there," he said. "So stop worrying about it."

"I want to go with you."

Joey downed his drink. "You can't—no way, understand?"

"No, I don't understand."

Joey slammed the glass on the bar top. "Goddamnit, drop it! Ain't she a little old to be your daughter?"

"Very funny, Joey. But you still haven't told me why I can't go over there with you."

"Because Nick's coming over. He wants to have a little chat with her."

"Now I've heard everything."

Joey wasn't listening as he hurried to the spare bedroom and closed the door. At one end of the wall-to-wall closet was a safe hidden behind a built-in shoe rack. Working quickly he raised the rack, opened the safe, and took out what he needed.

Tom Conti was talking with Teddy when Joey came out of the elevator.

"That's him," Teddy said.

"Okay, I'm gonna follow him. Ferris should be here any minute, tell him to wait here for my call."

Tom started after Joey, his step light. Finally, there was something he could do. He felt like grabbing Joey by the scruff of the neck and dragging him under the Boardwalk, where he could pound the truth out of him. Find out what was going on with Nancy and what had gone on with Frank. This punk had to know something about it. After all, he was close to Nick. And he'd been with Sal and Funzi on the Scolieri hit, which meant he had to know Allio.

As they reached the Palace's Boardwalk entrance, Tom's hand was within arm's reach of Joey's neck. He managed to restrain himself, following Joey across the jammed casino floor to a bank of elevators where several people were waiting. Joey turned in Tom's direction, but his eyes were hidden behind his fancy sunglasses.

When Joey stepped into the Penthouse Club elevator, Tom went along with him. The young operator in the splendid uniform smiled at Tom and Joey, his only passengers. Tom looked away. Joey stood with his arms folded across his chest, his head tilted back slightly as he gazed at the panel of flashing floor numbers.

"Penthouse Club," the operator said as the doors opened.

Joey moved quickly across the foyer and through the club's entrance, protected by a burly man in a tuxedo and two armed guards in police uniforms.

Joey stopped, spoke a few words to the tuxedo, then gave Tom a smile and a wave as he disappeared into the crowded room.

Tom swore under his breath.

"May I see your membership card, sir?" the tuxedo said.

"Will this do?" Tom said, showing him his shield.

"Philadelphia? Afraid that's not good enough, Lieutenant Conti. This is a private club, protected by the laws of New Jersey."

"I don't want to gamble," Tom said. "Just want to browse a little. Seems like an interesting place."

"Sorry."

As they talked, Tom was trying to follow Joey's progress toward the back of the room. A couple of times he saw Joey look over his shoulder and could have sworn he had a shit-eating grin on his face.

"Use your phone? One local call and I'll be out of here."

"Yes, sir," the tuxedo said, pointing to the telephone on the reservation desk, "but please make it short, you're blocking the entrance."

The moment Ferris came on the line, Tom said, "I'm at the Palace. Meet me in the foyer of the Penthouse Club soon as you can."

"On my way."

Joey was sure he had it made. The last time he looked back, that jerk cop was trying to muscle his way in — fat chance. Still, Joey had the cocaine. Should he ditch it? If he did, he'd have to go back to the condo for more, and the cop might be there again. He couldn't afford to waste any more time. He'd take care of that Conti broad tonight. Get it over with.

Ahead of him he could see the Fire Exit sign. He quickened his pace. People on all sides of him were saying hello, patting him on the back, or trying to whisper their desires into his ear; Joey kept smiling and moving, saying, "Later . . . not now . . . later . . . be right back . . . later—" By the time he shot through the fire door and hit the stairwell he was almost running.

"There you are," Tom said, grabbing Joey by the scruff of the neck and slamming him up against the wall.

"What the fuck you doing?" Joey screamed.

"Assume the position, punk. Spread 'em."

"Get your hands off me."

"Shut up," Tom said, patting him down. "For a minute there I thought you were going to disappoint me, but you ran true to form."

18

Joey sat on a folding chair in a windowless room, waiting for the questioning to begin. This was his first bust in Atlantic City. The skinny cop had read him his rights, and Joey had called Nick instead of a lawyer with the one telephone call he was allowed. Nick had told him to sit tight, Arthur Goodnough would be over as soon as they located him.

The room was about a third the size of Joey's bedroom closet. There was a beat-up metal table, a large mirror on the wall facing him, and the one chair he was sitting on. These guys didn't believe in wasting space or furniture.

Joey stared at himself in the mirror, straightened his tie, patted his hair around his ears, removed his sunglasses, pulled on the skin under his eyes, widened his eyes, smiled, and replaced sunglasses. If they were watching him through the mirror, he wanted them to know he was cool.

"Look at that conceited little prick," Ferris said.

"He knows we're watching him," Tom said.

"How about that suit?"

"It ain't polyester."

"How much you think it cost?"

"No idea," Tom said. "My tailor's Sears Roebuck."

"Look at the son of a bitch. Really thinks he's got it made, don't he? Walking around with five grams of cocaine and a syringe in his pocket like it was a pack of cigarettes and matches."

"That's how punks like him get to wear suits like that," Tom said. "I'll stick with Sears."

The two detectives sat on folding chairs facing the mirror. They were waiting for a lab report on the cocaine before starting the interrogation. Tom looked at his watch. At any moment some shyster lawyer would come waltzing in there with a writ and waltz right out with his client before Tom could ask him a single question.

"How the hell long does it take a lab to check out cocaine?"

Ferris shrugged. "This ain't Philly. I'll give them another buzz," he said, picking up the receiver. He listened, said "Thanks," and hung up.

"The coke's as pure as Ivory soap," Ferris said. "Fucking lethal."

"Amazing, I'd say. At least, I've never heard of anybody around here getting coke that pure."

"Nobody except this conceited little asshole. He must have some connection."

"So why's he carrying five grams of it around in a baggie like he's making a street sale? Who the hell's going to use it?"

"It'll curl their toes real fast."

"But whose toes?"

"Good question," Ferris said. "Let's go ask him."

Joey heard the door open and close but didn't turn his head. He watched them in the mirror as they took positions on either side of him, each perching on the edge of the desk.

Beanpole had a face like a clown Joey had known at Circus Circus in Las Vegas—big mouth, button nose, beady eyes. The other cop looked like he could walk through walls if had a mind to. Joyce was right, his face could have been carved out of a block of granite. Joey caught his eyes in the mirror and looked away. They were mean fucking eyes.

"Pretty impressive shit you're carrying around," Beanpole said. Joey could see the gold crowns in his back molars when he opened his mouth.

Joey shrugged.

"How's a little punk like you get pure shit?"

Joey shrugged again.

Beanpole leaned across the desk until his beady eyes were only inches from Joey's face. "Setting somebody up for a hot shot, were you?"

"Mind moving back?" Joey said. "Your breath smells like chickenshit."

Beanpole moved closer.

Joey reared all the way back in his chair. "You gonna book me? Do it. I'm not answering no fucking questions. You got that?"

Granite Face stood up and dropped a hand on Joey's shoulder. "Where were you last Thursday afternoon?"

Joey stared straight ahead. So this was what it was all about. Joey could feel his heartbeat slowing down. It was going to be easier than he'd thought. "None of your business," he said.

"No alibi?"

"I don't need no alibi."

"We've got a witness says you were in South Philly on Thursday afternoon."

"Bullshit. I was right here in town all day."

"Can you prove it?"

"I don't have to. You're the one has to prove it."

"It so happens I can," Granite Face said, increasing the pressure on Joey's shoulder. "You've been made on the Scolieri hit."

"Bullshit I have!"

"Eyewitness saw you blow him away. Saw your pals, too, waiting right there in a nice white Lincoln Continental."

"More bullshit," Joey said, trying to control his voice and facial muscles. "What pals?"

"Sal and Funzi. Sal was behind the wheel of the Continental. You like the picture I'm drawing so far?"

"Still feel like a wiseass?" Beanpole said.

"Bullshit."

"What've we got here, one-note Johnny?" Beanpole said.

"I'm not saying another word."

"I don't blame you," Granite Face said. "You don't sound too convincing. This guy sound sincere to you, Jim?"

"Sounds like he's full of that stuff he keeps mentioning."

"I think you're right. What I can't understand is how a guy that looks so smart could be so dumb as to blow away somebody with a shotgun in broad daylight and expect to get away with it in front of all those eyewitnesses. That's the sixty-four-thousand-dollar question. You know the answer to that one, Joey?"

"What do you want from me?" Joey shouted.

"A confession would be nice," Granite Face said.

"Somebody gave you a bum steer," Joey said.

Granite Face's hand tightened on Joey's shoulder as he slowly rocked the chair backward until Joey's feet were off the floor.

"You say a bum steer on the murder?"

"You're fucking right."

"We've got you by the nuts and you goddamn know it," Beanpole said.

"Listen carefully, now," Granite Face said. "This may be your only chance to make a deal that will deprive the Commonwealth of Pennsylvania of the pleasure of frying your ass. Once your lawyer shows up, your chance to plea bargain is gone forever. Believe me, we'll get the indictment — you think Sal and Funzi are going to let their future ride on your mouth? They'll get you out on bail and blow your ass away."

"Get off my case!"

"Now, you give us Sal and Funzi, and maybe Allio for good measure, and we'll give you a deal you can't refuse."

"Do I look like a fucking rat?"

"You look like a man who might want to save his ass. Not just from us, but from your pals. I'm offering you some options."

"Yeah, like what?"

"Can't be too specific right now on the time you'll have to do, but I can promise you it's going to be a breeze compared to what will happen if you go it alone."

"No way, I don't roll over for nobody. I don't want to talk to you no more."

"Don't be too quick to shut the door. Our deal includes protective custody. We'll get you in the government's witness program where you'll be safe from Allio and his gang. New identity, free transportation to wherever you want to live — a whole new life is waiting out there for you. What do you say?"

"I say you're nuts. I'm telling you, I was right here in town on Thursday, and I can prove it. You've got nothing on me. Period."

169

Granite Face stared at him, those mean eyes not even blinking. Joey was grateful for the shades. In a low hoarse voice, Granite Face said, "How about kidnapping?"

A shudder shot through Joey's body, and he wondered if Granite Face had felt it in the hand squeezing his shoulder. "You're really wacko, you know it?" he said. "Kidnapped who?"

Granite Face pulled the chair back until Joey was almost horizontal. With the other hand he yanked the sunglasses off Joey's nose. Now he was staring straight into Joey's eyes. "Nancy Conti," he said, his voice barely above a whisper.

Joey closed his eyes, turned his head away. "Let me alone," he yelled. "I got my rights same as everybody else!"

Granite Face seemed frozen for a moment, and Joey wondered if he was going to let go of the chair. Joey reached frantically for the edge of the table, but it was too far away.

"Where is she?" Granite Face said, his low hoarse tone more menacing than if he were yelling.

"I don't know what you're talking about. I never heard of this what's her name . . . this broad."

At that moment there was a knock at the door. When Beanpole opened it, Arthur Goodnough was standing there with a big smile on his face.

"Joey," he said, "fancy meeting you here. Ready to go home?"

Granite Face released his shoulder, and Joey jumped up. "Yes, sir."

Goodnough slapped a paper on the table. "A writ from Judge D'Ambrosio," he said. "You boys have heard of habeas corpus?"

"Got it on Sunday night, too," Beanpole said. "Good old Judge D'Ambrosio."

"Justice never sleeps," Goodnough said.

Granite Face banged his fist on the table. "You don't even know why he's here."

"No, and what's more, I don't care," Goodnough said. "He's going home. Tomorrow if you want to arrest him, be my guest. But you better have just cause. And you go through me. Is that understood?"

"Get out of here," Beanpole said.

"Come on, Joey, let's say good night to these good folks before the party gets too rough and certain public servants utter words in a moment of passion they'll later regret."

"They were giving me the third degree," Joey said, straightening his suit jacket. "Ain't that against the law?"

"It certainly is," Goodnough said, still smiling. "You can tell me all about it on the way home."

Following the call from Joey, Nick and Allio had gone into a huddle. Both men were puzzled by the arrest.

"Ever hear of anybody getting busted at the Penthouse Club for fucking carrying?" Allio asked Bartoli. "Get in touch with our contacts at the precinct. Let's find out what's going on. And call Arthur. I want Joey out of there pronto." Allio paused. "Who knows if this guy can stand up?"

Nick nodded. "Well, you know, I've had my doubts about him. These pretty boys are soft inside."

Allio waved a hand. "Let's not get carried away. Get Arthur down there. And get Joyce up to the suite. Tell her to stick with Nancy Conti until Joey gets back."

"Want Joyce to get a key from Larry?"

Allio nodded, wondering if Nick was right about

pretty boys being soft. Joey had done good work in the Scolieri hit, but that didn't mean he was strong enough to take the heat if it really came down hard. That was something he'd have to give serious thought to in the next few days.

After leaving his home in Colton, Frank drove to Tom's house. The house being empty, he entered with his own key, then called the precinct. Tom wasn't in. Convinced that Nancy was still a prisoner, Frank drove directly to Atlantic City. What better place to hide someone than an abandoned warehouse? He would begin his search there. He parked the Buick near the corner of Maine and Adriatic avenues.

On the drive over, Frank kept seeing little Ernie Stover in the middle of the street, emptying his gun like he knew what he was doing. Thank God that he didn't. Still one bullet had peeled paint above the windshield directly over Frank's head. Brave little guy. Who would have thought it?

Taking a crowbar and flashlight from the trunk, Frank walked around to the rear of Harper's Warehouse. He forced open a window with the crowbar and climbed inside. Using the flashlight as little as possible, he searched the rooms that lined both sides of the warehouse's large open space, listening at each door before rushing in, each time hoping to find Nancy.

He had nearly completed the search when he heard a car drive up in front of the building. The large overhead remote-controlled steel door rolled up; the lights came on. Frank slipped back inside the room he had just searched, leaving the door ajar so he could see who was coming in.

A black Ford LTD swung into the warehouse, and the door closed behind it. The four men in the car stayed inside talking for a while. Frank could hear their voices but not the words. There was laughter, and the driver, whose arm was hanging out the open window, banged his hand against the roof of the car.

"Bullshit," Frank heard him yell before he swung the car door open and got out. "You know, you're full of shit. I don't think you fucked her even once, never mind four times."

The man in the front passenger seat was the next one to get out. He was built like a linebacker and had the hard round face to go with the physique. "Hey, Tito, would I shit you," he called out.

Tito? Frank knew that name. He had been mentioned in several stories in recent years. He was Allio's cousin, Tito Iezzi, and the head of the state police had named him the mob's narcotics boss in testimony before a U.S. Senate subcommittee.

Tito waved his hands. "Forget it, man."

"No, no, wait a fucking minute," Linebacker said, coming around the LTD in front of Tito. "You wanna get your cock hard like a rock? Listen, I'm gonna tell you how to do it. You listening?"

"More bullshit," Tito said, shaking his head.

"No bullshit, man. Listen, all you got to do first thing when you get up in the morning is drink a half-dozen raw eggs in a glass of beer."

"You moron," Tito said. "That's enough cholesterol to kill a fucking elephant."

By now the other two men were out of the car and listening to the exchange with big grins on their faces.

"I'm healthy like a fucking horse," Linebacker said. "What're you talking about?"

"Don't you ever read nothing?" Tito said. "Everybody knows about cholesterol. That shit clogs up your veins, stops the blood from circulating, so one day it backs up in your head and blows all your brains out."

A horn sounded outside, and the men went into action. The overhead door began rolling up, and a black Daytona raced in, barely clearing the slowly moving door, tires squealing as it came to a bouncing stop only inches from the LTD's rear bumper.

The driver, a short Latino, jumped out and ran to see how close he'd come to the LTD's bumper. "Looka that, man," he yelled, holding up his thumb and forefinger to indicate a half-inch.

"Some day you gonna hit it," Tito said, going over to check the LTD's bumper, "and I'm gonna take it out of your hide."

"Don't worry, man," the Latino said, patting the Daytona's hood. "I know this baby like the palm of my hand."

Tito laughed. "You jackoff—got hair growing in there?"

As they talked, Linebacker and the other two were removing panels from inside the Daytona and its trunk, pulling out plastic bags containing a white substance Frank knew had to be cocaine.

"See this hand, man?" the Latino said. "Smooth as a baby's ass."

"Never mind your fucking hand," Tito said. "You drive too goddamn fast. You keep this up, you're gonna get your ass busted one of these days."

"No way, man. I got it all figured out. You know, using a little psychology. The cops see me going fifty-five in this hot Daytona they get suspicious. They say, this fucking spic must be carrying some shit, look how careful he drives, let's bust his ass. Now, I drive fast, they say, this fucking spic's show-

174

boating, forget him, he's gotta be clean."

"Very smart," Tito said, watching Linebacker and the others going over the Daytona. "How much longer?"

"That's it."

"How many keys?"

"Thirty-two."

"Okay, Juan." Tito handed the Latino an envelope. "Haul ass."

A few minutes later the same procedure was repeated, this time with a new Oldsmobile and a driver named Oscar who looked like a successful businessman.

The Oldsmobile left; the men threw the plastic bags onto a loading cart and wheeled it to the middle of the warehouse. Linebacker pulled a heavy drainage grate from the concrete floor, waited for his two helpers to stack the bags inside the opening, then replaced the grate. All four men got into the LTD and left.

As soon as they drove away, Frank turned the lights on. Certain now that Nancy wasn't here, he ran to the middle of the warehouse and pulled up the grate. Climbing down into the hole, he punctured each plastic bag with his crowbar, then climbed back up. At the far end of the large room was an oil drum with a pump on top. Frank filled a five-quart container standing next to it with oil, poured it in the drainage hole, found some newspapers, set them on fire, dropped them down the hole, and walked away as seventy-one kilos of high-grade cocaine went up in smoke.

Joyce unlocked the door to the Palace suite, switching on the lights as she went in. She stood in the foyer a moment, straining to hear the slightest sound. Nothing.

"Hello," she called. "Nancy? This is Joyce. . . . Are you up?"

She crossed the living room and stopped before the closed bedroom door. "Nancy? It's Joyce. You in bed . . . ? May I come in?"

She eased the bedroom door open. The room was dark, but from the light coming in through the doorway she could make out the outline of Nancy's body on the bed. Moving on tiptoe, she approached the bed, reached over, flipped on the bedside lamp—and saw Nancy's face.

"My God! Joey, I'll kill you if you did this." She leaned over the bed. "Nancy, wake up."

Nancy moaned, reached out for Joyce's hand. "Is that you, Joyce?"

"Yes, Nancy. Who did this to you?"

Nancy released Joyce's hand and pressed her hands against her face. "My husband isn't dead, is he? Joey said he was dead, but it's not true, is it? Please . . . Joyce, please, tell me he was lying."

Joyce put her arms around her, held her close a moment as she fought her own tears, then helped her sit up in the bed. "I'd give anything to be able to tell you it's not true, Nancy, but it is. He died in a plane crash Saturday night. I'm so sorry."

"Oh, my God! What's today?"

"Sunday night."

She held Nancy while she wept and found herself really feeling for Nancy's loss. She caressed Nancy's swollen face with her fingertips. "Did Joey do this to you?"

Nancy was still crying. "He tried to k-kill me. He's crazy."

"He won't hurt you anymore," Joyce said. "That's

a promise."

"I have to get out of here before he comes back."

"Come on, I'll help you."

"Are you sure nobody survived the crash?"

Joyce helped her out of the bed. "Yes, I'm sure."

"It's all my fault—"

"No, it's not. Now, please, let's get you dressed and out of here."

Joyce washed the dried blood from Nancy's face, got her dressed and out of the suite in five minutes.

They took the fire stairs to the thirty-eighth floor, the elevator to the casino floor.

"Walk behind me," Joyce said, as she hurried to the Pacific Avenue exit. Once on the sidewalk she hailed a cab, reached into her purse, and handed Nancy several hundred-dollar bills.

"Listen, Nancy, whatever you do, don't ever tell anyone that I helped you escape. It could mean my life. If it ever comes up, just say a maid opened the door."

Nancy hugged her, then sank back into the cab seat. "You don't ever have to worry about that. And thank you. I'll never forget what you've done."

Joyce leaned inside the cab. "And stay away from here."

"Oh, God, never again."

Joyce closed the door. "Take the lady home," she said to the driver, then waved at the cab moving into traffic. "Have a good life," she whispered as the taillights disappeared down the street.

Joyce stood staring up and down Pacific, with its flashy backs of casinos on one side and on the other its dismal array of parking garages and lots, tired motels, abandoned buildings with boarded-up or soaped windows, sleazy coffee shops, adult bookstores, and pawnshops with proprietors waiting behind walls of bulletproof glass—and for good reason. The street teemed with whores, pimps, muggers, pushers, and homeless lunatics released in droves from Ancora State Psychiatric Hospital in recent years.

Joyce watched as an elderly couple scurried from a parking garage with heads down, the woman desperately clutching her purse. "God," Joyce intoned, "what am I doing in this dump?"

19

Joyce sat with the cordless telephone in her hand a long time before dialing Nick's number. When she finally called him, she said, "Hi, Nick, this is Joyce. I'm over here at the Palace, but no one's in the suite. I wish you guys would let me know when you change plans."

"What the fuck you talking about? You telling me Conti ain't there?"

"I'm telling you no one's here. I've looked everywhere, which is why it's taken me this long to call you. I even checked the Penthouse Club, thought maybe she was gambling again—"

"Wait a minute. There's no way she could get out. She's gotta be there!"

"I told you, I looked everywhere. Anyway, the door wasn't even closed all the way."

"I don't believe this shit. You telling me Joey left the keys lying around or forgot to lock the door?"

"No."

"Then how the fuck—"

"How would I know? I wasn't even here. Maybe a maid let her out."

"No maid's got a key to that suite."

"Nick, I don't know, what can I tell you? She ain't here."

"Listen, you bitch, stay put. When Joey gets in, tell

179

him to call me right away. And while you're waiting, wipe the place clean. Understand?"

"Yeah, yeah, I understand. But why're you getting hot with me? What the fuck have I got to do with it?"

"Too much shit flying around here," he yelled, hanging up.

"Up yours, sweetheart," Joyce said, softly. She kicked off her shoes and stretched out, folding her hands behind her head. The only problem was, now she couldn't get after Joey for his treatment of Nancy. She'd have to watch herself.

Joey came through the door, guilt stamped all over his face. "What're you doing here?"

"Nick sent me."

"Listen, babe, I didn't mean to hurt her," he said, crossing to the bedroom door. "I caught the crazy broad calling that fucking cop, and when I tried to get the phone away from her, she jumped all over me. What could I do?"

"About what?"

"You've seen her, the bruises and stuff. That dumb cop just arrested me," he said, throwing the bedroom door open. "She'll be okay in a couple of days."

"Joey, what are you talking about. Where're you going?"

Joey snapped on the bedroom lights, rushed into the bedroom and out again. "Where the fuck is she?"

"Joey, she's not here. She was gone when I got here."

"You're crazy," he screamed, charging into the bathroom, then out. "Goddamnit, where is she?"

"How would I know? I just got here myself."

He took threatening steps toward her. "You set her loose!"

"Calm down, will you? Maybe you forgot to lock the door—"

He raised clenched fists over her head. "I'll kill you, you bleeding-heart bitch."

"Joey, cool it," she said, trying to stand straight under the threatening fists. "I called Nick, told him I thought a maid had let her out. He said for us to sanitize the place and wants you to call him right away."

"You fucking called Nick?" His whole body trembled as he lowered his fists. "Get out of here, get out of my sight!"

"Sorry you feel that way," she said, picking up her shoes and making as dignified an exit as she could manage.

As Joey paced around the room, his legs trembled and he could feel his pulse pounding in his temples. How long had Nancy been loose? Had she already talked to Granite Face? How else could he have known about the kidnapping? No, that was crazy. Granite Face had been fishing. Chances were Joyce had just released her. What Joey had to do now was find her and shut her up—permanently. Even if she got to Granite Face before he found her, corpses made lousy witnesses.

All he had to do was go to accounting and get Nancy's address from Dawn. If he hurried, who knows, he might even beat her home.

The Mark VII's digital speedometer was displaying its eighty-five-miles-per-hour limit, but Joey knew he was doing well over a hundred. Still, he was pressing down harder on the accelerator, demanding more. Fuck the cops. They were the least of his problems. If they thought they could stop him tonight, they were shit-out-of-luck. He wasn't stopping for nobody. If he pushed hard enough, maybe he'd get to her before she could talk to Granite Face. Joey was sure she'd go to him first, and he was probably still tied up with Beanpole in Atlantic City, the two of them dreaming up some other shit to throw at him.

Arthur Goodnough had been great. To think that Joey could have a fancy mouthpiece like Arthur getting him out of jail on a Sunday night, with a writ from an important judge like D'Ambrosio, that was strictly big time, a class operation, first cabin all the way. That's the way Joey planned to travel from now on. Nobody, but nobody, was going to louse up the trip.

Including the Conti broad. It wasn't her fault she was fucked up—nobody got themselves fucked up on purpose—but now it was down to a question of him or her, and that was no contest. Joey hadn't survived the streets of South Philly by worrying about the other guy. First and foremost, it was always yours truly. Sure, if it didn't cost him, he might worry about the other guy, assuming the other guy was worth it. He liked the Conti broad—that face and body had gotten to him—but how could a broad that looked so good be so unhappy all the time?

In the rearview mirror Tom could see the lights of Atlantic City shimmering in the misty night. Suddenly, a silver Mark VII shot by him doing a hundred-plus. Where was the highway patrol? The driver had to be insane. There was a time when Tom would have given chase, but he'd seen the mangled results of pushing insane drivers to the limit too often. This driver was already pushed beyond the limit—he was an accident waiting to happen.

"What do you think, Lieutenant?" the patrolman asked. "Smells like cocaine to me."

"It's cocaine, all right," Jim Ferris said, poking at the ashes with a stick. "Did the guy who called say anything about who stashed this stuff here?"

"Nah, he just said the place's being used as a distribution center for a cocaine operation — and that he's just set seventy-one kilos on fire."

Ferris nodded. According to the New Jersey Crime Commission, Harper's Warehouse was owned by Seagull, Inc., a corporation registered in the Bahamas. It being the commission's allegation that Allio was the exclusive owner of Seagull, Ferris had tried for the last five years, without success, to gather the kind of evidence that would hold up in court.

Seagull controlled other businesses in Atlantic City, several of which were involved in providing goods and services to the casino industry. And Allio lived on Seagull Lane. Ferris found it typical that Allio would let everybody know what a big wheeler-dealer he was, while making sure they couldn't prove it.

The patrolman was peering into the drainage hole. "How much money would you say went up in smoke here tonight?"

"Depends how many times the coke was stepped on, but if it's as pure as the stuff I saw tonight, millions out on the street."

The patrolman moved aside as Gino, the lab technician, stretched out on the concrete floor and reached into the hole with a small metal pan in one hand and a plastic bag in the other.

"Enough there to give me an idea of its potency?" Ferris asked.

"No problem, Jim," Gino said. "Have it for you in the morning."

"Thanks," Ferris said. "Think I'll go pay the anonymous owner a visit."

"And who might that be, he asked innocently," Gino said.

"Your paisan, Gino."

"Be sure to give him my regards. But if he's in bed — it's getting a little late, after all — don't wake him up. It might make him angry."

"Perish the thought," Ferris said.

Joey missed the Colton cutoff. When he realized his mistake, he slammed on the brakes and the Mark VII started fishtailing, bringing Joey's heart into his throat as he narrowly missed a half-dozen cars. Horns blared while he got the car back under control, easing it into the right lane for the next exit.

Starting to backtrack, he got lost. Colton wasn't a city — it was more like a string of housing developments and shopping malls. Joey found himself riding up and down streets called Cinderella Lane and Wishing Well Terrace, many ending in cul-de-sacs. He finally found the street he was looking for, which turned out to be another cul-de-sac. He spotted the Conti house and lowered the passenger-side window for a better look. The house was dark, but he noticed lights in a neighbor's house across the street. He pulled up to the curb in front of the neighbor's house, lowered his head for a better look, and saw a curtain move in a front window.

That was all he needed, a nosy neighbor. He pulled away from the curb, burning rubber to the intersection, swung left, and then slowed to a crawl while he tried to figure out his next move. The best plan was to

184

leave the car a couple of streets away and walk back to the house.

Except for that one neighbor, all the houses on the street were dark. Joey tried to look like he belonged as he sauntered down the sidewalk, his right hand in his jacket pocket, his fingers pressed against the cold steel of the Saturday night special. One shot behind the ear — maybe with a pillow to muffle the sound — and that would be it. Quick and painless.

His legs were moving funny, like he'd lost control over them, and he felt a chill on his shoulders. He shivered and raised the collar of his suit jacket as he stepped lightly across the front lawn toward the back of the Conti house.

The windows were steel frames that had to be unlatched from the inside and cranked open. The back door had a dead bolt. The sliding-glass door seemed his best shot. Grasping the handle with both hands, he tried to lift it off its track.

"Sonovabitch," he said softly. Being a burglar wasn't all that easy — who'd have thought this cracker box would be built like a fucking bank? He hadn't even brought along a screwdriver. The problem was, he hadn't had time to think it out; but in the back of his head had been the idea that all he needed was a credit card — slip it in, flip the latch like the cops and burglars on television, and you're in like Flynn — fucking piece of cake. But there was no space to slip in a piece of plastic here. This goddamn door opened inward, plus it closed against the frame.

Selecting what looked like a bathroom window, he picked up a rock, broke a pane, reached in, unlatched the window, and cranked it open. The space was just large enough for him to crawl in. Once inside, he carefully made his way in the dark until he was in the master bedroom. It was empty, the unmade bed cold

185

to his touch. He hurried through the rest of the empty house. Was it possible that she was still on the turnpike? Joey decided to give her another hour. If she wasn't here by then, he'd have to think of something else.

The Stovers were at their bedroom window again. For the past two hours they had been trying without success to reach Tom Conti on the telephone. Now they were sure that the burglar had returned to the Conti house. First alarmed by the squealing tires of Joey's Mark VII, they had stood watch behind the curtain until they thought they saw a man hurry to the back of the house. Then came the sound of breaking glass.

"Call the police," Ernie said. "I'm going over there."

"Ernie—oh, my God, be careful."

"I will, I will," he said, slipping into his loafers again.

"Don't forget your gun."

"Got it right here." He tapped the right pocket of his robe. "Tell the police I've gone over there. Don't want them to shoot me by mistake when they get here."

Arline kissed his cheek and hurried to the telephone while Ernie ran out the front door and to the back of the Conti house. He found the open window, thought about it a moment, then climbed through it and dropped to his knees. He took one step, tripped over his robe, falling headlong. He heard footsteps rushing toward him and he sat up, clawing at the pocket of his robe for his gun. When the harsh glare of a flashlight hit him in the eyes, he pulled out his gun and fired right at the beam. There was a loud click: his gun was still empty. The sharp explosion came a second later; Ernie felt a hot searing pain in his chest and knew that he had made a serious mistake.

Jim Ferris stopped the patrol car before the black iron gate and blew his horn.

"Yeah, who is it?" a gruff voice demanded from the speaker mounted on top of the wall.

Ferris stuck his head out the window. "Lieutenant Ferris, A.C.P.D. I want to see Tony Allio, police business."

"Got a warrant?"

"No."

"Just a minute," the voice said.

Ferris waited about two minutes and blew the horn again.

"I said just a fucking minute," the voice bellowed.

"I ain't got all night," Ferris called back.

"Yeah, you do. No warrant, no Mr. Allio."

"Tell him it's important."

"Hey, no tickee, no laundree, now fuck off."

"Wait a minute," Ferris said. "Tell him we've got a bag of ashes we'd like him to identify, found them in a drainage hole at Harper's Warehouse."

"Get out of here."

"Yeah, sure," Ferris said. "When he starts throwing one of his tantrums, tell him someone out there doesn't like him."

20

The cab driver waited while Nancy rang Tom's doorbell, then walked to the back of the house and knocked on the door. After a couple of minutes the driver honked, and Nancy came back to the cab.

"Take me to the third police precinct at Eleventh and Wharton," she said.

"You've got it, lady."

Nancy was so exhausted she could hardly keep her eyes open. Her head throbbed, her gums ached, her arms and legs trembled uncontrollably, her fingers tingled, her skin seemed an expanse of exposed nerve ends. She'd cried so much that she felt her eyes would turn to dust if she touched them. It was a familiar feeling, one she had experienced many times in her Valium-gin days. She hated it.

If she didn't find Tom at the precinct, she wouldn't be able to go another step. Joyce had told her of the local coverage of the plane crash and the photograph of Frank with Fuller. After Timmy's death, she'd thought she could never again be hurt so deeply, but she'd been wrong. Frank's violent death left her feeling desolate. She didn't know why he'd been on his way to San Diego, couldn't be sure it had anything to do with her—yet somehow she knew it had, that her weakness at the gambling table had precipitated whatever chain of events had led him to that dreadful end.

"Here you are, lady," the cabby said.

She looked at the meter, pulled out two one-hundred-dollar bills, handed them to him.

"I don't think I've got the change," he said, but she was already out of the cab and walking into the station.

The moment she came into the squad room, Johnny Brecato jumped to his feet.

"Nancy, what're you doing here?" he asked, his eyes searching her bruised face.

"Isn't Tom here?"

"Sit behind his desk, take a load off, you don't look too hot."

"Where is he?"

"On his way back from Atlantic City. Want to wait for him here? I'll have dispatch get him on the radio, tell him you're here."

"Thank you."

"Be right back."

She leaned back in the swivel chair and closed her eyes. She was having a hard time breathing; suddenly she started perspiring and her head began swirling. *Oh, my God, I'm going to be sick—*

She tried to get up. A moment later she clasped a hand against her mouth and looked around the desk for a wastebasket. There, on her knees behind Tom's desk, she threw up until she was too weak to return to the chair.

"Here," Brecato said, helping her to her feet. "I'm taking you to St. Agnes."

"I'm all right, please—"

"Sorry, but if anything happened to you while you're in my care Tom would never forgive me. Come on, let's go. I'll leave word for Tom to meet us there."

* * *

She didn't even protest being given another tranquilizer, an injection this time. She stretched out on the hospital bed and closed her eyes. She needed to clear her head of bad thoughts, and she cast about for a picture she could hold close to her heart. Gradually, she found herself floating away on that soft cushion of drowsiness where dreams come true. At first the image was blurred; she slowed her breathing, trying to coax it into sharper focus.

Suddenly there he was, the strapping young man she'd met on the campus of Syracuse University, and he was smiling as he walked up to her.

He said, "I've heard a lot about you."

"How could you? You don't even know me."

"You're wrong. I know all about you."

To Nancy he looked like a Greek god, tall and broad-shouldered, with clean-cut features and penetrating blue eyes. Catching her breath, she said, "I've never seen you before in my life."

"But I've had my eye on you a long time, have made numerous inquiries, and I'm happy to report that everything I've heard about you is bad—I mean, really, wickedly baaaad."

"Then why talk to me?"

A flash of strong, white teeth. "I prefer bad girls. I find them stimulating. Good girls are okay to take home to mother, but give me a baaad girl any old time for a good old time."

"I'll bet," she said, not knowing if she should act insulted or pleased, just knowing that she didn't want him to walk away without her telephone number.

He leaned forward and said, very seriously, "Do you know what the only thing is that worries me?"

"Bet I'm about to find out."

"What if some of the reports have been exaggerated, and you're not as bad as they say? I'm sure you can understand what a disappointment that would be to a man like myself who expects bad girls to live up to their notices."

She shook her head. "What have you been smoking?"

He shrugged. "The hell with it. I'll take my chances on you. What time shall I pick you up?"

"Is eight all right?"

She felt herself smiling at the memory, the first smile in a long time. She had smiled a lot that night, and over their years together until Timmy's accident. Something in her had died that morning, something so essential that it had destroyed her and now had destroyed Frank.

21

Nancy opened her eyes, sat up in bed, and looked around the hospital room. "Dad, how long have you been here?"

He smiled and took her hand. "Feeling better?"

"Yes, Dad." She hesitated a moment. "May I go home with you?"

"If the doctor says it's okay, you certainly can. In fact, I'd like that very much."

Her swollen face made her look like a little girl who has cried too much. Nor was what he could see of her eyes through the slits in the puffed lids encouraging. They were lifeless, reminding him of the eyes of so many of the victims of violence he'd encountered in his work. Last night, when the doctor had told him she wasn't in any danger, hadn't been raped, and would recover unimpaired, Tom had thanked God with all his heart and for the first time since he was a child cried like a child, uncontrolled and unashamed.

Tom had been in Nancy's hospital room since returning from Colton. He had responded to the call from the Colton police, had tried to console Arline, who was on the verge of total collapse. The cops investigating the homicide were of the opinion that Ernie had been killed while trying to prevent a burglary. Tom didn't argue with them. Nobody, however, had a convincing explanation for the disappearance of the Buick. "Of course,

192

the guy who stole the Buick could of told a friend about the place," the detective in charge had said.

Now Tom had a hundred questions he wanted to ask Nancy, but she looked in no condition to answer them. They could wait. And he certainly wasn't going to tell her that Ernie had been shot dead in her bathroom last night when Allio's men had come looking for her.

"You sure you feel strong enough?"

She squeezed his hand. "When is Frank coming home?"

"I don't know, Nance. A few days, I suppose."

"Will it be a closed coffin?"

"I assume so."

She gave this some thought. "How will we know if it's Frank in there?"

Tom rubbed his chin. "Good question."

She looked away. "That terrible fire. . . . I don't see how they can identify anyone."

"In such cases, they use dental records."

"It would be sacrilegious to bury a stranger in Frank's grave."

"I agree completely. We can insist on seeing the proof that it's Frank they've sent us."

She closed her eyes, covering her face with her hands. Tom was almost relieved when the telephone rang and Brecato told him to get over to the precinct right away.

The Third Police District in South Philadelphia included the intersection of Broad and Snyder, the heart of the Italian section, which meant that the bloody Mafia war was being waged in Captain Eugene Beal's bailiwick.

Each murder became a personal affront. More than once, in one of his frequent sessions with Tom, Beal had vented his spleen over the corpses being laid at his doorstep, as if somehow Tom's negligence were to blame.

Beal's goal, Tom knew, was to make commander of the South Detective Division before forty and police chief of Philadelphia by forty-five. After that, well, there was no telling where he'd wind up in this land of opportunity. At thirty-nine he had a year left to reach the first step on his ladder. Time was running out, the pressure was mounting.

Seated in front of Beal's huge desk, Tom wished he had a cigar, anything he could fiddle with while the captain delivered his harangue. Beal wasn't a screamer, a desk pounder, a foot stamper; his face didn't get red, the veins in his neck didn't bulge — he wanted to look cool when he let off steam.

"Tom, how many times have I talked to you about following channels, going by the book?"

Tom just nodded. He felt like he was seeing Beal for the first time. If he'd been handsome, which he wasn't, Beal could have been an educated clone of Joey Bucci. His suits were stylishly tailored, his shirts two-toned, his ties hand-painted, his shoes pointy high-heeled Italian boots. His long hair was styled rather than cut; his nails manicured and buffed and glossed. His personality matched his wardrobe: slick.

"Every time you guys break the rules, I get my ass chewed out by the chief. I'm getting damn tired of it. I'm here, in this office, at this desk, a good twelve hours a day for you guys. How many times have I told you guys to bring me your problems, that's why I'm here? Don't go off half-cocked — Tom, are you listening to me?"

"Do I have a choice?" Tom said. When he'd first walked into the office, Beal had expressed condolences, spouted a few cliches before launching into the business at hand. Even the murder of Ernie Stover in Frank's house had been dismissed as another dumb move by a nosy neighbor who should have reported the burglary to the police instead of pulling some macho stunt that got him killed.

"Do you have any idea, the slightest notion, of how much hell an attorney like Arthur Goodnough can raise when he goes upstairs with a legitimate complaint?"

"A lot, I suppose."

"You're not even warm, mister. I don't know what you were thinking of, I can't figure it out, it's beyond me. Going down to Atlantic City, to another state, on your own, investigating a murder that's none of your business, holding back information from the Round House, the very unit charged with conducting the investigation. . . . You know, the whole thing boggles my mind, I just don't get it. I've tried to understand your motivation, believe me, and the only thing I can come up with has to do with your age. Perhaps in your twilight hours as a policeman you're looking for some glory, a grand exit . . ."

If Tom hadn't had so many problems on his mind, he'd have laughed in Beal's face, but he had to get out of there before Beal got into high gear. Then the spiel could run all morning.

22

After spending the night in a motel, Joey lost no time heading back to Atlantic City. It was a beautiful September morning, with fleecy white clouds scudding across a cobalt blue sky. Football weather, the kind he'd loved when he was a wide receiver on his high school team. Weather like this brought back the fantastic passes he'd caught, the sensation of running full-out with the ball tucked securely in the crook of his arm, the fast cuts that left tacklers reaching for air, the sound of his pounding feet on the turf, the squeals and shouts from the bleachers as he crossed the goal line, the little dance and the big spike. . . .

Joey popped a Dave Brubeck tape in the cassette deck, lowered the Mark VII's front windows, and took a long, deep breath. Even on the goddamn expressway the air smelled great. In the rearview mirror, South Philadelphia was fading back the way tacklers had faded when Joey ran with the ball.

Goddamn! He was lucky to be alive. If that jerk's gun hadn't misfired, it'd be Joey dead on the bathroom floor. The stupid shit had to be crazy anyway, aiming a gun at him like that. Practically asking to be wasted.

He ejected the Brubeck cassette and switched the radio to a local all-news station. He listened through an international report dealing with the American hostages in Lebanon, something about relatives going to

President Reagan for help, but Joey's brain switched off until the newscaster said, "A bizarre development in Colton this morning when we return after these messages — stay with us."

"This is it," Joey shouted, pounding the steering wheel. "They just don't get any more bizarre. Come on, come on with the news!" The report when it came was not news to him except for the fact that the victim's gun was empty. Police called it a foiled burglary, and for that Joey was grateful.

But Joey's big problem was in Atlantic City, not Colton. No matter how much he tried to pump himself up, that lump of fear in his chest still felt like ice. What the hell was he going to say to Allio? He had to tell him something, try to anticipate what was likely to happen once Granite Face got into the act. If Nick —

Joey all but ran the car off the road. He'd been in such a hurry to get to Nancy that he'd forgotten to call Nick.

Nick, who had called Joyce at the Palace four times during the night, awakened her much too early in the morning from a Dalmane-induced sleep.

"Get him on the fucking horn right now, understand?" Nick yelled, nearly blowing her eardrum.

"I can't, damnit. He's still not here."

The sudden click didn't improve her mood. "Well, fuck you, too, you jackoff," she said, slamming the receiver down.

She rolled over on her side and closed her eyes. It had been a hard night, but a profitable one. The Palace had paid her five hundred dollars to entertain a cowboy from Amarillo called Slim. She wondered how many Slims there were in Texas. This one was a production number, from his cowboy boots to his cowboy hat —

which he never removed even when he fucked, standing up so as not to disturb it. Just as well, he came faster than a rabbit — by the time Joyce realized he was in, he was already out, zipping up his fly, a big shit-eating grin on his face.

He gambled like he fucked — fast and furious. Juice flowed through him like electricity through a transformer. After eighteen hours at a baccarat table, he looked as bright-eyed as the moment he'd walked in. Which was fine with Joyce. When the Palace closed at four, she'd had no trouble steering him to Donjo's back room, where he lost $28,000 in under an hour. Joyce's five-percent kickback added $1,400 to her evening's earnings, plus the two black hundred-dollar chips he gave her and the four she managed to steal, for a grand total of $2,500 — not bad for a night's work.

She debated taking more Dalmane, but before she could decide she was snoring. A half-hour later the door chimes started up. "They've got to go," she muttered, blinking at the digital numerals on the alarm clock, 10:28 A.M.: it had to be that dumb flatfoot. Who else did she know who'd be moving around at this ridiculous hour? She stood up, slipped into a negligee, and headed for the door. She'd let him know in language he could not fail to understand that this bullshit had to stop.

When she swung the door open, Nick pushed past her, followed by Sal. "Okay, where is he?" Nick demanded, moving toward the bedroom and Sal toward the kitchen.

"He's not here. Like I said on the phone."

"Yeah, yeah, sure," he said as he disappeared into the bedroom.

She followed him. "You're wasting your time, you know. I wouldn't lie to you."

"You sure you told him to call me?"

"I'm sure. But he was upset, you know, getting busted like that — they handcuffed him up there in the club's foyer. Everybody saw it. I mean, that's pretty damned humiliating."

Nick was looking at her as if she'd lost her mind. "Big fucking deal," he said, heading back into the living room.

Sal came in shaking his head. "He's not here."

"I don't get it," Joyce said. "What's happening?"

"Shut up," Nick said. "Get in the fucking kitchen and hustle some breakfast."

She laughed. "You've gotta be kidding — I can't cook."

"What the fuck," Sal said. "Don't you eat?"

"Sure. I can blend you some carrot juice or any other vegetable or fruit you'd like. I've got yogurt, wheat germ, bran cereal, mocha ice cream . . . let's see —"

"Got some oatmeal?" Sal asked.

"You mean that gummy shit you've got to *cook?*"

"What've you got for lunch?" Nick said.

"You planning on staying a while?" She was edging toward the bedroom.

"We're staying until he shows," Nick said.

"Look, anything you want, just help yourself. If you don't mind, I'm going to lie down. I've got a horrible headache."

"Go on, get outta here," Nick said. "Just looking at you gives me a pain in the ass."

The Mark VII pulled up in front of the black iron gate, and Joey sounded the horn.

"Yeah, who is it?" A voice spoke to Joey from a speaker mounted on top of the brick wall.

Joey lowered the window, stuck his head out. "This is Joey Bucci," he shouted. "I need to see Mr. Allio right away. It's very important. Can you tell him that?"

"Wait a minute," the voice said.

Joey remained with his head out the window. Had his hands not been clenched around the steering wheel, he might have crossed his fingers. If Allio agreed to see him, he had a shot. If not—

The gates swung open; Joey took another deep trembling breath and slowly let it out. The lump in his chest seemed to warm up just a little. He drove slowly, stopping when a guard walked up to the car, a rifle held low in both hands.

"Drive to the main entrance," the guard said. "Someone will meet you there."

Joey nodded and drove up the tree-lined drive, stopping in front of the stone steps that led to the mansion. Tito Iezzi was waiting for him.

"Leave the keys in the car, someone will park it. Come on, follow me, he's waiting for you." Tito paused and looked hard at Joey. "This better be fucking important, man. My cousin don't like for guys to come busting in here without an invite."

"It's important," Joey said.

He was beginning to sweat, Christ. He took his handkerchief out of his hip pocket and swiped at his face, ready to hide the handkerchief if Tito should turn to look at him. Tito led him down a couple of hallways, stopped before a door, knocked. Ugo opened it. At the far end of a windowless room, Allio was seated in a black leather executive chair, his feet propped up on the corner of a mahogany desk. Seated at a smaller desk behind him was a man working at a computer console. There were two unoccupied desks in the room, with typewriters and calculators; several file cabinets lined one wall, and there was a copier in one corner. Joey was surprised at how much the room looked like a regular business office.

Allio didn't get up, offer to shake hands, or take his feet off the desk. Joey stopped in front of the desk and forced a smile.

"I just got in from Philly," he said. "Thought I'd better come tell you what I've been doing. It's kind of important."

"Ugo, call Nick, tell him and Sal to haul ass back here," Allio said, his eyes not leaving Joey's. "So what's up?"

Joey nodded slowly as though he were trying to decide something. "Could we talk private?"

Allio laughed. "There's nothing you fucking know, or will ever fucking know, they can't hear. Now, what's up?"

Joey swallowed. This had to come out the right way first time out. There wasn't going to be any rerun.

"Well, Tony, I swear — word of honor — I don't know how that Conti broad escaped from the suite. I know damn well she was locked in when I left to come see you at Donjo's. And I had my keys with me. Hell, there's a record of them at the precinct, they took inventory of all my shit over there."

Allio's intense stare remained on him. "So you're telling me it's a mystery?"

"It's a mystery far as I'm concerned. What happened back there at the Palace while I was being booked I have no way of knowing."

"So where've you been?"

Joey nearly reached for his handkerchief. "I went looking for her."

"Yeah?"

"I was gonna get some shit in her like you wanted, but she wasn't home."

"But somebody else was, right? Somebody who ended up dead."

"A nosy neighbor, came through the bathroom win-

201

dow, for Chrissake. He tried to kill me, aimed right at me and pulled the trigger, but his fucking gun was empty. So I shot him and got the hell out. Nobody saw me."

"What's wrong with you? Can't you fucking do anything right? I'm beginning to think you're a big mistake."

"I'm sorry," Joey said. "I did my best. Give me a chance to make it up to you."

"Know what I do with mistakes?"

Joey shook his head.

Allio said nothing. Instead, he picked up a pencil and rubbed his thumb across the eraser.

Frank was parked on Seagull Lane, on the other side of Atlantic Avenue, facing the ocean and Allio's compound. He'd been there for hours, his frustration mounting as his search for Nancy seemed to lead nowhere. By the time he got to Seagull Lane, he'd run out of places to search. It was possible that she was inside the compound, but the longer he waited, the more he began to doubt it. All he knew was that he would have to do something soon.

The compound was a busy place. Everything from pickup trucks to sportscars to limousines went in and out, all day long. Finally, at dusk, the black LTD came through the gate and turned right on Atlantic, heading toward town.

It was Tito, and he was alone. Frank got directly behind him. Traffic was light in Longport, but he knew it would get heavier as they passed through Margate and Ventnor and neared the strip of Boardwalk casinos. At Providence Avenue Tito turned right, then left on Pacific.

He stopped in front of the Tropicana, leaned to his

right, motioned to a man standing near the casino's entrance, and drove away the moment the man got in. Stopped only a car length behind Tito, Frank immediately recognized his passenger as the "linebacker" from last night's visit to the warehouse.

The casinos went flashing by, but Frank didn't see them. Next thing he knew he was back on Maine, the LTD coming to a stop across the street from Harper's Warehouse. Frank quickly killed his headlights. His was the only car on the street other than Tito's. He wasn't more than thirty feet behind it, but in the darkness he could barely make out the LTD's outline.

They were there only a few seconds before Linebacker opened his door and the LTD's dome light came on. Linebacker leaned inside a moment, exchanged a few words with Tito, closed the door, and sprinted across Maine. He stopped when he reached the sidewalk, looked up and down, then disappeared behind the warehouse.

Frank grabbed the crowbar on the seat next to him, got out of the car, and hurried toward the driver's side of the LTD.

He was in luck. Tito's window was open. Tito was a big man, at least six feet tall and topping two hundred pounds. But in one fluid motion Frank opened the door and, using the crowbar as a garrote, pulled Tito's flailing hulk from the car and dragged it across the sidewalk — across sand dunes, across the old Boardwalk, and out into Absecon Inlet. When Frank stopped, he was standing in two feet of water.

Tito was no longer flailing. Frank released the crowbar; Tito sank into the water. He came up gasping and spitting, his eyes wild.

"Wha . . . what . . ."

Frank bent over, grabbed him by the hair, and pulled him up until their faces were almost touching. "Where are you holding Nancy Conti?"

"Wha . . . what . . . man . . . what the fuck . . . you talking about . . ."

"You heard me, you son of a bitch, where are you holding Nancy Conti?"

Tito was getting his wind back and with it his courage. "Let go of me, motherfucker—"

Frank reached up with his foot, stepped on Tito's chest, and pressed down until he was completely submerged, keeping him there until the bubbles stopped coming. Then he lifted his foot and pulled Tito out by the hair.

Water bubbled out of his mouth and nose. "You crazy motherfucker," he gasped, trying to wrench away from Frank's grip. "What the fuck's wrong with you? You nearly drowned me."

"I'll finish the job if you don't answer my question," Frank said.

"Go fuck yourself!" Tito shouted, twisting like a fish fighting at the end of a line. "Let go of me—"

"Where are you holding Nancy Conti? I'm not going to ask you again."

"Motherfucker!" Tito screamed. "I'll kill you . . ."

Frank looked down at Tito and saw the angry face of Allio threatening to send Nancy back in pieces.

He reached down, grabbed Tito's head with both hands, and twisted it until he heard the sound he was waiting for.

23

Opening the bedroom door a crack, Tom took another peek at Nancy. She lay on her side, knees drawn up, arms folded against her chest, head resting on her hands. She hadn't moved an inch in the ten or so hours since coming home from the hospital.

Tom tiptoed to the kitchen. He poured himself another cup of coffee and sat there at the table, drumming his fingers.

When the telephone rang, he grabbed the receiver. It was John Fuller at the Colton bank.

"Mr. Conti, can you drop by here in the morning?"

"Why? What's on your mind?"

"Well, let's do it on the phone." Fuller cleared his throat. "It's about Frank. A reporter called me yesterday. I have no idea how he got his information, but he claimed Frank was skipping the country with embezzled funds when he was—"

"What are you talking about?" Tom shouted.

"Let me finish. The reporter knew the exact amount: one hundred and forty-two thousand five hundred dollars. We checked our records, and that is precisely the amount Frank embezzled with phony loans on Friday, the day he left."

"Frank never stole a nickel in his life," Tom said, trying to keep his voice down.

"That's what I told the reporter," Fuller said. "But

now, having verified the amount, I've no choice but to get back to the reporter with the facts, which he asked me to do. He needs my corroboration for his story."

"Wait a goddamn minute," Tom said. "Something's crazy here. Who's this reporter? Give me his name?"

"Sorry, he came to me on a confidential basis."

"I don't care about that," Tom shouted. "This is my son's reputation you're playing with. Can't you see what's going on here?"

"The money *is* missing," Fuller said. "And Frank did make out the phony loans and cash the checks."

"Look, Fuller, if Frank took the money, it wasn't for himself. Now, I need a very big favor. Give me forty-eight hours to get to the bottom of this before you talk to the reporter."

"How can I? He's already got the story."

"The hell he has. Without your corroboration he's got nothing."

"I'm sorry, but I really don't see how I can—"

"Look at it this way," Tom said. "If Frank had the money with him, it went up in smoke. You give me forty-eight hours, and I'll personally guarantee to make good your loss."

There was a long pause. "All right," Fuller said finally. "I'll try to stall him."

Lying in the large bed next to Joyce, Joey had so much on his mind that for the first time in his life he was unable to perform. He couldn't believe it. No matter what she did, he remained limp—a failure that was as devastating as anything that had happened over the past few days. It was like some crazy jinx had suddenly grabbed him by the throat and wasn't going to let go until he was dead.

At least Joyce was a good sport about it.

"Don't let it drive you to suicide, lover," she said lightly. "Sooner or later it happens to the best of studs."

"Easy for you to say. You can always lube your box."

"It's only a sometime gland, lover; most of the time it's just the tube you use to relieve your bladder."

"Yeah, that's what you think. That's the family jewel, babe, and don't you ever forget it. And it's connected right to my brain. Now I'm gonna worry about it every time I've got to get it up."

"Better not," she said softly. "That's a stud's kiss of death."

This, without any question, had been the worst week of his life. And the way things were going, it sure as hell wasn't looking to improve any time soon.

"Your aunt's in bad shape," Rocco Iezzi said, his own face gray. "You know, Tito was her favorite. Jesus Christ, Tony, it's gonna put her in her grave."

"What the fuck's going on?" Allio screamed, pounding the card table where a moment before he'd been playing poker with Nick, Sal, and Funzi. "Last night it was the coke, tonight it's Tito. Them motherfuckers are gonna pay—believe me, Uncle. There's gonna be blood in the fucking street tomorrow."

"Who did this?" Rocco cried. "Just tell me, Tony, I'll tear his heart out with my bare hands myself."

"Think it's one of our fucking mules?" Nick said. "That fucking Juan's got a big mouth. Tito told me about him. A fucking wiseass."

"Who brought the stuff in Sunday night?" Allio asked.

"Juan and Oscar."

"Hit them," Allio shouted, again pounding the table, "and get their connection, too."

In days to come, the mutilated bodies of six known

drug traffickers, including Juan's and Oscar's, would be found stuffed in trash bags that were left on the shoulders of country roads to make sure they were quickly discovered and that Tony Allio's warning was understood by all concerned.

Tom couldn't sleep. He felt like getting up, but decided that would only make it worse when he got back to bed. Better to close his eyes and try to think of something pleasant. God, it'd been years since anything really pleasant had happened in his life. He tried to remember things he'd done with Frank when he was a boy. That was it. There was the day he brought home the boxing gloves. Frank couldn't have been more than nine, tall for his age but skinny — wiry, actually, and fast as lightning. Tom tried to explain the fundamentals of boxing, a little footwork, how to lead with his left, to jab with it, holding the right in reserve for an opening — and first thing Frank did when they squared off was nail Tom with a round-house right that nearly broke his nose. His eyes closed, Tom thought he could still feel the pain of that punch.

"You're bleeding!" Frank had cried out, more elated than worried.

Tom allowed Frank his brief moment of satisfaction, then snapped a left jab to his nose. When Rachel came out to see how the boxing lesson was progressing, both father and son were sitting on the ground, their heads tilted back, holding bloody handkerchiefs to their noses.

Tom stretched, smiled at the memory. A moment later he heard a noise coming from the direction of the kitchen. He sat up, waited to hear the sound again. Someone was knocking at the kitchen door. He got up, slipped his gun out of the belt holster lying on a chair, walked quickly to the kitchen, placed the gun on the sink countertop, and opened the door. A tall man was standing there in the darkness.

"Pop, it's me," Frank said.

Part Three
The Trial-1988

24

It snowed during the night. Now the wind had come up, and it was blinding cold on the steps of the Atlantic County courthouse. Yet the press horde was out in full force when the three white limousines with the black windows came up the street.

Inside the first limousine, Tony Allio and Arthur Goodnough sipped coffee from Styrofoam cups. The lawyer was laying out the strategy for the day. Allio listened, unsmiling. Two weeks into the trial—a week to select a jury and a week for the prosecution to present its case—and to hear Goodnough tell it, everything was coming up roses.

"So now it's our turn at bat," Goodnough was saying as the limousine plowed its way through a snowbank toward the sidewalk. Allio shook his head. "We got no reason to think they'll lay off of us the way you laid off of them. I still don't understand why you didn't cross-examine them. Shit, you didn't even object to anything they said!"

"Sure I did. When Nancy Conti said Joey had told her of your involvement, I objected on the grounds of hearsay and it was sustained. But the point to bear in mind here, Tony, is that I didn't dignify their story by making more of it than it was. Believe me, Nancy Conti was skating on the edge of total collapse, ready to unload a flood of tears that could have swept the jury right along in the tide."

"That's not the way I saw it," Allio said. "She looked in fucking control to me."

"Don't you see how quickly the jury would turn against you if they thought I was badgering a classy dame like that? As for the husband, forget it, there's no way you're going to budge him. That's one hard nut to crack. And the more we pound on that story, and the more he holds to his guns, the more truthful it begins to sound to the jury."

Goodnough paused to adjust his granny eyeglasses. "Take my word for it, Tony, I learned long ago not to go head-to-head with guys like Frank Conti. One wrong word and they bury you."

"Well, maybe," Allio said, "but I kept hoping you'd rip into them—you know, tear them to pieces, make them look like fucking idiots up there."

"Tony, trust me on this one. Using a little strategy here. You've got to play it close to the vest with a guy like Mike Butler. He's been district attorney a long time—"

"That piece of shit!" Allio shouted, spitting into his empty coffee cup.

"Then there's his deputy, Margot Sodana."

Allio laughed. "Are those bazooms for real?"

"So I'm told. But don't let the tits fool you. She's a killer, goes for the jugular every time."

Allio suddenly leaned forward. "Look at them motherfuckers, willya?" he said, waving a hand toward the reporters who were already pressing against the car even before it had come to a full stop.

"Treat them nice," Goodnough said. "They're *our* motherfuckers. They love you. You're the local hero."

"I'll tell you one thing," Allio said. "I'm the biggest fucking man ever come out of these parts."

"That you are. Come on, let's get out there and give

them a big smile and a little bullshit."

"How about a little smile and big bullshit?"

Goodnough laughed. "Let's save the big stuff for the court. Besides, you think I want to freeze my balls off? It's fucking twenty below out there. We're going to make this fast and painless."

From an upper window in the courthouse, Frank and Nancy watched the ritual that had repeated itself without variation every morning of the trial. Arthur Goodnough came out of the first limousine and held the door open for Allio, who waved and smiled as the reporters quickly closed in around him and his lawyer. Nobody paid any attention when the other two limousines pulled up and unloaded Joyce, Joey, Sal, Funzi, Nick, and their lawyers.

"Look at him," Nancy said, pointing to Allio. "He looks like he doesn't have a care in the world. Like he knows something we don't."

Frank's arm tightened around her waist. "Don't let him get to you," he said. "He'd look like that on his way to the gas chamber."

"Those eyes, the way he stared at me the whole time I testified . . ." She shuddered. "If anyone can be said to have evil eyes, he does."

"That's old Sicilian bullshit," Frank said. "He's been practicing that evil eye all his life."

"I saw the way he looked at you, too, when you testified. He never took his eyes off you."

"I know."

"And you looked right back at him. I tried, but I couldn't do it." She shuddered again. "I'll be glad when this is over."

"So will I," Frank said. "It won't be long now. At least, the worst is over. We've been on the stand, told our story, now it's their turn. Sure, they'll deny everything, but I think the jury will believe us."

"God, I hope so."

After Nancy had gone to bed last night, Frank had talked with Tom in the living room of a safe house that was guarded by a detail of U.S. deputy marshals.

"Looks real good," Tom said. "You and Nancy did a terrific job on the stand. There's no way that jury didn't believe your story."

Frank nodded. "Yes, but win or lose, after this is over we're going to be stuck in this witness protection program—have to spend the rest of our lives looking over our shoulders."

"Frank, we've already had that conversation, five months ago. Let's not have it again."

Frank stood up, walked behind the sofa, and put a hand on his father's shoulder. He didn't want to think about that conversation, much less repeat it. When he learned what they had done to Nancy, he'd been half-crazed with the need to exact his own punishment against Allio.

"Listen, kiddo, this ain't Vietnam," Tom had said. "It's a jungle out there, all right, but a hell of a lot more complicated than the one in Southeast Asia you roamed around in. You kill people here they call it murder and fry your ass, no matter how righteous you feel about it."

"So, tell me, Pop, how *do* you stop an Allio? So far, the law hasn't done such a great job."

"Exactly my point," Tom said. "With you and Nancy as witnesses, believe me, we've got a shot."

"Yeah, what kind?"

"For openers, extortion, kidnapping, embezzlement, conspiracy to smuggle drugs into the country—I mean, it's not ironclad, but it's a shot. If we win, we can put these people away for a long time. In my book that's a lot smarter than going out like a crazy Rambo and getting your ass shot off."

"And if we lose?"

"Well, we're still within the law," Tom said. "Let the law take its course. That's what I've represented all my life. I know, there are too many laws and not enough order, but we win some."

25

"All rise."

Judge Malcom Swift swept into the room with his usual flourish, black gown swirling as he turned to climb the steps to his throne. "Be seated," he said, then smiled broadly, his black cheeks glistening, emphasizing the whiteness of his false teeth. "Good morning, ladies and gentlemen. I trust you all had a pleasant weekend. Mr. Goodnough, are you ready for the defense?"

There were five lawyers at the two defense tables, but the judge and everybody else in the courtroom knew that Goodnough was in charge. As District Attorney Mike Butler had told his deputy, Margot Sodana, "It's gonna be another one of Goodnough's seminars in the round for mob mouthpieces."

Goodnough stood up. "Yes, Your Honor. At this time, I would like to make my opening remarks to the jury."

"Very well. First, Mr. Goodnough, I want to address the jurors. Ladies and gentlemen, as I pointed out before Mr. Butler presented his opening remarks, the prosecution gets the first opportunity to address you because the state has the burden to prove guilt beyond a reasonable doubt. Then it is the defense's turn, which usually follows immediately upon the prosecution's statement. In this instance, however, Mr. Goodnough deferred making his statement until he was ready to present his defense. Remember what I said. Opening remarks are not evidence. Evidence is what you get from the witness stand or from exhibits that come in during the course of the trial or from stipulations—that's when the attorneys agree that something is a fact. It is from those facts, that evidence, that you will determine whether the defendants are guilty or not guilty. Now, Mr. Goodnough, you may proceed."

Goodnough walked briskly to the jury box, his movements deliberate, his demeanor serious. "Good morning, ladies and gentlemen. For five months now we've all been told, time and time again, in the newspapers, on television, over radio and back fences, in barrooms and at sporting events, in all the places that people congregate across this great land of ours, and by every means of communication known to man, that my client, Tony Allio, has committed a whole multitude of crimes. Let's see if I can enumerate them all: kidnapping, extortion, assault and battery, embezzlement, drug trafficking, conspiracy—oh, well, why waste your time with fiction when we can talk about facts. The fact is that Tony Allio has never met that woman sitting over there, the prosecution's chief witness, Mrs. Nancy Conti, had never laid eyes on her until the day she walked into this court and proceeded to tell this most incredible story—you look surprised, ladies and gentlemen. Imagine Tony Allio's surprise, if you will, when faced with such monstrous allegations.

"And then there is the prosecution's other chief witness, her husband, Mr. Frank Conti, the honest banker, the great war hero—oh, yes, let us not forget that for one moment."

Goodnough strolled down the length of the jury box, then turned and shot a glance in the direction of Frank Conti. "Yes, the confessed embezzler himself," he said, twisting his lips as if the words left a bad taste in his mouth. "And a man in an unhappy marriage looking for a way out — but more about that later. Mr. Conti, we are told, was a former schoolmate of Tony Allio's. But that was over twenty years ago, and in all that time since Mr. Allio graduated from South Philadelphia High School, as will be shown in this court, he never once laid eyes on this man, this witness with the fertile imagination. Have you ever in your whole life been asked to believe such a story? Have you ever seen the likes at the movies? I mean, ladies and gentlemen, it's a fabrication that truly boggles the mind — even the mind of a lawyer as experienced as myself. I thought I had seen and heard everything in my thirty years before the bar, but I tell you quite frankly this one takes the grand prize.

"Now, I'm sure you've noticed how quiet I was while Mr. Butler orchestrated this fabulous theatrical scenario. I felt like a first-nighter on Broadway, afraid even to cough. How could anyone interrupt such a magnificent production?

"Take a look at Mr. Butler, the state's celebrated prosecutor — take a good look, ladies and gentlemen, at this great stage director, who acts in his own plays. Who struts on the stage like William Shakespeare's Hamlet, beseeching his players to 'speak the speech I pray thee, trippingly on the tongue, for if you mouth it, as many of your players do . . .' and so forth and so on. And, yes, they did speak trippingly, didn't they. And he's proud of them. And well he should be. You saw how happy he was during their performances. Well, I ask you, why not? Do you have any idea how long Mr. Butler has waited for just such a moment in the national spotlight — oh, yes, believe it, this case is grist for the national media mill. If he wins the case, perhaps he'll get his picture on the cover of *Time* or *Newsweek,* or both.

"But there's a catch. He needs a conviction, doesn't he? You can't be a loser and a star. And to be a winner, he needs you. Yes, ladies and gentlemen, he needs you desperately. With your help, and the witnesses' help, he's going to bag this so-called big-time kingpin of organized crime. Makes it sound like Chicago in the Roaring Twenties, doesn't he—Al Capone, 'The Untouchables.'

"Some people, ladies and gentlemen, because of their ethnic origins and the neighborhoods they grew up in and the associations they inherited in those neighborhoods—and sometimes because of a mistake or two made when they were young—become fair game in the press and are endowed with a reputation they can never shed. Men like Mr. Butler tilt at these paper windmills until they find people like the Contis to pave the way for them. The Contis can make him famous. Make him attorney general of New Jersey, perhaps even governor of our great state.

"So that is what is at stake here, ladies and gentlemen, the future of that man in the governor's mansion and the imprisonment of Tony Allio, or the freedom of Tony Allio and the failed bid of Mr. Butler—who, win or lose, will still have his freedom.

"My responsibility as an officer of this court, ladies and gentlemen, is to make sure that you get beyond this snow job—I mean, my gosh, they've shoveled more snow in here than God ever delivered outside—my responsibility is to see that you get all the facts. You will meet Joyce Kresse and Joey Bucci and many others, and they will speak to you and will look at you, and you will look at them and judge them on the facts, not on some grandiose scenario that insults your intelligence. And when this case is over, ladies and gentlemen, you will go back to the jury room to deliberate and, therefore, as honest jurors, will find that there is only one verdict you can return, and that is a verdict of not guilty. Thank you very much."

As he walked back to the defense table, Goodnough glanced at Nancy, adjusted his tinted John Lennon eyeglasses and winked at her. She looked quickly at Frank, who had caught the wink. Throughout Goodnough's remarks, Nancy had held Frank's hand, her grip growing so fierce that his hand felt numb.

"Son of a bitch," Mike Butler whispered to Margot Sodana.

Margot shook her head. "Better hold tight, Mike," she said. "We're in for another one of Goodnough's slippery rides."

"Thank you, Mr. Goodnough," Judge Swift said. "Call your first witness."

"I call Joyce Kresse."

Joyce kept her eyes straight ahead as she was sworn in, then focused on Goodnough the moment he approached the witness stand. "Ms. Kresse, do you reside here in Atlantic City?"

"Yes."

"Directing your attention to late August of last year, do you recall meeting Nancy Conti?"

"Yes, I do."

"Where did you meet her?"

"At the Boardwalk Palace."

"In the casino?"

"Yes."

"In the regular casino or upstairs in the Penthouse Club?"

"Downstairs, in the regular casino."

"Can you recall the exact date?"

"Not exactly, but I'm sure it was during the last week of August, last year. A Wednesday or Thursday, I think."

"Yes, the indictment charges that the alleged kidnapping of Mrs. Conti began on Thursday, August twenty-seventh."

"So I've been told."

"Did you kidnap Nancy Conti, Ms. Kresse?"

"No, sir!" Joyce said.

Goodnough smiled. "I understand, believe me. Now, please, could you tell us how the meeting came about?"

"Well, Joey Bucci and I happened to be sitting next to her at a blackjack table."

"Is that the same Joey Bucci who is a defendant in this case?"

"Yes."

"Do you see him here in court?"

"I do."

"Please point to him and describe what he is wearing."

He's the good-looking man in the blue suit sitting at the second table over there."

"Mr. Bucci, will you stand up, please?"

Joey stood up and looked directly at the jurors.

"Thank you," Goodnough said. "Ms. Kresse, was that your first meeting with Nancy Conti?"

"Yes, but I had seen her gambling before."

"Pretty heavy gambler, was she?"

Butler jumped to his feet. "Objection, speculation."

Goodnough turned to look at Butler, then turned back to the jury and shrugged. "Judge, I'll rephrase the question. How much did she bet on each hand at the various times you observed her?"

"Oh, anywhere from five black chips to ten or more, and sometimes a lot more."

"Could you tell us the value of a black chip, please?"

"Yes. A hundred dollars."

"Well, is that pretty rich for your blood? How much

do you usually bet?"

Joyce smiled for the first time. "Five or ten dollars is my limit."

"Okay, let's pick it up again where you first met her. Tell us in your own words what happened."

"Well, she started talking to Joey, made some comment, said that her luck really sucked—"

"*Sucked?* Is that the word she used?"

"Oh, yes, I remember that distinctly. She was losing quite a bit of money. I know she signed a five-thousand-dollar marker—"

"A marker?"

"It's like a note—for a loan, you know. The pit boss gave her the money, and she signed for it."

"Can anybody ask a pit boss for five thousand dollars and just sign his name on a note?"

Joyce laughed. "Not hardly. You have to establish what they call a credit line. It's a courtesy that's extended to high rollers."

"High rollers. Yes, I've read about them. They're the big gamblers that get the red-carpet treatment, is that right?"

"Yes."

"Did you have anything to do with her credit line?"

"No."

"Who, then, would have to approve her credit line at the Boardwalk Palace?"

"I don't know, the credit manager, I suppose."

"Do you know Larry Walsh, the credit manager at the Palace?"

"No, sir."

"You recall, don't you, that Nancy Conti testified in this court that you are the one who arranged for her credit line?"

"That's really weird. I don't know where she got that idea."

"You didn't do it?"

"Absolutely not. I don't work for the Boardwalk Palace."

"That is strange, indeed," Goodnough said, cupping his chin. "All right, so what happened to the five thousand?"

"She lost all of it in about thirty minutes. So she said she ought to take a break and asked Joey if he'd join her in a drink at the bar. Joey told her he was with me, and she said, 'Fine, bring her.' So we went to the bar, but before we could order drinks she suggested we go to her suite."

"Her suite?"

"Yes, she kind of bragged about it, said she was being comped by the hotel—which, you know, is another courtesy extended to high rollers. So we went up in this private elevator, and before we even got to the room it was obvious to me that she was zeroing in on Joey."

"Objection, Your Honor," said Butler, "that's pure speculation."

"Yes, I'll strike it. The jury is advised to disregard the observation 'she was zeroing in on Joey.' Continue, Mr. Goodnough."

"Leaving the zeroing-in aside, what happened in the suite?"

"She sat next to Joey, kept looking in his eyes, then she said we ought to see the bedroom. There was a huge round bed with a mirror above it and mirrors on the sides. She laughed and said the bed was big enough for the three of us. I finished my drink and left. I never saw her again."

There was considerable stirring in the jury box.

Goodnough turned to face the jurors and pressed both hands against his forehead. "Pretty heady stuff," he said to no one in particular, then abruptly turned to look at Nancy, who stared right back at him, her face blank. "To the best of your recollection, Ms. Kresse, describe the suite for us. How many rooms?"

"Bedroom, living room, a small alcove with a bar, and a bathroom."

"How many phones were there, to the best of your recollection?"

"Several, I suppose, but I only recall two. One on the bar and a wall phone in the bathroom."

"When you left, tell us, did you have trouble at the door?"

"What do you mean?"

"Did you need assistance of any kind in opening the door or turning the lock?"

"No, Mrs. Conti had her own key and she'd let us in, but I let myself out. I mean — well, I didn't like her suggestions, so I left. By that time she and Joey were already in the bedroom."

"You heard Mrs. Conti testify, did you not, that there were no phones in the suite?"

"Yes, I did, but I didn't understand it. It was just a regular suite. Nothing different that I could see."

"Nothing special about the locks?"

"Nothing that I saw."

"You heard her testify, did you not, that she was locked in the room and couldn't get out for five days — until a maid, mind you, inadvertently let her out?"

"I heard her testimony, but I honestly didn't understand it. All I know is, I had no trouble leaving."

"Could you find that suite again?"

"I doubt it. When we went up with her I wasn't paying any attention, and I left in sort of a hurry and certainly had no intention of ever returning, that's for sure."

"I take it you were a little angry?"

Joyce nodded.

"Speak up, Ms. Kresse, the court reporter can't hear

a nod. Were you angry because Joey Bucci stayed behind?"

"Yes, well, let's say I was disappointed."

"Thank you, Ms. Kresse. Your witness."

As Goodnough walked back to the defense table, there was the sound of a cough from the jury box and then silence.

"Cross-examination," Judge Swift announced.

Margot Sodana stood up, leaned over for a final word with Butler, and walked to the stand. "Ms. Kresse," she said in a soft voice. "Where do you reside in Atlantic City?"

"The Ocean Towers."

"Pretty ritzy address. Do you rent, or do you own your own condominium?"

"Rent."

"How much does that set you back a month?"

Joyce shrugged. "I don't know."

"What do you mean you don't know? Are you being kept — are you somebody's mistress?"

"Objection."

"Your Honor," Margot said, turning to the judge, "I am entitled to explore Ms. Kresse's character — after her Victorian protestations under Mr. Goodnough's skillful guidance."

Judge Swift smiled. "Overruled. Answer the question, Miss Kresse."

"I live with Joey Bucci. Some months I give him money, and some months I don't."

"Well, let's see if I can help you along. According to the management at Ocean Towers, the rent on that apartment is forty-five hundred dollars a month. Does the amount surprise you?"

"No, it's a nice place."

227

"Do you work, Ms. Kresse?"

"Of course. I'm a real-estate broker."

"Really? I thought you were in, shall we say, another line of work."

"Objection, badgering the witness, Your Honor." Goodnough remained seated at the defense table, his voice low but each word so carefully articulated that he could be heard in the farthest corner of the room. "I move to strike this vicious indulgence in character assassination through insinuation, Your Honor."

"Granted. The jury will disregard that last remark."

"Your Honor," Margot said, "I have a right to an answer from this witness."

"Then rephrase your question, Miss Sodana."

"Ms. Kresse, where do you do your real-estate brokering?"

"Atlantic Shores Realty."

"Do you own the company?"

"No."

"Do you know who owns the company?"

"I think it's Seagull, Inc."

"You think? You didn't know how much rent your keeper over there paid, and now you don't know who you work for? I must say, you move around in a pretty vague little world."

"Your Honor, I—"

"Sustained," Swift interjected. "Kindly spare us your opinions, Miss Sodana."

"Let me enlighten you, Ms. Kresse. According to the New Jersey Crime Commission, Seagull, Inc. is a Bahamian corporation owned exclusively by none other than Tony Allio, our celebrated defendant, your anonymous boss."

Goodnough was on his feet. "Objection, Your Honor, speculation. The New Jersey Crime Commission is a private, nonprofit organization that has no legal status."

"Sustained. The jury will disregard it."

"Do you sell a lot of real estate, Ms. Kresse?"

"I sell my share."

"Name one property you've sold in the past twelve months."

Joyce bit down on her lower lip and glanced over at Goodnough.

"Don't bother looking at Mr. Goodnough," Margot said. "He can't help you here. You've had your lessons, you're on your own on this one."

"I can't think of any right now."

"Well, let's make it easy. Name one you sold in the past twelve years."

Joyce shook her head. "I'm just a little rattled, can't think straight right now."

"Well, if it should come to you later on be sure to let us know. Now, Ms. Kresse, I apologize, but I must ask a few questions about your work in a field other than real estate. Have you ever worked as a prostitute in Atlantic City?"

Joyce raised her voice a couple of octaves. "Never!"

Margot shook her head. "How about in Las Vegas?"

"Never!"

"Dallas?"

"Never!"

"Your Honor, what is this?" Goodnough said in a bored tone of voice. " 'Twenty Questions'?"

Swift scratched the back of his neck and looked at Margot Sodana. "Miss Sodana, you either have foundation for this line of questioning or you don't. I suspect you don't, so let's get on with it."

Margot flushed and turned back to Joyce. "Your Honor, please, I would like this witness to be reminded of the penalty for perjury."

Goodnough jumped to his feet. "Intimidation, Your

Honor."

"Let's not get excited, Mr. Goodnough," Swift said. "What do you have in mind, Miss Sodana?"

"Your Honor, I'm prepared to bring into this court a number of men — and women, I might add — who will testify that this witness is a prostitute, an expensive one but a prostitute nonetheless."

Swift looked down at Joyce. "Ask your question, Miss Sodana."

"Ms. Kresse," Margot asked, "have you ever worked in any place at any time as a prostitute?"

"Well, look, I've been out with men who were generous and gave me presents that I accepted. I never asked for anything."

"That's not the point," Margot said. "I'm talking here about sex for money, big money."

"Well, that's your version. I never looked at it that way."

"Ms. Kresse, what I find extremely disturbing about you is the contrast between your performance under Mr. Goodnough's direction — so positive, so clear-headed, so swift with the answers, such an impeccable memory — and now suddenly you're so tentative, so confused, so vague. Isn't that a little bizarre? Or is it just plain convenient?"

Joyce shrugged. "I don't know what you're talking about."

"Oh, but I'm sure you do," Margot said.

"Your Honor," Goodnough said, "what is this, a debate? I object —"

"Save it," Margot said, "I've had it with this witness, no more questions."

As was their practice during court recesses, the prosecution team had gathered in a courthouse conference room. There were large pizza cartons on the table, but only Margot was still eating. Frank and Tom were drinking coffee, Nancy a 7-Up, and Butler had taken the last bite of a sandwich he'd brought in a brown paper bag just as he had every day of the trial.

"Good going, Margot," Tom said. "It looked bad there for a while, but I think you discredited her."

"I don't understand it," Frank said. "Didn't she kind of fold pretty fast?"

Nancy nodded. "She was forced to testify the way she did when Goodnough questioned her, but I don't think her heart was in it."

"What do you mean?" Frank asked.

"I think when she saw a way of helping us that wouldn't get her in trouble with Allio, she took advantage of it."

"That's giving her a lot of credit, for reasons I don't understand," Butler said.

"Pardon me, Nancy," Margot said, "but is there something between you and Joyce that you haven't told us?"

"No, I told you she wasn't involved in any of this. Sure, she arranged for my credit with the Palace, but she was always a friend and had nothing to do with my being held prisoner."

Butler raised his eyebrows. "Well, all I got to say is that we were in deep shit until Margot stepped in and burst her balloon."

Margot laughed. "The truth is, I didn't have a soul I could bring in there who would testify to having had sex with her."

"Don't you think I knew it?" Butler said. "You had me worried. What if she'd called your bluff?"

"We'd have had to get our asses out there pounding the pavement for some of her old tricks."

"Our asses, and a lot of other asses, have already

231

been there," Butler said. "Christ, all we got was a lot of gossip, up and down the Boardwalk, but no solid evidence, nothing that would pass Swift's litmus test. Nobody wants to come into this court and testify against Allio."

"Except us suckers, right?" Frank said.

"Wait a minute," Butler said, "you and Nancy did a great job, but we're doing our part, too. Now, remember, Pretty Boy's going to take the stand this afternoon, and Goodnough's sure to give us one of his little soft-shoe routines. Nancy, don't worry about Joey. We wouldn't be here if I didn't think we could nail him. We're a little weak on corroboration, but your testimony, both of you, was first-rate, really convincing." He looked at his watch. "It's time to go in—except, Nancy, you don't have to. You've given your testimony. The bullshit level in there is likely to reach an all-time high this afternoon."

"It will take more than that little creep to keep me out of the courtroom," Nancy said, taking Frank's hand. "Come on, co-chief witness, let's go listen to another sleazy fairy tale."

As he waited for Goodnough to begin the questioning, Joey straightened his tie, then slowly turned his head until he was looking directly at the jurors. When he flashed a smile, four of the women and one man returned it.

"Ah, Mr. Bucci—or may I call you Joey?"

"Sure," Joey said. "That's my name."

"Joey, do you know the other defendants in this case? I mean other than Joyce Kresse."

"No, sir . . . Well I do now, but I didn't know them before the indictment, not personally that is."

"Okay, that's fine. What about Joyce Kresse? Do you

share an apartment at Ocean Towers with her?"

"Yes."

"Who pays the rent?"

Joey laughed. "Joyce really gave me hell at lunch today. She didn't know I was paying forty-five hundred a month. From time to time, she gives me a thousand or two toward the rent, and she pays the utilities, buys the food. It's a good arrangement."

"What kind of work do you do, Joey?"

"I'm a junket operator."

"Could you tell us what that is?"

"I bring high rollers to the various casinos in private planes and limousines, make sure they get the red-carpet treatment."

"Does that pay pretty well?"

"Yes, I get a percentage of their losses."

"Was Nancy Conti one of your high rollers?"

"No, no." Joey smiled, shaking his head. "She's a pretty big gambler, but not in that category. I'm talking about millionaires, people from South America, the Middle East, Japan, Texas—"

Goodnough laughed. "Texas, another foreign country heard from. Well, Joey, that was very interesting, but I think we'd better move along; I know His Honor will appreciate it. So why don't you tell this jury exactly how you came to know Nancy Conti."

"Well, it's like Joyce said this morning, we were playing blackjack at the same table and we struck up a conversation. She was losing a lot of money, but I've got to hand it to her, she was cool about it. You know, like money was going out of style, a sort of who-needs-it kind of attitude. Anyway, she asked us to her suite. I remember in the elevator she kind of made a little pass, so I got the idea—knew right off what she had in mind."

"What kind of a pass?"

Joey looked at the jury and dropped his eyes. "Her

hand touched me in front here. Kind of a little priming action, you know, so by the time we got to the suite, we were both a little excited. Well, she is an attractive woman, after all, and I'm a man."

Goodnough smiled. "Ideal combination."

"The only kind in my book. Anyway, while we were having a drink, she took my hand and led me into the bedroom. Joyce got miffed when Nancy invited her to join us. She just got up and left."

"I see. Now, could you tell us, to the best of your recollection, how many telephones did you observe in the suite?"

"Three. One in the bedroom, one in the bathroom, one on the bar."

"Do you know if they were operational on the evening in question?"

"Yes, when we first got there I used the one on the bar to check in with my answering service."

"How about the lock on the front door. Anything unusual?"

"Just a regular lock, far as I could tell."

"Joey, this is important. Did you kidnap Nancy Conti?"

"No, sir. I've never broken the law in my life. Well, I've gotten a couple of speeding tickets, but that's all."

"Fine, Joey. Now, think this over carefully. Did you, in any way, detain Nancy Conti against her will?"

"What do you mean? That was her suite, not mine. If you want to know the truth, I got out of there fast as I could."

"What do you mean, Joey?"

"I mean after we did it, you know—"

"You mean after you were intimate with Nancy Conti?"

Joey nodded. "Yes, but just that one time."

"Oh? Why only once?"

"Well, for one thing, I had to fly to Cleveland the next morning to arrange a junket."

"How long were you gone?"

"I left on Friday morning, August twenty-eighth, and got back late on Saturday, the twenty-ninth."

"Joey, aren't those the exact dates that you were supposed to be holding Nancy Conti prisoner in that suite at the Boardwalk Palace?"

"That they are," he said, pressing his lips together. "How ridiculous can you get, right? I told the cops, but they wouldn't listen to me."

"Do you have any proof you were in Cleveland during those dates? Airline tickets, hotel bill?"

"I used a private plane, and you've got the manifest and my hotel bill at the Cleveland Biltmore."

Goodnough smiled. "Your Honor, I'd like to enter these in evidence."

"So ordered," Swift said.

Butler was on his feet. "I'd like to see them, if I may."

"Of course," Goodnough said. "I have a copy for you."

"Oh, Christ," Butler said, flipping the documents across his desk.

"Mr. Butler!" Swift said.

"Sorry, Your Honor."

"Proceed, Mr. Goodnough."

"Now, where were we? Oh, yes, we were in the bedroom, and you had just had sex with Nancy Conti. So you left because you had to get up early in the morning to fly to Cleveland."

"Yeah, and also — well, after we finished, you know, she got some cocaine, made lines on the dresser and sniffed a couple of them up her nose, then handed me the straw. That's when I said, 'No way, José, good-bye and good luck,' and took off. I don't like coke heads."

"Objection!" Butler shouted.

"On what grounds?" Swift demanded.

"On the grounds that there has to be a limit to the number of lies one of these trained parrots can recite before this court with impunity."

"Mr. Butler, that opinion of yours is *not* grounds for objection."

"Judge, can't you see these people have been coached within an inch of their life."

"Mr. Butler—"

"Your Honor, that man sitting in the witness chair was arrested on Sunday, August thirtieth, with five ounces of hundred-proof cocaine in his possession."

"Mr. Butler, I'm not going to warn you again. Sit down. You'll get your chance on cross."

"Your Honor," Goodnough said, "I move to strike Mr. Butler's remarks as grossly unfair and prejudicial to my client and this witness. And to me personally, Your Honor."

"So ordered," Swift said, turning to face the jury. "You will please disregard Mr. Butler's outburst."

Goodnough turned back to Joey. "Were you arrested with cocaine in your possession?"

"No, sir," Joey said, looking directly at the jury. "That cop sitting over there behind the DA's table, Tom Conti, picked me up on August thirtieth and planted that stuff on me—"

"Objection, Your Honor," Butler shouted. "Speculation. Move to strike it from the record."

"Judge, the witness is just trying to set the record straight here. Mr. Bucci was indeed picked up for questioning. It's his contention that the illegal substance was planted on him to justify bringing him in. To date, Your Honor, no evidence has been produced by Detective Lieutenant Tom Conti—who, by the way, is a Philadelphia cop with no jurisdiction in Atlantic City—to establish probable cause. Nor are there any arrest records of the detention. They just hauled him in for questioning, and when they didn't get what they wanted, they tossed him out. As you no doubt have noticed, Your Honor, cocaine possession is not part of the indictment here."

"There are reasons for that omission, Your Honor," Butler said.

"Mr. Butler," Swift shouted, swiveling his chair to face him. "I will tolerate no further disruptions in this court."

On that high point, Goodnough concluded his examination. "Your witness," he said.

"Your Honor, it's getting late," Butler said. "May we recess until morning? I'd rather not have my cross-examination interrupted."

"All right," Swift said. "This court stands in recess until nine o'clock tomorrow morning."

26

When court reconvened the next morning, Butler was eager to begin his cross-examination of Joey. Yellow pad in hand, he approached the stand.

"Mr. Bucci," he said, "if you don't mind, I'm not going to call you Joey. It's such a boyish little name for a man in your position."

Joey shrugged. "Call me whatever you like, makes no difference to me."

"Fine, Mr. Bucci. How long have you known Joyce Kresse?"

"Seven, eight years."

"Is she one of your girls?"

"What do you mean?"

Butler moved to the side of the stand so that he stood between Joey and the jury box. "You know exactly what I mean, Mr. Bucci."

Joey looked at the jury over Butler's head. "No, I don't."

"Hard to believe," Butler said, scratching the back of his neck. "A guy like you, living in a fifty-four-thousand-dollar-a-year apartment, entertaining high rollers, riding around in limousines, wearing two-thousand-dollar suits . . . A sweet life — right, Mr. Bucci?"

"Your Honor, is that a question or a speech?" Goodnough said.

"Get on with it, Mr. Butler," Swift said.

"Sorry, Your Honor. It's not every day that I get to stand next to a millionaire playboy. What I meant, Mr. Bucci, is that we know Joyce Kresse is a prostitute, and what I want to know now is whether she's *your* prostitute. Is she in your stable?"

This time Goodnough was on his feet. "Your Honor, outrageous allegation."

"Judge, this man's character, or lack of it, could scarcely be more pertinent to the truth or falsity of his statements under direct examination. I beg the court's indulgence."

Swift waved his hand to silence Goodnough before he could respond. "Answer the question, Mr. Bucci."

Joey shook his head. "What's a stable? You make it sound like I run a racetrack. I don't have no stable. Period. Whatever Joyce does is her business, understand. I don't pry in her affairs, and she don't pry in mine."

"Are you telling this court that prostitutes don't work for you, or have never worked for you?"

"Think what you want, I gave my answer."

"I accept that, Mr. Bucci, as an admission."

"You're trying to trip me up. I'm just not going to argue with you. Think whatever you like. I told you that woman made a play for me, and it's the truth."

"All right, Mr. Bucci, let's move on. Do you know Larry Walsh?"

"The name's familiar."

"Let's see if I can help you. He's the credit manager at the Boardwalk Palace."

"Yeah, I heard of him, but I never met the man."

"You don't have a credit line at the Palace?"

"No, I'm not a gambler."

"So you never met Larry Walsh, is that correct?"

"That's correct."

"How about the other defendants in this case. How long have you known Mr. Allio, Mr. Sabato, Mr. Bartoli?"

"Just a few months," Joey said. "Just since my arrest."

"Excuse me, are you saying you didn't know them before your arrest in this case?"

"Oh, I'd heard of them, I'd seen them, but I didn't know them personally. Not to talk to, you know."

"Mr. Bucci, you keep surprising me. Would you care to rethink your answer?"

"Badgering, Your Honor," Goodnough said. "The witness has already answered this question, it is on the record, he testified in direct examination that he did *not* know Mr. Allio, Mr. Sabato, or Mr. Bartoli."

Swift waved the objection aside. "Mr. Bucci, answer the question."

"I'm telling the truth, Your Honor. I never met or talked to any of these gentlemen until my arrest." Joey paused, turned, smiled at the jury. "And I don't work for Seagull, either."

"So glad to hear it," Butler said. "May I remind you that you are under oath?"

"You don't have to, I know I took an oath to tell the truth. And I resent your implications." Joey looked directly at the jury. "I'm not lying."

Butler opened his yellow pad and took out a small stack of 8-by-10 photographs. "Mr. Bucci, I show you this photograph, and I ask you if you recognize any of the people in it?"

"What's going on here?" Goodnough said, jumping to his feet. "Your Honor, permission to approach the bench."

"Stay put, Mr. Goodnough," Swift said.

"Your Honor," Butler said, ignoring Goodnough, "they happen to be police surveillance photographs that show Mr. Bucci in the company of the defendants, all of whom he has denied knowing in direct and cross-examination. The photos are all dated, Your Honor, and all of them were taken well before the indictment."

"Judge, I object strenuously."

"On what grounds?"

"Irrelevancy, improper impeachment."

"Your Honor, this testimony is critical."

"Overruled. Proceed Mr. Butler."

"Exception, Your Honor."

"Noted."

"Mr. Bucci, please identify the people in this photograph," Butler said. "But first tell us where it was taken."

Joey swallowed hard. "Caesars."

"At a boxing match, right?"

"Yeah."

"Okay, let's name them. I see you're all in the front row, ringside—going first class, as usual."

"You've really got a smart mouth," Joey said.

"Mr. Bucci," Swift said, "no bantering. Answer the question."

"Yes, sir. Well, there's Funzi Cocchiaro . . . Sal Sabato . . . Tony Allio . . . Nick Bartoli . . . myself . . . Larry Walsh . . . Rocco Iezzi . . . and Donjo, I don't know his real name."

"All right, here's another photograph, where was this one taken?"

"At Donjo's."

"You with the same people again?"

"Yes, except Mr. Iezzi isn't there."

Butler turned to Swift. "Your Honor, I have several more photos here that show this defendant in the company of the other defendants and Mr. Walsh, all of whom he denied knowing in this court. After this trial, I will ask this court to cite Mr. Bucci for perjury—"

"Hey, wait a minute," Joey said, turning to the judge. "I forgot. In my business, I meet so many people, it's hard to remember them all. So I made a mistake. That's not perjury."

"Mr. Bucci, there's no question pending. Continue, Mr. Butler."

"At this time I would like to enter the photographs in evidence and then let the jury see them."

"So ordered. Continue."

"Mr. Bucci, earlier, in direct examination, you told Mr. Goodnough that Detective Lieutenant Tom Conti planted cocaine on you to justify a false arrest."

"Yes," Joey said, raising his voice, "but I wasn't arrested. I was picked up for questioning. Why can't I get this through your head? I've never been arrested."

"Well, you were arrested in this case, otherwise you wouldn't be on the witness stand, would you?"

"You know what I mean."

"Was Lieutenant Conti alone when you were . . . picked up?"

"There was another cop with him, I don't remember his name, something like Fairy, I don't know."

Butler turned to face the courtroom. "Will Detective Lieutenant Jim Ferris stand up."

When Ferris stood up, Butler said, "Is he the one?"

"Yeah, that's him."

"Thank you, Lieutenant, you may sit down." Turning to Joey, Butler said, "Did you know that Lieutenant Ferris is the head of the local organized crime unit?"

"So, what's it got to do with me?"

"You say they picked you up for questioning; what did they question you about?"

"Crazy stuff, I don't remember."

"Listen, Joey, you can tell us or I can put Lieutenant Ferris on the stand and he can tell us."

Joey shot a glance at Goodnough. "It was off the wall," he said, "something about a murder in Philadelphia."

"Whose murder?"

"Your Honor, objection, no proper foundation, irrelevant, inadmissible, way out of line. Your Honor, how far afield can this rogue elephant roam before he's tethered?"

"Your Honor, may counsel approach the bench?"

The two attorneys stood before Swift, who leaned forward, lowering his voice. "Mr. Butler, I'm not letting you open this can of worms. We have enough issues before this court without tracking in everything you can find on the police blotter. Get back to the witness and stay within the parameters of this indictment."

Butler looked at the jury, shrugged, walked back to the prosecution table. "I've no further questions for this witness."

Swift banged his gavel. "We will recess until one-thirty this afternoon."

"Motherfuckers, what the fuck's going on . . ."

Goodnough leaned back in the limousine's cushions to wait out the storm. There was a time when Allio's tirades had frightened him, but by now he knew how to handle this pint-sized hoodlum with the gargantuan ego. All you had to do was nod agreement, look serious or sad, whatever the occasion called for, and let him wind down. Then give him some good news. And if you didn't have any good news, make some up real fast.

"Let's not be premature," Goodnough said when Allio reached into the small refrigerator for a club soda. "We're going to win this case hands down. Sure, we took some body blows with Joyce and Joey, but you've got to expect that in any trial. The other side is not asleep—believe me, Sodana is one of the sharpest investigative lawyers in the business. And we took chances with Joyce and Joey. What were the odds that they'd pop up with surveillance shots of Joey with you guys? I didn't know they existed, and, as you know, I'm pretty well connected downtown. I knew there was nothing on the record about Joyce's prostitution, and I assumed they couldn't find a trick dumb enough to testify. They may not have, you know. I suspect they got away with a bluff."

"Butler and Sodana made them both look like fucking liars, goddamnit."

"Well now, Tony, I don't think it hurt us all that much. The jury was impressed with their direct testimony. I don't think they're going to forget it."

"Listen, I better not lose this fucking case, that's all I've gotta tell you."

"Tony, we're doing fine," Goodnough said. "Would I shit you?"

"Not if you're smart," Allio said, giving Goodnough a hard stare. "The question is, would you shit yourself."

When court reconvened after lunch, Goodnough breezed through a gaggle of witnesses summoned to confirm Joey's presence in Cleveland at the time the prosecution claimed he was in Atlantic City holding Nancy prisoner: the pilot of the private plane; the room clerks who checked Joey in and out of the Biltmore; two Cleveland gamblers who flew on the plane with him; and the plane's flight attendant, a statuesque blonde who said she spent Friday night with him in his Biltmore hotel room. Under cross-examination, the stewardess managed to slip in the information that she had known Joey for two years and had spent the night with him at least a dozen times. She described him as gentle and loving, the kind of man whose bed any woman would be happy to share.

The next morning Goodnough called a surprise witness, Charlotte Mackey.

"Your Honor," Butler said, "may counsel approach the bench? This witness was not on the list that the defense gave to the prosecution. Counsel for the defense is not complying with the discovery procedure."

"Your Honor, she's a reluctant witness," Goodnough said. "She was located only last night on the basis of information uncovered yesterday."

Swift shrugged. "What's the fuss, Mr. Butler? The defense is not required by law to supply the prosecution with its witness list."

"Yes, but they gave me one and left her off it. Who is this woman?"

Goodnough smiled. "Why don't I call her to the stand so we can all find out who she is."

"Please do," Swift said, leaning back in his chair.

Charlotte Mackey was tall and slender, with straight coal black hair, classical features, and a creamy complexion. After being sworn in, she sat down, crossed her long legs, and folded her hands in her lap. Her eyes, dark as her hair, flashed as she faced Goodnough, but her voice was soft when she answered his questions. She testified that she was divorced, had no children, and worked as a buyer for a Philadelphia department store.

"Ms. Mackey, have we ever met before last night?"

"No, sir."

"Have you ever met any of the defendants sitting at the two tables over there? Mr. Allio, Mr. Sabato, Mr. Bartoli, Mr. Bucci, Ms. Kresse?"

"No, sir."

"But I did talk with you last night."

"Yes."

"And you agreed, although reluctantly, to testify here today after I explained to you the importance of your testimony in rectifying a terrible injustice that was being committed in this court—is that correct?"

"Yes, sir."

"All right, Ms. Mackey. Do you know Frank Conti, the gentleman sitting over there just behind Mr. Butler."

"Yes."

"Could you describe for us your relationship with Frank Conti."

"We are friends."

"Ms. Mackey, may I remind you that you are under oath."

Charlotte Mackey seemed to have trouble swallowing.

"Would you like some water?"

"Yes, please. This is very difficult for me. I've never been in a courtroom before."

"Just relax," Goodnough said. "We're going to give you all the time you need to answer these questions. Just tell us the truth, that's all we ask."

"Yes, sir, I will."

"Bailiff," Swift called, "bring the witness some water."

As the bailiff scurried for a glass and the water carafe, Charlotte Mackey struggled to compose herself. Handed a full glass, she quickly drank it all down.

Goodnough gave her a smile. "Feel better now, Ms.

Mackey?"

"Yes, thank you."

"All right, now, what was your relationship with Frank Conti?"

"He was . . . my lover."

There was a loud murmur in the courtroom, and Swift banged his gavel. "Order," he said, again banging the gavel, "order, order. Proceed, Mr. Goodnough."

"And how long was he your lover?"

"Well, I haven't seen him in about five months, since a little after the plane crash in San Diego, but before that we went together for about a year."

"Goddamnit," Frank Conti shouted, jumping to his feet. "I never saw that woman before in my life. This is incredible."

"Sit down," Swift ordered, banging his gavel.

Butler stood up halfway in his chair and motioned for Frank to sit down.

"No further outbursts," Swift said, "or I'll have you ejected from this court. Do you understand?"

Frank nodded and looked at Nancy, who took his hand and pressed it against her cheek. "It's all right," she whispered. "We're just going to have to sit here and wait this nightmare out."

Tom reached over and gently touched his son's shoulder. "I'm sorry," he said.

"What the hell is this?" Butler said to Margot.

"Talk about a ringer," Margot said. "Mike, we need time on this one."

"Tell me about it. Let's have a list of your contacts in Philadelphia. We're going to need them."

"Please, tell us, Ms. Mackey," Goodnough said, "were you in love with Frank Conti?"

She bit into her lower lip in a valiant effort to keep back the tears, but they flowed anyway. Goodnough handed her his handkerchief, and she dabbed at her eyes.

"Were you in love with Frank Conti?"

"Yes, I was," she said in a little girl's voice.

"And was he in love with you?"

"Objection. Speculation."

Before Swift could rule on the motion, Goodnough said, "Did Frank Conti ever say he loved you?"

"Yes, many times."

"How do you know he was being truthful when he said he loved you?"

"He wanted me to go away with him."

"Go away with him? Go where?"

"Mexico."

"But Frank Conti is married, Ms. Mackey."

"I know, but they didn't get along. He told me his wife was gambling and drinking and running around and he was tired of it. He hated his job, he just wanted to get out from under — you know, get away from it all, start over again fresh in a new place, with me."

"Did you agree to go with him?"

She nodded, again wiping at her eyes.

"Ms. Mackey, the court reporter can't hear a nod."

"I'm sorry. Yes, I agreed, but later I changed my mind."

"But why? You say you loved him."

"I know. I did love him, but he came to see me the day he left for San Diego and opened this briefcase and he had so much money in there, he said it was nearly a hundred and fifty thousand. I got scared. He didn't say he stole it, but I knew he must have because the poor man was always broke, his wife gambled away every cent he ever had and then some."

"I see," Goodnough said, turning to look at the jurors. "So you were afraid that if he got caught you

248

might become implicated as an accomplice?"

"Yes," she said, pausing to drink from the fresh glass of water the bailiff had brought her. "There were also his plans, they scared me too."

"What plans were those?"

She cleared her throat and recrossed her legs. "Well, he said he'd laundered drug money at the Colton bank and thought that he could earn a living doing that in Mexico. Maybe go down to the Caribbean. I'm afraid my love wasn't strong enough, I got cold feet."

Goodnough nodded. "That's understandable. Was that the last time you saw Frank Conti?"

"No, he called me on a Sunday, I think it was the day after the plane crash, and he wanted me to join him in San Diego. I was shocked. I thought he was dead. It was on television and in the newspapers, and there he was on the telephone. At first I thought it was some crank playing a sick joke. But Frank laughed and said it was him all right and that he had it made." She paused. "He said something real strange."

"What was that?"

"He said that God had finally done something for him. You know, given him a chance at a new life. He called it his second life. And he said he wanted me to be his first wife in his second life. It was getting a little too spooky for me. I refused to join him, and the next day, in the middle of the night, he showed up at my place and begged me to go with him. I mean he practically got down on his knees. But by then the whole thing had gotten too bizarre for me. I told him I didn't want to see him again. And that was it. I never saw him again until I walked into this courtroom."

"Thank you for coming here today and telling your

story to this jury of twelve honest men and women, who have a complex task ahead of them. I know it was difficult for you, but justice is always worth the effort, no matter the price we have to pay. God bless you. Your witness, Mr. Butler."

"Your Honor," Butler said, "I respectfully request a forty-eight-hour recess so that we may check out this woman's story."

Goodnough was on his feet. "Your Honor, I see no reason for a lengthy delay simply because Mr. Butler doesn't like what Ms. Mackey had to say about his chief witness. He's had five months to prepare his case. I think it's a little late in the game to go back to square one."

"I agree," Swift said. "Request denied. Your witness, Mr. Butler."

As Butler approached the witness stand and the now fully composed Charlotte Mackey, Allio leaned forward, caught Frank's eye, and, with his fingers close to his face, pantomimed the firing of a gun.

Part Four
The Payoff — 1988

27

It was a lovely day for a walk. A warm breeze was coming in from the Gulf Stream. Having come to Key West directly from snowbound Philadelphia the day after the trial, Nancy had yet to take the cloudless skies and gentle sunshine for granted.

They had rented a small cottage in the Old Town section, and within three days of their arrival Frank found a job as a construction worker on a hotel going up near Flagler Avenue and Atlantic Boulevard. It was back-breaking work, wheel-barrowing wet concrete up steep ramps, and she felt sorry for Frank, but he actually seemed to love it — his step was light when he got home, even though she could tell from his face that he was exhausted. After all, Frank hadn't done anything physical in nearly twenty years. Now he was working side-by-side with twenty-year-olds.

After dinner every night they sat in an old canopied swing, set between tall coconut palms in the backyard, enjoying their coffee and looking up at the stars. They took long walks, holding hands, Nancy loving it and wishing it could go on this way forever. It was like awakening from a long nightmare and finding yourself in a new beautiful world.

Nancy had been to Key West before. When she was nine years old, she had come to visit a grandaunt and granduncle who lived in what they called a shotgun house. Built back in the 1880s for Cuban cigar workers, the house had a long hallway connecting to several bedrooms — which they rented to fishermen whenever they could — and a large all-purpose room at one end. They were poor, but Nancy had loved every minute of the two months she had spent here with them. Nearly every day she fished off the long pier with her granduncle, and what they caught they had for dinner that night and lunch the next day.

Her walk on this lovely day took her to Duval Street, where she window-shopped. She stopped a long time in front of Fast Buck Freddie's, admiring the strange assortment of quality merchandise being offered by a store with such a dubious name. Tourists crowded the street, most dressed in beachwear, eating hot dogs and licking ice cream cones; others rode by in the Conch Train and the Old Town Trolley, all apparently having a wonderful time.

When she got home with two bags of groceries in her arms, Neil Andrews was parked in front of the house, waiting for her. It was through the bureaucratic magic of Andrews, an inspector with the U.S. Marshal Service, that they were now Frank and Nancy Ciotti, with new birth certificates, driver's licenses, Social Security numbers, credit cards, and manufactured histories. In charge of the Federal Witness Protection Program in Philadelphia, Andrews had taken an instant liking to Frank. Both men were Vietnam veterans, Andrews having served with the marines in some of the fiercest action of 1968.

As Nancy approached the car, Andrews got out. "Looking beautiful, as always," Andrews said, taking the groceries.

"When did you get in?" she asked. "Been waiting long?"

"Around four-thirty. Had to come to Miami, so I

thought I'd hop down for a visit with my favorite couple. How's it going? Frank got a job yet?"

They went into the house, and Andrews sat at the kitchen table while Nancy made coffee and told him about Frank's job.

"That's great," Andrews said. "A couple of months on a job like that, and he'll be like a kid again. If I could afford it, I'd like to do something like that myself. But the pay—God, what's he getting, minimum?"

"No, he's earning almost ten an hour. We can get by on that, although this town's pretty expensive."

"Yeah, it's turned into a real tourist paradise," Andrews said. "Not like when you were here as a kid, right?"

"It was just a small town then."

"This can be a good place for you and Frank. You can start a new life here. I know one thing that hasn't changed, people on the island mind their own business. How do you like it so far?"

"It's a little early to tell, but so far we love it. It has a sort of seedy tropical elegance."

When Frank came in from work, he seemed genuinely pleased to see Andrews. They shook hands, and Andrews stepped back, putting his hands on his hips as he looked Frank over.

"I'd say this place agrees with you," he said, "in fact, with both of you. You two look great. Come on, get ready, I'm taking you out to dinner.

The Lobster House on Front Street overlooked the harbor and shrimp docks.

"Go out there in a boat," Andrews said, "hang a left and ninety miles south you run into Cuba. A lot of fishermen around here who went to Mariel during the Cuban boat lift got their boats red-tagged."

"What does that mean?" Nancy asked.

"Confiscated. For carrying illegal passengers."

"I'm sure it's still going on," Frank said.

"You're not kidding," Andrews said. "The Keys have long been a way station for all kinds of smuggling. During prohibition it was rum from Cuba. Today it's cocaine and marijuana from South America. Boats and planes land regularly on the Keys."

"It's hard to believe," Nancy said. "It's seems so peaceful here."

When the waiter came for their orders, Andrews selected the wine, but Nancy poured 7-Up into her wine glass.

"Heard from your dad?" Andrews asked.

"Talked to him last night," Frank said.

"I saw him before I came down here. Looks like he's taking the outcome of the trial harder than you."

"I doubt that," Frank said.

"Those miserable bastards," Andrews said. "I still can't believe they got away with it. You can't imagine how much I hate those sons of bitches. They're worse than any gook I ever killed. Allio and his bums wouldn't have lasted a day out in the bush—right, Frank?"

"What I think is that I don't want to think about it."

Nancy reached over and touched Frank's hand. "He's right," she said, "the past is gone, finished, it's history. What we're doing here is building for the future."

Joey hung up the phone, hurried to the spare bedroom Joyce used as an exercise room. "Hey, babe! Guess what, the man himself—not Nick, not Sal, not any of his other flunkies—just personally called to invite me to his place for a celebration dinner. How about that?"

Joyce, wearing only bikini panties, was lying on her back, lowering both legs to the floor for the twenty-third time. "Terrific," she said between clenched teeth.

"God, I love it when your body's all wet and shiny," Joey said. "Even your nipples sweat. Christ, you look good enough to eat."

"You already did that," she said. "So when's this shindig?"

"Sunday noon, after church, that's when they have their big spread. We did that at my house, too, when I was a kid. It's an old Italian custom, kind of a Catholic thing, too, I suppose."

"You mean to tell me that little shit goes to church?"

"I don't know, maybe. I hear his mother, Chiara, is very devout, goes to mass every morning and is in thick with the priest. She gives the church lots of money, and the priest says a mass for Vincenzo every week."

"Yeah, well, it'll take more than masses to drag that old fart out of hell."

"Do you know this is my first dinner invitation? Christ, you ought to see the place. I'm telling you, it's one big fabulous . . . I don't even know what to call it — estate, mansion, whatever, it's the greatest. Some day, babe, I'm gonna have me a place like that — hey, don't laugh, I'm serious."

"Why not?" Joyce said. "All it takes is money. Big junket operator like you, should be a piece of cake."

Joey grinned. "When I said junket operator, Butler nearly shit his pants. Babe, we did a hell of a job for Tony in that courtroom. That's why the invite. It was touch and go there for a while, but now, you know, I'm really part of the team."

"You better be careful. He's probably got a crematorium in his backyard, and nobody will ever hear from you again."

"What the fuck are you talking about? I was *great* in that courtroom."

Joyce sat up. "Great? Goddamnit, Joey, wake up!

Butler and Sodana made us look like world-class liars. If it hadn't been for Charlotte Mackey, we'd all be in the slammer."

"Hey, she'd have looked like a world-class liar too if Butler had gotten the goods on her the way he did on us. If anybody fucked up, it was Arthur. He's the one who told us to deny everything. Anyway, this invitation is something special, believe me. You'd be included except Tony don't want women around when he gets together with the guys."

"Thank God for little favors," Joyce said. "If you were smart you'd stay the hell away from there."

"Are you fucking crazy? You can't say no to Tony Allio."

"Why not?"

"Because he don't like it."

She reached for a towel on the floor and dried her arms and shoulders. "I've got Allio up to here," she said, tapping her hand under her chin. "That beady-eyed little prick and his goons were in Goodnough's office the whole time the chinless marvel was priming me for my fucking debut."

"So what? They were there for me, too."

Joyce climbed on the Lifecycle and started pedaling. "Joey, they're not your friends, any of them. Especially Allio."

"Ah, fuck it," Joey said on his way out of the room. "I can't talk to you anymore.

28

On Sunday morning, Chiara, Dorotea, and Stella
went to early mass. There was so much to do before
noon. Antonio wanted everything perfect for the *avvocato*. Chiara had enjoyed the trial, particularly the part
where the *avvocato* had made fools of those crazy people
with their *stupido* story and that *repulsivo* district attorney and his assistant with the *poppas* on her like a *vacca*.

On the stove a huge pot of meat sauce was simmer-
ing, filling the kitchen with its spicy aroma while the
women worked. Chiara was buttering loaves of garlic
bread for the oven, Dorotea was washing lettuce, Stella
was setting the banquet table in the baronial dining
room with its walk-in fireplace and massive antique
furniture.

At twelve o'clock sharp, the guests, who'd had drinks
and antipasto in the library, followed Allio into the dining room and began looking for their name cards. Allio
seated himself at the head of the table, his back to the
mammoth fireplace, Goodnough to his right. At the
other end of the table sat Vincenzo, Allio's seventeen-
year-old son. Lined up on both sides of the table were
the three uncles, Rocco, Raulo, and Rufo; Raulo's son,
Arrigo (he called himself Hank), who had replaced the
late Tito as narcotics boss; Donjo, Larry Walsh, Sal Sabato, Funzi Cocchiaro, Ugo Failla; Pasco Zito, the local prostitution boss; Kid Blast, a loan-shark collector
and former heavyweight boxer once managed by Allio

whose real name no one seemed to remember; and Joey Bucci.

As soon as they were seated, Chiara, Dorotea, and Stella brought in chafing dishes of meat sauce, followed by steaming bowls of spaghetti. Allio was talking when Stella placed the pasta in front of him. Still talking, he picked up a fork, reached into his bowl, then pulled back.

"What the fuck is this gummy shit doing here?" he screamed at the top of his voice. Lifting the bowl in one hand like a shot-putter, he hurled it across the room, missing Stella by inches as she was retreating toward the kitchen.

Conversation resumed its flow; wine bottles made their rounds.

"How's your pasta?" Allio called to his son.

"It's okay, Dad," Vincenzo said.

"Are you sure?"

"Its good, Dad, really."

"Goddamn woman will never learn that unless you get it under cold water right away this shit keeps cooking," Allio said to no one in particular.

Chiara rushed in from the kitchen. "Don't worry, Antonio, I got more cooking, I bring it right away."

"Okay, Ma, just make sure it's the way I like it. And I want you to do the veal dish yourself."

Chiara patted his arm. "Don't worry, I take care of everything."

"And get Stella in here to clean this shit up."

"Sure, Antonio," Chiara said, "she come right away. Now, leave everything to me. Enjoy your dinner with your nice friends."

Joey emptied his wine glass and quickly refilled it. Maybe Joyce had the right idea. This guy was as unpredictable as a two-dollar pistol. One wrong word and he could blow up in your face. The fact that no one had reacted impressed Joey almost as much as Allio's display of temper. They must have seen so many tantrums one more didn't mean anything to them. Or to Allio. One moment he was screaming and the next he was talking and laughing with Goodnough as if he didn't have a care in the world.

"Hey, everybody," Allio called, tapping his wine glass with a spoon. "Fill your glasses, let's drink a toast to our great barrister, the one and only Arthur Goodnough."

"Thank you, my friends," Goodnough said. "Here's to freedom."

"And to surprise witnesses," Allio said. "Except, you son of a bitch, you had me on the ropes there until the last round. When Joyce and Joey got all fucked up, I could see the cell door closing."

"Don't be too hard on them," Goodnough said, winking at Joey. "They accomplished what I wanted—created confusion in the jurors' minds. Through that little opening wedge, I was able to drive the big one home with Charlotte."

"Yeah," Nick said. "Tell us about Charlotte."

"Great fucking legs," Sal said. "How'd you like to have them wrapped around you?"

"Yeah, Arthur, how about her phone number?" Funzi said. "I'll give her a friendly call when I get back to Philly tomorrow."

"Sorry," Goodnough said, "but Ms. Mackey no longer resides in your friendly city. She has departed, I'm happy to report, for parts unknown. And, I might add, to the great consternation of that fearless detective Tom Conti, who seems most anxious to find her."

"The timing was perfect," Allio said. "No wonder you was so fucking cool when I was steaming—you had Swift in the bag all along, right?"

Goodnough gave Allio a shocked expression. "What are you implying?"

Allio laughed. "You son of a bitch."

"We're talking trade secrets here. Does a magician say how the rabbit got in the hat?"

Allio reached over the squeezed Goodnough's arm. "Thanks, buddy."

Goodnough's eyes, magnified behind the thick lenses, turned serious as he looked at each man around the table. "Tony, when the freedom of my good and dear friends is at stake, I never take chances."

After dinner, as the men headed into the parlor for cigars and brandy, Nick pulled Joey aside.

"Come with me," he said in his gruff voice.

"What's up?"

"Shut up and move your ass."

Joey nodded, hurrying to keep up with Nick's long stride. "Everything okay?" he asked.

"I told you to shut the fuck up."

Joey swallowed and reached for his handkerchief.

Nick opened a door, waved Joey into Allio's office, and closed the door behind them. Allio was sitting behind his desk, his arms folded on the desk top, his chin resting on his hands. His dark eyes drilled Joey, who shifted uneasily but kept his mouth shut.

"I waited six months," Allio said, suddenly leaning back in the large leather chair. "I let Arthur handle the case, didn't want to rock the boat, but now I want some fucking answers, understand?"

"Sure, Tony," Joey said.

"How did Nancy Conti know about me? You told her, didn't you?"

"No way," Joey said. "I never said your name in front of her, I'm not that stupid. Maybe, you know — I've given this some thought — maybe Butler put her up to it, to sharpen up his case."

"Bullshit."

"Why not? It makes sense."

"Don't fuck with me."

Joey looked down at the floor. Those crazy eyes were making him dizzy. "The only other explanation—" he paused and wiped his upper lip, "maybe Joyce told her. I mean, they were pretty tight. I know goddamn well I locked the door when I left, and no maid had a key to it. So how'd she get out?"

"Joey, you just said the magic words." Allio crooked his finger. "Come here," he said, "bend over the desk, I want you looking at me when I talk to you."

When Joey leaned forward, Allio grabbed his necktie and pulled down until they were eyeball to eyeball. His eyes boring into Joey's, Allio raised his right thumb and slowly moved it forward until it rested on Joey's nose. "Ice her," he said.

Joey's eyes widened.

"You heard me. Ice the bitch."

The pressure against Joey's nose made his eyes smart. "Tony, I'm not sure she did it, I was only guessing."

"Hey, it's either you or her. Nobody else was in that fucking room, right?"

Joey closed his eyes and tears rolled down his cheeks. "Damn, Tony, she was great in the courtroom."

"Don't give me that bullshit."

"Tony . . . Jesus, man, I love the broad. Give her another chance, please, Tony. She been with me a long time. I need her, you know—"

"Hey, no more talk, just do it, capisci?"

When Joey nodded, Allio released him. Joey straightened up and made rapid swipes at his eyes with the handkerchief.

"Don't fuck it up."

Joey pressed his fingers against his temples. "I won't," he said, his words barely audible.

29

Joey stood beside the bed, watching Joyce sleep. She was such a quiet sleeper. Never tossed or turned, much less thrashed around the way he did. Her face looked so serene, like whatever was going on inside her head was peaceful.

It seemed that all the women he'd known were great sleepers. Most of them could sleep all day if left alone. What was it about women that made it so easy for them to escape into sleep, just conk out and be out of it while he awakened a half-dozen times every night, thinking about all his problems at a time of night when there wasn't a goddamn thing he could do about them?

Christ, things had gone from bad to worse. What in the hell was he going to do about Joyce? He'd been agonizing for days. There was no getting around it. Sooner or later, and it had better be sooner, he was going to have to deal with it.

Why hadn't he kept his stupid trap shut? Maybe Allio hadn't made up his mind about Joyce until Joey put her neck in the noose. But what choice had Allio given him? What it had come down to was her neck or his.

How long had he known Joyce? How many times had they done it? Maybe he didn't love her, not the way people talked about love, but she was the best person he'd ever known and he liked her more than anyone he knew. This wasn't Bobby Scolieri, where you closed your eyes and pulled the trigger. This was personal.

During the night he had awakened next to Joyce in their large bed, a light coming through a slit where the drapes parted, casting strange shadows on the walls, reminding him of when he was a kid and afraid of the dark. In the mirror over the bed he could barely make out the outlines of their bodies. Joyce was lying on her back, dead to the world. Could he have put a pillow over her face and snuffed out her life while she struggled to live? He shuddered. Maybe he could get somebody to do it for him—no, he might as well forget that idea. There was no subcontracting in this business.

Joey pushed the remote button, and the drapes slowly opened to bright sunshine. At least the weather was with him. He leaned over and brushed a tangle of red hair out of Joyce's face.

"Hey, babe, wake up," he said, running his hand inside the covers.

Joyce moaned and barely opened her eyes. "Ohhh, hmmm, that feels good," she murmured, stretching. "A little lower . . ."

Joey hesitated, his hand between her breasts—one last fuck, he thought, seriously considering it for a moment, then pulling back. "No time for monkey business," he said. "Get your ass out of bed, we're going for a ride."

Her eyes opened wide. "A what?"

"Hey, it's Sunday afternoon, the sun's shining, the roads are clear, let's take a ride down the coast, maybe Cape May. I know a great restaurant there, we'll have dinner, how about it?"

She sat up and looked at him. "What's gotten into you?" she said. "What's up?"

"What do you mean, what's up? It's a beautiful day, just thought you'd enjoy taking a ride. Don't you want to come?"

"That's a first," she said, "you taking me for a Sunday drive like Joe Schmo. What is it, you got some business down there?"

Joey gave that some thought, then laughed. "Damn, you read me like a book. Yeah, I got a little business, but nothing that's gonna interfere with our dinner or anything."

"Is it business for Allio?"

"No way, babe. I'm taking your advice on him, gonna keep my distance from now on. You're right, I think the guy's practically psycho. He's got mood swings you wouldn't believe."

"There's nothing bad you can tell me about that little prick I wouldn't believe."

"He treats his wife like shit."

"He treats everybody like shit. Glad to see you coming to your senses — finally."

He nodded. "I know, it took me a while to wise up, but the guy's too heavy. Come on, get dressed, we don't want to miss any of this sunshine."

Joey was unusually quiet, preoccupied with some business he refused to discuss. The champagne had made Joyce lightheaded, and the drone of the engine and the headlights bouncing in the darkness of the deserted road soon lulled her to sleep. She had lowered the seat, and her head was resting against her shoulder, putting a strain on her neck that she alleviated by moving her head from side to side every few minutes. She dreamed about her mother, just bits and snatches that didn't make sense, but it occurred to her that when her mother died she was younger than Joyce was right now. It was a disturbing thought, and she opened her eyes.

It took a moment for it to dawn on her that they had left the main highway and were moving slowly along a narrow road cut through a heavy grove of pine.

"Where are we?" she asked, sitting up straight, rubbing sleep from her eyes.

"Avalon," Joey said.

"Joey, we're in the woods."

"Hey, relax," he said, "I'm cutting through to the parkway."

"What for?"

"It'll be faster."

"What's the matter with you?" she said. "There was nobody on the road, you had it all to yourself."

"Nah, you were sleeping," he said. "Must have been an accident ahead, there was a real jam-up."

She leaned forward, peering out the windshield. "This can't be the road to the parkway. I know this area. If we're at Avalon, the only road that goes to the parkway is the one to Swainton, and this sure ain't it."

The engine suddenly died. "Oh, shit," he cried, "what the fuck's wrong now?" He pulled to the side, braked to a stop, popped the hood, and got out to look at the engine.

"This's ridiculous," Joyce shouted. "What do you know about fixing a car?"

"I know plenty," he called back. "Come here, I'll show you. I just found the trouble."

"Joey, just fix it and let's get out of here. The place gives me the willies."

"Come on, take a look," he said. "I'm not fixing it until you look at it."

"Oh, shit," she cried, throwing the door open. "It's fucking freezing out here. Hurry up, will you?"

Joey was standing in front of the headlights. As Joyce came around the open door, she saw his arm go up—and, then, the gun in his hand. The scream she heard was hers.

* * *

There was a blinding flash. She felt something hot in her mouth and a vicious searing pain in her right cheek. The next thing she knew she was running in the woods with snow up to her knees, falling down and scrambling back to her feet, bumping into trees and bouncing off, and all the while, Joey shooting and screaming, "Stop . . . I wanna talk to you! Come back here, stop, willya . . . don't be afraid, Joyce — talk to me, for Chrissake! Stop!"

She kept running until she couldn't hear the shots or the screaming. When she felt the blood in her mouth, she spat and touched her cheek. There was a hole in it. The first shot must have gone through her open mouth and out through her cheek without touching anything else.

"Joey!" she cried, the tears streaming down her face, "WHAT HAVE THEY DONE TO YOU?" Then, in the distance, she heard the Lincoln's engine start and fade away.

Tom scrubbed the kitchen sink. The madder he got, the harder he scrubbed. The Scolieri investigation wasn't getting anywhere. After Frank and Nancy left for Key West, Tom had gone back to work on the Scolieri murder, looking for that one little break that would lead him not only to Joey but eventually to Allio himself. But that was a long shot. If only there were something he could do to heat up the gang war, give it a little push, maybe Allio's number would come up.

Unfortunately, Captain Beal was watching him like a hawk; with retirement just around the corner, Tom had to be careful. Under Beal's order, he'd turned over everything he had on the case to Mooney and McGeary at the Round House, for all the good that would do.

As part of Frank's plea bargain on the embezzlement charge, he'd returned to the Colton bank the $100,000 he'd brought back from San Diego. Tom had raised the extra $42,500 by taking a mortgage on his house.

"Its not fair," Frank had said. "You're ready to retire. You don't need that extra expense."

"I won't even notice it," Tom said. "The world is full of people with mortgages, it's the American way of life. Besides, I'm also going to keep up the payments on your house for a while. The mortality rate in Allio's occupation is pretty high these days. Who knows, the other side could get lucky and you two might be back here sooner than you think."

The telephone rang. Tom quickly dried his hands, then picked up the receiver.

At first, between the sobs and the curses, he couldn't make out what Joyce was saying. Then he got it: Joey had tried to kill her, Joyce had escaped and was holed up at the Avalon Motel.

"Stay there, wait for me," Tom said. "I'll be there as soon as I can."

"Please hurry," she said. "I'm afraid they'll come looking for me."

"Don't open the door to anyone until I get there," he said. "Listen, it's going to take a while. You're not exactly across the street."

"I know," she said, "but hurry."

"I will. Now be brave, hold tight till I get there."

Tom grabbed his coat and left the house. As the car raced down Broad Street, he decided that the longest route would be the fastest. Take the Atlantic City Expressway to the Garden State Parkway, down to Swainton, then across to Avalon. With luck he'd make it in record time.

* * *

At seventy-four, Doctor Sam Moceri had a limited practice. He hadn't made a house call in more years than he cared to remember. So when the telephone rang at three in the morning, he reached for it with a shaking hand, convinced that something terrible must have happened to his daughter or his grandchildren.

When he heard Tom Conti's voice, he was so relieved he had to work at sounding annoyed about being awakened from a sound sleep in the middle of the night.

"Goddamnit, you know I don't make house calls," he said when Tom asked him to come right away.

"I know, Sam, but I really need you. Believe me, I wouldn't call at this hour unless it was critical."

"So what's the matter with St. Agnes's emergency room, or the paramedics?"

"Sam, when was the last time I called you in the middle of the night?"

"I'm telling you," he said, "it better be life and death, that's all I've got to say."

Joyce was sitting at the kitchen table, holding a wet facecloth against her injured cheek. There were red circles around her eyes.

"He didn't want to come, did he?"

"Well," Tom said, "he's getting old and it's a little past his bedtime."

"I can't believe what that bastard Joey tried to do to me," she said, starting to cry again.

"The way I see it," Tom said, "Allio gave Joey the contract. I don't think Joey had any choice in the matter."

"Are you *excusing* him?"

"Not at all, just trying to analyze it. Allio can't be sure who released Nancy. This way he gets one to kill the other, leaves him only one to deal with."

"Jesus, I hope that little rat fink Joey gets his real

soon. I can't believe he'd do that to me, after all these years — God, I was scared. It was so dark and cold out there, and I could hear the shots and his footsteps, and he was yelling crazy stuff, it was a living nightmare."

There was a knock at the kitchen door. "It's okay," Tom said, opening the door. "Come in, Sam."

Sam Moceri reminded Tom of the wizened little men he had seen on a trip to Sicily years ago. They spent their days in the piazza, sitting on boxes and broken chairs, their sunken eyes gleaming like vultures' eyes.

"So what've we got here?" he said, dropping his medical bag on the table.

Joyce tried to smile. "I've got a hole in my cheek," she said.

"Hmmmm," said Moceri, pushing a Q-tip through the hole. "You do this, Tom?"

"That's not funny," Tom said.

"Wasn't meant to be," Moceri said. "This looks like a gunshot wound."

"That's what it is, all right," Tom said.

"And I suppose you don't want it reported?"

"Not tonight, I don't."

"When you do, remember to cover me."

"You don't ever have to worry about that, Sam."

Moceri turned to Joyce. "How tough are you, little lady?"

"Very. Wait a minute — why do you ask?"

"Gotta take a couple stitches here."

"Will it leave a scar?" Joyce asked.

Moceri cackled. "Vanity, vanity, all is vanity."

"Very funny," Joyce said.

"Don't worry yourself." He took out a needle and thread. "Do I look like a butcher?"

"Do I have to answer that?"

Another cackle. "Relax, little lady, while I give you a cute little dimple."

"Please, hold my hand," Joyce said, reaching for Tom's.

Moceri looked up at Tom. "You gonna tell me what happened here?"

"Nothing happened here," Tom said.

"So how did she get this?" he asked, as he carefully began stitching. "She didn't put a gun in her mouth, that I can tell you."

Joyce squeezed Tom's hand. "That fucking hurt," she said when Moceri was done.

"If my mother was here," Moceri said, "she'd wash your mouth with soap."

"If your mother was here, she'd be too old to pick up a bar of soap."

Moceri looked at Tom. "She's got a smart mouth, this one. No wonder somebody put a bullet in it."

"Didn't shut her up, though, did it?" Tom said.

"Maybe I should sew it shut while I've got the needle and thread handy," Moceri said with a straight face. "Someday, Tom, you'd thank me for it."

Tom could feel himself flushing. "What're you talking about, you old coot?"

"If only I was a couple years younger, I'd show you what I'm talking about." Moceri put his equipment back in his medical bag and winked at Joyce. "Who does he think he's kidding, right?"

She winked back at him.

"You're some looker," Moceri said, picking up the bag. "I was his age, I'd blackmail you into my bed. I could blackmail her, couldn't I, Tom? Something illegal went on here tonight, right?"

"Good night," Tom said, "and don't let the door hit you in the ass on the way out."

"That's the thanks I get for getting dragged out of my warm bed in the middle of the night."

Joyce stood up. "Thanks for the compliment and the

272

dimple," she said, kissing Moceri on top of his bald head.

Joyce lay in Frank's old bed and stared up at the ceiling. Dawn was breaking; her cheek was throbbing, and she was still awake. Every time she closed her eyes, she found herself in the woods again, running for her life. In that engulfing darkness she had faced certain death, and it terrified her in a way she could never have imagined. She had never wanted to live more than at that moment when she was sure she was going to die.

How could she have been so wrong about Joey? She'd known he was vain and self-centered, that he admired Mafia guys, their money and power. But his biggest problem, she now realized, was that he was weak. Too weak to say no when Allio laid it on the line.

This whole thing was Allio's doing. That horrible little man wanted her dead, and who on earth could stop him from getting what he wanted? Not Joey, for sure. Not the police, whose track record was pathetic. Tom Conti was the most likely prospect, and Tom was an old man.

On the ride in from Avalon, she'd told him everything she knew about Allio's operation. Besides the usual rackets—loan-sharking, prostitution, drugs— there was Allio's stranglehold on several key unions, including casino security guards, hotel and restaurant employees, bartenders. A strike of those unions could close down a casino's operation anytime he gave the word. Allio used this clout to force the casinos to purchase goods and services from corporations he controlled through offshore holdings. Her information was hearsay, of course, most of it from Joey, nothing that would hold up in court. Even Goodnough's coaching her, in front of Allio, to lie about her testimony was protected under the attorney privilege. The fact was, she knew nothing that would buy her entry into the witness protection program.

Finally, she couldn't stay in bed any longer. She came out into the hallway and walked to Tom's bedroom door. She listened a moment, then slowly opened it. It creaked; she froze in the half-open doorway, peeked in to make sure he was asleep, then crept across the room to his bed. Lifting one end of the covers, she carefully slipped beneath them. He was lying on his left side, his back to her; she sidled up to him, pressing her body into his. She could feel his warmth radiating against her chilled flesh.

Slowly, stealthily, she lowered her hand along his side, ran it across his hips to his hard flat stomach, reaching down until she had him in her hand.

Tom groaned and straightened his legs; she could feel him getting hard immediately.

"My God," he moaned, "what are you doing?"

"Shusssh," she whispered.

For a Monday, Donjo's was unusually crowded. Patrons were lined up three-deep at the bar, and the topless dancers were in full jiggle. Joey stood at the back of the room, surveying the action, trying to decide what he was going to tell Nick. He could see Nick and Sal sitting in Allio's reserved booth. At least Allio wasn't there.

All day Joey had kept away from his apartment, afraid Joyce must have gone to the police. In late afternoon he'd called the Ocean Towers security guard, who told him Joyce hadn't been around and no one had been asking for him. Obviously, she hadn't gone to the police. Maybe she wouldn't. Maybe she'd just hide out until the heat cooled.

This latest fiasco was just plain ridiculous. That fucking Saturday night special—piece of fucking shit. Only six goddamn feet away when he fired—point-blank, for Chrissake. He could have sworn he hit her right in the head. Still she ran away—Jesus, she ran like a fucking deer in snow up to her ass. It was all that lousy aerobic and Lifecycle shit she did every day.

So what was he going to do? Run? Hide? Take the heat? Or lie like a bandit? Damn, it was hot in this fucking joint. Joey reached for his handkerchief. Son of a bitch! Why was he always sweating? Made him feel like a motherfucking wimp. He wiped his upper lip and forehead and tucked the handkerchief in his inside breast pocket, keeping it handy for the next sweat session.

Putting a smile on his handsome face, Joey strode across the room and slipped into the booth next to Nick. "Hi, what's happening?" he said. "Busy fucking night for a Monday."

"Where the fuck you been?" Nick asked. "Tried to reach you all day."

Joey's heart sank. "Yeah, what's up?"

Nick leaned forward. "Where's Joyce?"

Joey swallowed. "She's dead," he said, lowering his voice. If she didn't go to the cops and stayed in hiding, that was like being dead. If he told Nick she'd escaped, his ass would be in a sling and they'd get some guys out on the street looking for her.

"Yeah? As of when?"

"Last night."

Nick turned to Sal. "What do you think of that?" he said.

Sal got up and slipped into the booth next to Joey, sandwiching Joey between the two of them. "Joey, why didn't you call last night?"

Joey bit his lower lip. "I was pretty low, didn't feel like

talking to nobody."

"Joey, you better not fucking lie to us," Nick said.

"I'm not, I swear on my mother's head. She was my girl, goddamnit. How would you feel?"

"Where's the body?" Nick said.

"I buried her in the woods near Swainton."

Sal grabbed his arm. "Buried her? What'd you use, a fucking blowtorch?"

"I mean in the snow," Joey said.

"How'd you kill her?"

"Shot her."

"Where?"

"In the head."

"How many times?"

"I emptied the clip, seven times I think, I didn't count."

Nick leaned back in the booth. "Where's the gun?"

"Gone. I threw it away."

"Where?"

"In the ocean, at the end of Steel Pier."

Nick stared at him a long time. There were small beads of sweat on Joey's face, but he resisted the urge to go for his handkerchief.

"You better be fucking straight, man," Nick said. "One more fuck-up and you'll be gone, too. Capisci?"

30

This time Jim Ferris had a warrant when he and Tom went to arrest Joey for attempted murder. Tom had told Ferris everything except where he'd hidden Joyce. For one thing, he was afraid of leaks in Ferris's office; for another, he felt funny about saying that she was staying with him. Especially after what had happened when he found her in his bed. That was something he wasn't about to tell anyone.

The flesh was weak. He'd always known that but had never thought of himself that way. He'd been faithful to Rachel all those years, and after she'd gotten sick and sex was out of the question, he'd written off that part of his life for good. He certainly wasn't going to go out looking for it, that was for damn sure. No senior citizen centers for him. Now and then a wet dream, maybe, but that was beyond his control. So this morning was more than a surprise, it was a revelation. The advanced age of sixty-five — married over forty years, a cop all his life — was a bit late to find out how little you knew about the mysterious pleasures of sex. That Joyce was a piece of work. He'd never known women like her existed outside of books.

They had been sitting in Joey's living room all evening, waiting to arrest him the moment he came in. If he ever decided to come in, that is. There were enough reasons for him not to.

"What are you grinning about?" Ferris asked.

"Nothing," Tom said, his expression turning serious.

"You looked like the cat that ate the canary," Ferris said. "What happened last night when you picked up Joyce?"

"Nothing," Tom said, bristling. "Just what I told you."

"It's okay," Ferris said. "You don't have to tell me anything personal. After all, it none of my business."

"There's no business to tell."

Ferris started singing, "There's no business like monkey business, like no business I know —"

"Get off it," Tom said, trying not to smile. He got up and walked to the large window and looked down at the lighted Boardwalk. He saw little hurrying figures, bent over against the wind coming off the black ocean.

"What's keeping him?"

"He'll be along," Ferris said. "He's not going to leave all this expensive clothing and jewelry behind, not to mention the loot or the cocaine he's probably got stashed in that closet safe."

"What do you suppose he told Allio?"

"Maybe he's dead, Tom. Botching a murder is a pretty heavy fuck-up."

"In that case, we've got a long wait," Tom said.

The phone rang. It was Teddy, calling from the lobby.

"He's on his way up," he said, and hung up.

On the way back to the apartment, Joey played and replayed his conversation with Nick and Sal. Was he off the hook? He told himself yes, but the piece of ice in his chest said no. He didn't like the way Nick and Sal kept looking at each other while he told his story. Those guys would be suspicious of a deathbed confession from their own mother.

Why couldn't they trust him? After what he'd done for them—hitting Scolieri on the fucking street, in plain sight of everybody. How many guys could do that? Keep their cool like that? Allio himself had been proud of him, had told Nick to talk to him with respect, that he was one of them now. So where was the respect? How many more would he have to kill before he gained their respect for longer than ten minutes?

Now it was Joyce they'd wanted him to hit, his best girl, the only woman he'd ever really cared anything about. Did they give a shit? The family had a zillion hitters, why couldn't they have given the contract to somebody else? It was like they enjoyed making him suffer. That fucking Nick had to be behind it. He'd had it in for Joey from the moment they met. He was so ugly, a fucking gorilla—maybe he was jealous of Joey's looks. What broad would ever put out for a guy like that unless he paid for it? That was Nick's problem, why he was so fucking mean—no loving, just a lot of bought ass.

Who would they want him to hit next? He hadn't gotten this far to end up a lousy hitter—it was the political clout and raw power and respect of a made guy that appealed to him. He wanted the flunkies bowing and scraping when he entered a casino. He wanted to be a heavyweight.

As Joey inserted the key into the lock, he wondered what Nick and Sal were telling Allio at this very moment. He pushed the door open, reached out for the light switch, stepped into the room—and the door slammed behind him. Startled, Joey turned and bumped into Granite Face, who grabbed him by the scruff of the neck, spun him around, slammed him up against the door.

"Assume the position, punk. Spread 'em."

Joey turned his head and saw Beanpole standing behind Granite Face, grinning like a fucking idiot.

"You don't have any rights here," Joey said. "This is my apartment, you're invading my privacy. I wanna call my lawyer."

Frisking him, Granite Face quickly found Joey's Saturday night special.

"What've we got here?" he said, handing the .25 caliber automatic to Beanpole.

"An Astra Firecat. A little old lady's popgun."

"Big enough to kill you," Granite Face said, taking out his handcuffs. "Get your hands behind your back. Jim, read him his rights."

While Beanpole read Joey his rights, Granite Face snapped on the handcuffs.

"Come on, let's go," he said, opening the door and pushing Joey out into the hall.

Nobody said a word while they rode down in the elevator, walked through the lobby, drove away in the police car. Joey figured they were trying to sweat him with the silent treatment. At the police station, Joey was taken to Beanpole's office. Granite Face closed the door and removed the handcuffs.

"Sit," he said.

"What am I," Joey said, sitting down. "A fucking dog?"

"I'd like you a lot better if you were."

"Wait a fucking minute. What's this all about?"

"Where have I heard that before?" Beanpole was scratching his head to simulate deep thought.

"Funny," Joey said. "Come on, you guys, why the bust? You got a warrant?"

Beanpole showed Joey the document. "See what it says here? 'Attempted murder.' "

Joey clenched his teeth. Goddamn her. Why couldn't she have gone to some hick cop in Avalon?

"Look, I'm not talking to nobody, understand? I

want my attorney, and that's all I'm gonna say, period."

Granite Face's expression changed. "That was a dirty deal, Joey, trying to kill Joyce. How could you do that?"

"He's a snake," Beanpole said. "That's how."

"I don't know," Granite Face said. "I don't think it was his idea. In fact, I don't think he really wanted to do it."

"Really? What about that hole he put in her head?"

"What are you talking about?" Joey said, his hopes rising. "Is she dead?"

"No, Joey, she's alive and ready to testify against you," Granite Face said.

"So what's fuckface talking about? He said I put a hole in her head."

"The bullet went in her mouth and out through her cheek," Granite Face said. "Now, Joey, we know this wasn't your idea. We know Allio put you up to it. Work with us, Joey, and we'll work with you. You're a young man, you don't want to spend the next twenty years in prison. That's a long haul."

"Yeah," Beanpole said, "a guy with your looks, they'd be killing themselves over your ass. You want to become some black stud's old lady? You're gonna spend a lot of time on your knees."

"Shut up!" Joey screamed. "I don't want to hear it. I got my rights."

"Just a minute," Granite Face said. "You've got your rights to remain silent, and we've got our rights to talk to you, to tell you what you're up against. Let me ask you a question—now you don't have to answer it, just listen. What are your options? We'll let you call Goodnough and he'll bail you out, get you out there on the street where they want you. What do you do then? Run? How long do you live? Do you think Allio's gonna trust you to keep quiet?"

"No way, José," said Beanpole. You're the boy who can put him away, not only on this one but also the Scolieri hit. On the street, you're dead meat. I wouldn't give two cents for your chances. Wise up, listen to what we're telling you."

"There's another option," Granite Face said. "Cooperate with us, and we'll see what we can do about getting you into the government's witness program. That's your best shot."

"Your only shot. I'd grab it if I was you."

Joey knew they were right, but singing just went against the grain. He couldn't see himself on the witness stand testifying against Allio. On the other hand, he couldn't see himself serving twenty years. He needed time to sort out his options.

"Hey, cut the bullshit and book me."

"It's your funeral, punk," Beanpole said.

"Go ahead, make your call," Granite Face said, picking up the receiver. "Let's see how long it takes Goodnough to get here."

"Forget it," Joey said. "I'm not calling nobody. Just book me and get off my back."

Tony Allio was in a foul mood. After the trial, he had Federal Expressed photos of Frank and Nancy to every Mafia family in the country, with an urgent plea that everything possible be done to locate them. This was followed with personal calls to the bosses, again urging them to make it top priority. So far nothing.

Now he was discussing the matter with Goodnough. "How about hitting some of your old buddies in Washington for a favor?"

"That was a long time ago, Tony. Christ, I was at Justice when Bobby Kennedy was AG."

"And you worked with the organized crime task force, right?"

"Yeah, but most of the guys I worked with have long

gone into private practice. There may be a few left, but they're probably in some other division now. It's a mammoth bureaucracy, believe me."

"Wait a fucking minute," Allio said. "What I'm hearing is a lot of maybes and probablys. Find out, make a fucking call."

"Tony, that's not the way it works. First, those guys that are left are really into the system by now, working toward their pensions—glorified clerks, you know, making peanuts. They hate guys like me for getting out and making a buck defending clients they don't approve of. Second, the witness protection program is a separate unit, tied in with the Marshal Service, and the lawyers in Justice have no access to those files. Believe me, something as sensitive as the new identity of an individual in the program is top secret, known only to the people actually involved in that individual's protection. That's why, Tony, after all these years, they haven't lost anybody in that program."

"Yeah, well, that's all going to change. I know two fuckers they're gonna lose, you better believe me."

"Then we're going to have to find some other way."

"You telling me you can't help?"

"Tony, I'm telling you it's not the way to go about it."

"Arthur, I want them," Allio screamed, his face twisting. "Don't you fucking understand? I wanna take a bath in their fucking blood, that's how bad I want them. Am I getting across to you?"

"Tony, I'll try, but I've got to be extremely careful."

"Go ahead, be careful, just get me some results. *Capisci?*"

The telephone rang, and Nick picked it up. He listened a moment, hung up. "They've got Joey downtown again," he said.

Joey hadn't been in the holding cell twenty minutes before Goodnough showed up with a writ of habeas corpus. At first when the guard told Joey his lawyer was waiting for him, Joey refused to leave his cell. The son of a bitch had gotten to the jail in record time. Allio had to have an important connection down here, a fact that could make Joey's jail cell even more dangerous than the street. Joey had read numerous stories about prisoners hanging themselves in their cells. He'd never believed one of them.

"Well, what's it gonna be?" the guard said. "You staying or leaving?"

"I'm leaving," Joey said, following the guard to the reception area.

"Hello," Goodnough said, greeting Joey with a smile. "They treat you all right?"

"Sure," Joey said. "How'd you get here so quick?"

Goodnough blinked and his magnified eyeballs reminded Joey of an owl. "Well, actually, I was already down here on other business when a little birdie whispered in my ear. So I called our good friend, Judge D'Ambrosio, and got this little piece of paper that says you're a free man. How about that?"

"That's terrific," Joey said, trying to sound enthusiastic. "Have you told Tony?"

Goodnough looked him straight in the eye. "No, you want me to?"

"No, that's okay, I'll tell him."

"Fine," Goodnough said. "Why don't I drop you off at the compound."

"Thanks, appreciate it."

As worried and preoccupied as he was, Joey couldn't help stopping to admire Goodnough's white Rolls-Royce.

"That's a beauty," he said, with genuine enthusiasm. "Real class. What year is it?"

"This year's model, just traded my old one in."

"Jesus," Joey said, getting in the passenger seat, his hands caressing the soft leather, "how much it set you back?"

"It lists at one forty," Goodnough said as they began gliding down the street. "I know it's a lot of money for a car, but it's a magnificent piece of machinery, a work of art, you might say. Last you a lifetime if you take care of it, and it always looks elegant, no matter what its age."

Joey nodded. "I guess I could buy one if I really wanted to," he said, "but I never got around to it. Jesus, I can't even hear the fucking engine."

Goodnough turned on Atlantic Avenue, heading toward Longport. "You know what they say, Joey, all you can hear is the clock ticking, or words to that effect."

"You're not kidding. Hey, turn down Pacific, willya? Want to see what the action's like tonight."

"Joey, traffic's always a mess on Pacific."

"I know, but do me a favor, okay?" Joey laughed. "I want some of my pals to see me in this Rolls."

"Sure, Joey," Goodnough said, turning the car. "Anything for a friend."

"Even got a fucking phone? Hey, can I use it?"

They were almost directly in front of Ocean Towers when Joey made his move. Grabbing the cellular phone in the console between the seats, he swung with all his might, striking Goodnough across the bridge of the nose. Goodnough slammed on the brakes, and Joey jumped out of the Rolls and ran like a deer into his apartment building.

Tom was exchanging a few last words with Ferris when the phone rang. Ferris picked it up, listened a moment, said, "Oh, shit," and slammed it down.

"What's up?" Tom asked.

"Son of a bitch. Joey's gone already."

"Gone where?"

"Goodnough picked him up a half hour ago."

"Jesus Christ," Tom said. "I thought they were going to call you when Goodnough got there."

"So did I," Ferris said, slamming an open palm against his desk top. "So what do we do now?"

"Let's hit his apartment and, if he's not there, the compound. He's probably at one or the other."

"Wherever he is, I hope he's still breathing."

Sweat kept trickling into Joey's eyes, and he kept wiping at it with his knuckles as he tried to work the combination on the closet safe. When the door finally opened he reached in and pulled out three plastic bags of cocaine, four jewelry boxes, several stacks of paper currency. He dumped everything into the open suitcase on the floor, hurried into his bedroom and began stuffing Armani suits into a large garment bag. When it was full he zipped it up, flung it over his shoulder, picked up the suitcase, and dashed out of the apartment. The rest of his stuff could rot.

Alone in the elevator, he kept his finger pressed against the button for the subterranean level his Mark VII was parked in, his eyes glued to the panel, terrified that it would light up and someone would slow his progress by getting on. Coming back to the apartment had been a gamble, but he couldn't see himself leaving everything behind.

The elevator came to a stop and the doors opened. The garage's fluorescent lights made it look spooky. Joey hesitated a moment, took a deep breath, and ran for his car. He was alone in this vast concrete catacomb, his footsteps echoing eerily, his breath catching in his throat, his vision blurred with sweat.

He let out a deep breath when he reached the Mark VII, dropping the bags and digging into his pockets for the keys.

"Joey," a voice called from the darkness, "going somewhere, sweetheart? In a hurry, are you?"

Joey dropped the keys. "Who is it?"

"Look behind you, Joey."

Joey spun around. Sal sprang up from behind the car parked next to the Mark VII.

"Surprised?"

Joey tried to let his breath out slowly. "Yeah, Sal."

"Look who's with me."

Funzi stood up. He was laughing so hard tears were running down his face. "Hey, Joey, you shit your pants, baby?"

"Of course not."

"Man, you looked like you saw a fucking ghost."

"What do you guys want?" Joey asked, his eyes darting back and forth.

"Don't even think about it," Sal said. "You wouldn't get ten feet before a bullet caught up with you."

"I'm not running."

"So what do you call this?" Sal said, pointing to the bags.

"Goodnough just bailed me out," Joey said. "Told me to get out of town till he gets things straightened out with the courts."

"Well," Sal said, "that's different. Listen, before you leave town your good friend Tony wants to give you a little farewell party. Come on, sweetheart, put your shit in the trunk and let's go. Funzi will ride in your car with you, and I'll follow in mine."

Joey's legs were trembling so hard he could barely stand up. "I don't think I can drive," he said. "I don't feel so good."

Funzi stepped up and grabbed Joey by the seat of the pants.

"He's clean," he said. "Thought sure he shit his pants. Come on, pick up your fucking shit and keys and get behind the fucking wheel. Don't give me no more fucking shit."

Joey picked up his bags and keys, got in the car, waited for Funzi to get in, started the engine, and drove slowly out of the garage.

"Where are we going?" he said.

"Harper's Warehouse, Maine Avenue, know the place?"

"I've seen it. Is the party there?"

"Sure," Funzi said, "it's a great place for a party. Plenty of space, you know."

Joey hated Maine Avenue. At the farthest eastern end of the island, it was one of the sleaziest parts of town. Abandoned warehouses, burned-out and boarded-up buildings, rubbish-littered vacant lots, crumbling houses with cardboard-covered windows.

Harper's Warehouse looked deserted.

"Drive up to the door and blow the horn," Funzi said.

The large door rolled up and Joey drove in, followed closely by Sal. The door rolled down, but the warehouse remained dark.

Joey's heart was hammering so hard he wondered if Funzi could hear it. "There's nobody here," he said.

"Leave your lights on and get out. It's time to party, baby."

Joey stepped out of the Mark VII and looked around.

"There's nobody here," he said as Sal and Funzi came up behind him.

"Sure there is. Look out there." Sal pointed in the direction of the headlights' beams.

Then Joey saw them, Allio and Nick walking slowly

into the headlights, legless torsos with distorted faces floating toward him.

"Hi, Tony, Nick," Joey called, raising his hand in a tentative greeting.

There was no answer. The distorted faces bobbed closer.

"Sal and Funzi said you're giving me a farewell party," Joey said, his voice cracking. "Where's everybody?"

Behind him, Joey could hear Funzi trying to suppress his laughter. The floating torsos were beginning to have legs, moving a little faster as they got closer. Then, suddenly, they were directly in front of him.

"Joey," Allio said, his dark eyes burning into Joey's, "you fucked up once too often."

"Tony, please . . . don't say that. It wasn't my fault, you gotta give me another chance!"

"Remember what I told you about mistakes?"

"Please, for the love of God, don't do it. Tony, I'm a big money-maker—you'll see, I'll make a lot of money for you. I've got great contacts . . ."

"It's too late for that shit," Allio said, releasing the switch blade on the knife in his hand.

The snap of the blade hitting the handle made Joey cry out in fear. Next thing he knew, something warm was running down his leg. "Oh, Mother of God . . . Tony, please don't . . . oh, I'm sorry . . ." He dropped to his knees in front of Allio.

"Get him on his feet," Allio barked.

Sal and Funzi each grabbed an arm, pulled Joey up and held him there.

"Tony, for the love of Jesus, can't you—"

"Sure, I can, motherfucker," Allio said, plunging the knife into Joey's stomach.

"Oooooooh . . . You fucking . . . killed me. . . ." Over the knife hilt, Joey made the sign of the cross.

"Hail, Mary, Mother of God . . . pray for us sinners now and at the — oh, God, it fucking hurts —"

Allio ripped upward with the knife. Joey's eyes turned inward, and his mouth went slack.

"Don't look so pretty now, do you?" Allio wiped the knife against Joey's Armani suit. "Let the cocksucker drop."

When they released him, Joey sank to the floor in a sitting position, then slumped onto his back. His glazed eyes seemed to be staring into space. Allio knelt beside the body, placed his fingers against Joey's throat, found no pulse, then opened Joey's jacket. Nick took out his gun, pressed it over the heart and fired.

Sal and Funzi quickly stripped the body, stuffed the clothes into one huge plastic garbage bag, the naked body into another. When they were finished, they dumped the bags in the trunk of the Mark VII. Later that night they'd drop the clothes in a dumpster and leave the Mark VII in the long-term parking lot at the Philadelphia airport. It would be several weeks before the body was found.

On the way back to the compound with Nick, Allio grabbed his arm.

"Jesus, I just got a great idea," he said.

"Yeah, what?"

"I know how to find the Contis. We can't get to them, so let's bring them to us."

"What do you mean?" Nick asked.

"I mean, let's flush them out."

31

Tom woke up to a familiar aroma—freshly brewed coffee and burnt toast. He sat up, ran his fingers through his hair, and yawned. "Can't expect her to cook, too," he said as he reached for his shorts on the floor next to the bed. This had to be the strangest week of his life. And certainly the most exciting in many a year. That woman was insatiable, not to mention incredibly inventive.

Tom got his robe from a chair across the room, slipped it on, and padded barefoot down the stairs to the kitchen.

"There you are, sleepyhead," Joyce said. "Better hustle or you'll be late for work."

Tom took one step into the kitchen and stopped dead in his tracks. Joyce was wearing a lacy apron and absolutely nothing under it.

"I'd cook you some eggs, but it's been such a long time I've forgotten how. Besides, you don't want eggs, all that cholesterol, and bacon's full of nitrates, stick to wheat toast and cereals. And get us some decaf coffee, will you?"

Tom nodded, averting his eyes as he hurried to the table and sat down. Christ, he was getting hard just looking at her in that getup. The top part of the apron wasn't large enough to cover her breasts, and the bottom barely covered her bush, which he could see anyway through the sheer material. As for the back view, well, that was one hundred percent exposed. She opened the refrigerator door, bent over to get something, and Tom saw everything, the whole shooting match. He struggled to bunch the robe up over his erection. God, he'd forgotten what it was like to be horny. This woman was enough to drive a saint to orgasm.

She closed the refrigerator door, poured orange juice from a carton, and brought Tom a full glass. "Here, honey, quench your thirst."

"Thanks," Tom said.

"Oh, oh, what's this you're hiding under your robe? Let me see."

Tom picked up the orange juice and gulped it straight down. "Tastes good," he said.

"Now, just a little minute here," she said, her hands busy. "Hey . . . see what *I* found!"

Tom closed his eyes.

"It's okay," she said. "You can look at it, it's yours."

Tom looked down at himself.

"See, the poor thing's crying," she said, taking him in both her hands, one on top of the other. "Does that feel good, honey?"

"Not bad," Tom said, sucking in his breath.

"Would you like me to make it feel better?"

"I don't know if I can stand anything that feels better."

"Hold on now, the fun's just started." She straddled him, her hand guiding him inside her. She kissed him passionately and then pulled away, her tongue moving across his cheek, down to his neck, up to his ear. He shivered as she began moving her hips sideways and up and down.

"Come on," she whispered into his ear, her breath hot, her tongue wet and penetrating, "let's fuck our heads off."

The moment she said that, Tom came.

Almost directly across the street, Hank Iezzi and Ugo Failla were waiting in a stolen van, Ugo wearing a white ski suit and a ski mask.

"What time is it?" Ugo asked.

Hank looked at his wristwatch. "Eight-thirty-six."

"And this is the sonovabitch who leaves for work at eight sharp every morning?"

"Maybe he's not going to work today," Hank said.

"Why the fuck not?"

"How the fuck would I know? What's the matter, you getting antsy."

"Oh, shit, that's a stupid question," Ugo said. "You wanna do this fucking job?"

"Hey, take it easy, I was only kidding."

"Take it easy, my ass. You cased the job a fucking week, man. You telling me this is the first time he's late?"

"You got it. There's always a first time, right?"

"Ah, fuck."

"Hey, you wanna call it off? Just say so. But don't ask me to explain it to Tony."

"What's this, your morning to be stupid? It's going down if I have to go in the fucking house."

"You won't," Hank said. "The motherfucker's finally coming out."

Before the words were out of Hank's mouth, Ugo was jogging across the street. He was there before Tom had even closed the front door, a brown paper bag in his right hand.

"Hey, motherfucker," he called, raising the paper bag, "you forgot something."

Tom turned to face him. The bag exploded as a half-

293

dozen shots rang out. Tom grabbed his throat, spun around, toppled down the steps head first. Before Tom's head hit the sidewalk, Ugo was back in the van. A moment later, it had disappeared around the corner.

Dressed in Tom's robe, Joyce came out of the house, screaming. Passersby and neighbors came running, but she was the first to reach him. She dropped to her knees, lifted his head from the sidewalk, cradled it in her arms.

"You poor sweet man," she cried, rocking on her knees.

A knot of people had circled her, all staring down, but she was unaware of anything except her own despair. The last man who had shown her any kindness was dead. And she, in some inexplicable way, felt responsible.

32

Police cars lined both sides of the street, taking up all the parking spaces. The private cars of other cops were double-parked, creating a congestion that defied solution. Traffic cops blew their whistles and shouted to no avail. Policemen had come en masse to honor one of their own.

Inside the funeral home, mourners were queued up, awaiting their turn to view the open flag-draped coffin that was flanked by an honor guard of four lieutenants in dress uniforms.

Guarded by Neil Andrews and a detail of U.S. marshals, Frank and Nancy had just arrived from Key West and were viewing the body for the first time. Frank stared at the man in the satin-lined box. He was wearing Tom's blue suit, the hair was combed the way Tom had combed his hair, the features were Tom's, the hands folded across the chest held Tom's worn rosary, the third finger of the left hand bore Tom's wedding ring—but he was so clearly a stranger, someone impersonating his father. This was not the man Frank had hugged and kissed at the airport only a few weeks ago. This was not the man who had cared for a wife with a dehumanizing affliction without once complaining or giving up, the man who over a beer had told his son of his love for a young English girl. No. The man in the box was someone else, a someone who would be buried in this box while Frank's father stayed alive in his son's memory.

Frank had his arm around Nancy's waist. Feeling her tremble, he maneuvered her away from the coffin and over to the two metal folding chairs reserved for them at the head of several rows of chairs.

Sergeant Johnny Brecato offered Frank his hand. "Frank, Nancy, my condolences—a terrible loss, to you and to the department. Your father and I worked together so many years I can't even count them. He was a great guy to work with, the best. The finest, toughest, fairest man I ever knew. He was—"

Captain Beal elbowed Brecato out of his way. "Frank, only got a minute, I wanted to extend condolences to you both. The department has lost one of its best—and only months away from his retirement. Not that he was all that hot about the idea. In fact, he hated the thought of retiring. Well, the department looks after its own. We're going all out to give Tom a grand send-off. We're having a bugler to sound taps, an honor guard, the works. Afterward there's the reception at the Elk hall—Tom's house isn't big enough to accommodate the crowd we expect."

"How's the investigation coming along?" Frank asked.

"All homicides are investigated by the Round House. If you're interested, I suggest you go talk to Captain Thompson over there. Now, if you'll excuse me, I'll take my leave. Don't want to hold up the line any longer."

The moment Beal turned to leave, Brecato took Frank's arm. "Listen, Frank, this morning in Atlantic City, Allio, Nick, Funzi, and Sal strutted up and down the Boardwalk in ski outfits. They were laughing and having a ball. It's the first time any of the sons of bitches ever wore a ski outfit in public. They're really rubbing it in."

Before Frank could respond, Sam Moceri came up and threw his arms around Frank. There were tears in the little doctor's eyes. Frank was grateful for the interruption. It would give him time to compose himself, get his voice back under control. The anger gripping him was so intense that it was choking him.

33

From his prone position on the snow-covered knoll, Ugo Failla had a clear view of the grave site no more than five hundred feet away. Still wearing the white ski suit, he was invisible in the snow as he awaited the arrival of the funeral cortege. He had already adjusted the scope of the high-powered rifle that lay at his side wrapped in a white towel.

The wind had come up since he'd arrived about an hour ago, and Ugo was getting cold. The thermal underwear and turtleneck sweater under the parka were not enough to protect his chest. Even his hands in the heavy mittens and his feet in the fur-lined boots were starting to feel numb.

He watched as the workmen finished their preparation of the grave site and left in their truck. Then Ugo was alone in Sacred Heart Cemetery. He sat up and rubbed his knees, which also had gone numb. He shivered and swore at the sun timidly breaking through a gray sky. It had snowed in the night, and the wind was whipping the snow around. Enough to interfere with his aim? He unwrapped the rifle, stretched out on the ground, wound the sling around his arm and sighted the flower-ladened burial plot. No problem. The scope cut right through that shit. It was like he was standing right over there.

"Come on, you motherfuckers," he muttered, "bring

me your fucking heads."

Grim-faced policemen stood at attention as police pallbearers removed the flag-draped casket from the hearse and started up the snow-covered path. At the grave site, a bugler sounded taps and everybody bowed their heads. Then Father Alaimo began the ceremony.

Again Frank stood with his arm around Nancy's waist, his face drained of color, his free hand clenched tightly at his side. The priest droned on; Frank could feel Nancy's knees weakening. He glanced down and saw in her hand the red rose she wanted to lay on the casket before it was lowered into its final resting place.

Suddenly, Frank's attention was caught by a movement on a distant knoll. His eyes narrowed as he focused on the object. It stopped moving. Frank's arm tightened around Nancy's waist.

In the scope Ugo saw the man's face clearly, saw the grim expression as he stepped away from the woman and stared in Ugo's direction, giving Ugo the eerie feeling that the man could see Ugo as clearly as Ugo was seeing the man—Ugo knew the man's name was Conti, but names had no meaning for him. All he had to do was squeeze the trigger, and the man would never see anything again. But Ugo had his orders. He moved the weapon slightly to his right and squeezed the trigger.

The object moved again, and there was a glint of reflected light, followed immediately by a flash and a puff of smoke.

"Look out!" Frank shouted, pulling Nancy to the ground with him.

When he looked down at Nancy, the top of her head was gone.

Frank screamed, pulled her body into his arms, and crushed her against his chest, the scream shaking his throat, seemingly trapped there.

Ugo saw the woman's head come apart, saw the man pulling her to the ground—too late. What incredible power. The slight physical movement of crooking his finger had caused the death of another human being.

He watched the man holding the woman, rocking her dead body in his arms. A beautiful woman, young, most of her life ahead of her. Hundreds would mourn her death. And not one of them would ever know that he was the one responsible, the one who had given them this secret pleasure.

Even killers like Allio didn't understand the power they paid him so handsomely for exercising. They didn't even know that money had nothing to do with it, that if nobody paid him he would do it anyway. How could they possibly understand? With men like Allio the act of murder was always corrupted by other motives, money or revenge or jealousy, motives that blocked out the pure essence of it.

Ugo pushed himself to his knees—the man was running across the cemetery toward the knoll. "Holy shit!" Ugo tried to stand up and fell, his legs too numb with cold to obey his brain. He couldn't even feel them. He hit them, striking furiously up and down each leg, trying to stimulate circulation. He had to get the hell out of there. This motherfucker could run. The fucking cops would be after him next.

Ugo left the rifle and staggered crazily on legs that felt wooden to the stolen Oldsmobile parked a hundred yards away. Hanging on the open door, trying to catch his breath, he saw that the man had gained the top of the knoll and was still coming toward him at full speed. He fished the car keys out of his pocket, slipped in behind the steering wheel.

At that moment the man, obviously aware that he couldn't reach the car in time, veered to his right, slipped and fell, got up and ran toward the cars and limousines parked along the roads that meandered through the cemetery. Some of the drivers were waiting inside their limousines, engines running for warmth.

As Ugo shot past, he saw the man reach inside a limousine and pull the driver out as if he were a rag doll.

"Jesus H. Christ!" Ugo adjusted the rearview mirror and saw the limousine start after him. There were sharp turns ahead; he kept both hands on the wheel as the Oldsmobile slipped and slid and skidded, banging against snowbanks, fishtailing into turns, going down the road half the time sideways.

Finally, he hit Broad Street, which was straight as an arrow but congested with midday traffic. Ugo barreled through the traffic, the limousine right on his tail. He had an automatic in a shoulder holster inside his parka, but no time to take it out. It took all his strength and attention to keep the Oldsmobile on the road—this was no time for an accident. There was no way he could outrun this guy. Or outfight him. He looked like one mean motherfucker.

At Moyamensing Avenue he swung right, heading for Penrose Avenue and the George C. Platt Memorial Bridge. From there he had no idea where the fuck he was heading. All he knew was that he had to keep moving until the maniac behind him either crashed or gave up.

As he neared the entrance to the Platt bridge, the limousine banged into the Olds's rear bumper. Ugo nearly lost control. "Motherfucker," he screamed, unzipping his parka and pulling out the automatic, "I'll kill you."

Ugo looked in the rearview mirror; the limousine wasn't in it. He glanced at the sideview mirror and saw that it had drawn almost even with him. Aiming the automatic across his chest, he fired through the window just as the man swung the wheel of the limousine, sending it careening into the Olds. Ugo screamed when the Olds jumped the sidewalk and crashed through the guard rail. He was still screaming as he plummeted through space toward the freezing waters of the Schuylkill River.

George Napoli had been the mortician for both Frank's paternal grandparents, for his mother, for Timmy, for his father, and now for Nancy.

Frank had been five the first time he came to the Napoli mortuary, crying for his grandfather. Mr. Napoli had picked him up so he could see his grandfather lying in his coffin, and for weeks Frank had nightmares about his grandfather and the mortuary. What Frank couldn't understand was how anyone could work with dead people. And Mr. Napoli was such a jovial man, always smiling, always so proud of his work.

"I'll pay for repairs," Frank said when he brought the limousine back to the mortuary.

"Forget about it," Napoli said, holding on to Frank's hand. His voice was soft, his face serious now. "Christ, I can't believe what's happened here. The cops are looking for you, this thing's been running on TV all day. They still haven't fished that car out of the river. Glad you got the dirty bastard—I'm telling you, I've never seen the likes of it. Oh, God, your poor wife. What a tragedy."

"I want to see her," Frank said.

"Later, Frank, we're not finished working with her yet. She's still on the table."

"I want to be alone with her."

"It's not a good idea, Frank. Come back later, when she's ready for viewing."

"I don't know if I can come back," Frank said. "I just want to hold her hand and say good-bye while I still have the chance."

"Okay, Frank, I think I understand," Napoli said, nodding his nut brown bald head. "Give me a few minutes."

Frank waited in Napoli's office. Behind the desk was a large crucifix flanked by gold-framed paintings of the Virgin Mary with baby Jesus in her arms and one of the Sacred Heart of Jesus. He stared at the paintings without seeing them.

Napoli came back and led Frank to the embalming room. Nancy lay under a white sheet on a stainless-steel table. Only the face, from her chin to her eyebrows, was exposed, and it was almost as white as the sheet. Frank reached under the sheet for her hand, cold and stiff; bent down and pressed his lips against it. Then, being careful not to disturb the white cloth covering her head, he pressed his cheek against hers. "It's my fault, Nancy," he said. "All of it is my fault, please forgive me. I love you, I'll always love you. Good-bye, my love. Wherever you are, I hope you're with Timmy."

Seven hours later, he drove past Allio's Seagull Lane compound.

34

Frank slowed the car down to give himself time to remember the compound's layout. At the next lane he turned left, drove to the end of it, made a U-turn, and brought the Buick to a stop next to the utility pole that supplied power and telephone lines to the compound.

Satisfied that the street was deserted, he stepped out and quickly climbed on top of the Buick. His face and hands were covered with black camouflage grease. He was dressed in black karate-gi pants, a black sweatshirt that concealed a flak jacket, black running shoes. On his hip was a fourteen-inch blue steel double-edged knife in a black leather sheath; on his head, a black wool cap. Infrared night goggles hung from his neck; wire cutters were tucked into his waistband.

Chiara sat in a rocking chair next to her bed, having spent most of the day watching for local news briefs. Spending that much time in front of the television reminded her of the three days she had spent glued to the set when President Kennedy was shot. Vincenzo had been glad the young president was dead, but Chiara had felt sorry for his wife and the two small children. Besides, she liked Kennedy, he seemed like a good family man. She had seen pictures in magazines of little John-John playing under his father's desk in the president's office while his father discussed *importante* matters of state with men almost as *importante* as he was. She wished Vincenzo had been a good father, like Kennedy. She knew Mrs. Kennedy never had to wash the president's feet or run to the basement for wine all night long or cut up his food for him. Chances were she didn't even have to cook.

Although Chiara had refused to believe that her son had anything to do with the kidnapping of the Conti woman—a belief reinforced by the jury's acquittal of all the defendants—in the courtroom she had found herself sympathizing with Nancy Conti. There was something about the woman's gentle demeanor that appealed to Chiara. She was certain that somehow Joey Bucci was to blame for everything. He couldn't be trusted—he was too *bello*, too *effeminato*. Sometimes pretty boys were *misogino*. She had known some in her village. What surprised her the most was that Antonio had not punished Joey for having caused him this *terribile cimento*.

She had been wanting to talk to Antonio about this matter for a long time. It was not fair that her son and his family should be put through this *cimento* by someone who was practically a stranger. She particularly resented Joey's invitation to the celebration dinner. His presence had offended her. And now this *terribile crimine*—Joey again, she suspected. Would her son once more be blamed by the police? She stood up, her mind made up. She would talk to Antonio right away.

Allio motioned for Nick to turn off the television.

305

The shooting at the cemetery and the crash into the Schuylkill had dominated local newscasts throughout the day. Frank Conti had been identified as the driver of the limousine that had deliberately rammed the Oldsmobile. The Olds had been fished out of the river, but the unidentified driver was still missing. The theory was that the current had carried his body into the Delaware River, in which event it might never be recovered.

Allio clapped his hands. "You can bet your ass that motherfucker's really hurting now!"

"I tell you," Nick said, "this Conti prick went fucking berserk at the cemetery."

"That's why I had Ugo get the wife first," Allio said. "You know, you kill him first, what the fuck, when you're dead, you're dead, you don't hurt no more. Think he's sorry now he fucked with me?"

"Teach him a lesson he won't forget in a hurry," Funzi said. Allio nodded. "Yeah, let him live with it a couple more days. Let him get a good taste of it, then we'll hit him before the Feds get a chance to tuck him away again. Too bad about Ugo, though. He was a good worker."

"The best," Nick said.

"You should have seen him when he hit the cop," Hank Iezzi said.

Allio got up. "I'm going to bed." He paused at the open door. "Hank, I'm giving you the Conti contract. But Nick, I want you there to back him up. Can't afford another fuck-up."

"No problem," Nick said.

"Don't worry about me, Tony," Hank said. "I can handle it."

"You two help him out," Allio said to Sal and Funzi. "Okay, get to work on it, we'll talk about it in the morning."

"Good night, Uncle," Nick said.

" 'Night, Tony," the others said.

Allio waved his acknowledgment, closed the door, and walked up the hallway toward his bedroom at the rear of the house.

"Antonio, wait a minute," Chiara called. "I want to talk to you. *Importante.*"

Then the lights went out.

It was a moonless, starless night. With the power line cut, it was now pitch-black inside the compound that had been brightly lit with floodlights. Frank climbed down the utility pole, paused a moment on the roof of the Buick, then vaulted over the wall. The instant he hit the ground, the knife was in his hand. Before moving on, he donned the infrared goggles. Everything came into focus in a reddish glow, but he himself was invisible.

As far as Frank was concerned, he was in a denied area, and within it were targets for extermination. His survival depended on his ability to kill the enemy before the enemy ever knew he was there.

Keeping close to the wall, he moved toward the entrance gate and its guards. Through the infrared glasses he could see the heat radiating from their bodies—which was appropriate, considering their imminent journey to hell.

The two guards had left their stations on either side of the wide gate and were discussing the problem created by the power outage.

"Fucking Edison," one guard was saying. "What the fuck we supposed to do now? No phone, no lights, no power to open the gates."

The other said, "You know, this ain't the first time this's happened when I've been on the job."

"How'd you handle it?"

"Sat tight. Took it easy. Sooner or later the power comes back on."

"Yeah, what the fuck, it ain't our fault."

"Hey, got another butt?"

"Come on, man. I thought you fucking quit."

"Whatta you mean? Except for the couple I bummed from you, I ain't smoked in three days."

"Here, you cheap bastard, you didn't quit smoking, you just quit smoking your own."

As the guard reached for the cigarette, Frank decided the two men were not important enough to interfere with his mission. Sheathing the knife, he walked around them, passing not more than six feet away.

Four men sat around a card table in Allio's library, their faces lit only by the single candle in the middle of the table.

"Why not hit him at the church?" Hank said. "He'll be coming out right behind the casket."

"Great," Nick said. "I know this guy with a house across the street. You know him, too — Sam Brozzetti, owns Sam's Diner on Broad. His wife works with him, so the house's empty all day."

"Is there a second floor?" Sal said.

"Yeah," Nick said. "It's perfect. Got a straight shot at the motherfucker when he comes down the church steps. Be out of there in one minute flat."

"Sounds like the ticket," Funzi said.

"Let's check it out tomorrow. When's the funeral, Nick?"

"Couple of days, I guess. Hank, call Napoli tomorrow, get the date and time of the service."

"No problem. Gonna get a key to the Brozzetti

place?"

"I know where he hides the spare."

"How come?" Funzi said.

Nick laughed. "Been fucking his wife, Anna. She knows—"

"Wait a minute," Hank said, sitting straight up. "You hear anything?"

"No. What?" Nick said.

"I don't know. Sounded like a window sliding up."

"What the fuck, you getting jittery already?"

Hank shrugged. "I don't know, must be the wind. Or I'm hearing things."

"Speaking of hearing things, how about using a silencer?" Funzi said. "That way nobody'll know where the shot came from."

"I like that," Nick said. "Hit the motherfucker in the gut, and they won't even know he's been shot until we're at Donjo's having a beer."

"I could use one now," Funzi said. "How about it, Hank?"

"Coming right up." Hank pushed his chair back.

"Here, take the candle so you don't break your fucking neck in the dark," Nick said.

"Thanks." Hank picked up the candle. "Be right back."

When Hank placed the candle on the bar top and turned around to open the refrigerator, Frank leaned forward and blew the candle out.

"What the fuck!" Nick called out. "What're you doing, for Chrissake? This place's dark as the insides of a rat's ass."

In one smooth movement Frank grabbed Hank by the hair, pulled his head back, and slit his throat. The only sound was a soft gurgle as air escaped from his lungs through the rush of blood, until a voice called out.

"Hank, wake up, light the fucking candle." That had to be Funzi.

"Yeah, what're you waiting for?" That was Nick.

"You think maybe he's trying to scare us?" Funzi again.

They all laughed.

Frank turned to face them. Seen through the goggles, the heat radiating from their bodies made them look like huge pulsating blobs of protoplasm, movie aliens pulsating before they disintegrate. Which, at the moment, was all they were to Frank: less than human beings, less than animals, less than the gooks who had slaughtered his buddies and hung their mutilated bodies in the trees. At least the gooks were soldiers, fighting to eliminate an enemy that was killing and mutilating them. Allio and his thugs killed and maimed for other reasons.

Frank moved across the room, stopped behind Funzi, who sat between the other two.

"You won't have to come to the funeral," Frank said. "I've come to prepare you for yours."

Three radiating blobs bounced up in their chairs.

"What the fuck!" Sal said.

"Jesus Christ, it's Conti!" Nick said.

"Motherfuck—"

That was as far as Funzi got before the knife severed his vocal equipment. In seconds Frank had slashed to his right with the knife, catching Sal under the ear and slicing downward.

Nick flew up in his chair, his knees banging against the table, toppling him backward. He landed on his back, rolled over on his stomach, and began crawling like a crab.

Frank stepped on his neck, jamming his face into

310

the carpet.

"Please," Nick cried, "don't hurt me . . . I didn't have nothing to do wi—"

Frank plunged the knife into his back and through his heart with such force that the point stuck into the floor, pinning Nick to the carpet.

Allio didn't like getting buttonholed by anybody, not even his mother. When she got wound up, she could be a fucking talking machine. She'd been ranting like a crazy woman about the Kennedys and Nancy Conti and Joey and the trial.

"I tell you, Antonio," she was saying, "that Joey is the *colpevole*, the one who kidnapped Nancy Conti, and I think he killed her at the cemetery."

"Ma, I just told you for the hundredth time, don't worry about Joey."

"I do worry."

"Ma, he's gone—gone, gone, gone—for good. Capisci? So forget about him, willya?"

She wasn't listening. "You are too kind, too *di buon cuore.*"

Allio threw his hands up. "Ma, I've been accused of a lot of things, but softhearted ain't one of them."

"But you are, Antonio. When you was just a little boy, you cry when your papa hit me. Sometimes you get so mad you want to kill him." She found his hand in the darkness and patted it. "No, you got good heart, you are good boy, you love your mama and you are good to her. Not like your papa."

"Look, Ma, that's ancient history. Now, good night, okay? I wanna go to bed."

"Okay, but you remember what I tell you. That Joey will bring you trouble if . . ."

Not more than ten feet away, Frank waited. Targets—even in denied areas—did not include women and children. The major had seen things differently. Frank remembered the old woman and two children he had saved—and the times in the hospital in Guam when that memory saved his sanity.

Chiara felt with both hands for her son's face, kissed him on the cheek.

"Buona notte," she said.

"Yeah, Ma, good night," he said, backing away, retreating up the hall.

"Don't forget what I tell you about Joey," she said, turning and carefully feeling her way down the hall, passing not more than a few feet from Frank, who was plastered against the wall.

Frank heard a door open, close, and then a sudden bellow from the front of the house. Allio stopped and spun around.

"Mr. Allio! Oh, Jesus God, somebody come quick!"

Frank saw the bouncing beam of a flashlight at the front end of the long hallway. For a second he was silhouetted in its beam.

Allio jumped back. "Who's there?" The words came out in a choked whisper.

"It's me," Frank said, moving closer.

"Get away from me!" Allio backed up, his hand moving inside his jacket.

Footsteps pounded up the hallway, a voice filled with fear and revulsion reverberated off the walls. "Everybody's dead—murdered, Mr. Allio. Come quick."

Frank spun, delivered a karate kick that caught Allio high in the chest. He spun again; this time the kick struck Allio in the forehead. Allio fell backward, hit the floor hard in a sitting position but with a revolver now in his hand.

Frank dived headlong, out of the bouncing light beam, just as Chiara came out of her room and up the hallway toward her son.

"Antonio, what is it? Are you hurt?"

Frank reached out, caught her leg, and pulled her down just as Allio fired. "Stay down!" he ordered.

"Let me go," she cried, hitting at him with both hands. "What have you done to my Antonio?"

The guard with a flashlight was getting closer. Allio fired again, and the guard hit the floor, fell on his flashlight. "I'm shot!" he yelled. "Jesus Christ . . . what's going on here?"

"Ma, where are you?" Allio screamed.

"I'm here," Chiara cried out. "I am holding—"

Frank clamped his hand over her mouth; she bit it. He clenched his teeth but kept his hand over her mouth. Chiara twisted and bucked with a strength that astonished him. He had to get on his knees to hold her down.

Allio fired in the direction of the noise caused by Chiara's scuffle. Frank felt the bullet rip into his flak jacket and rolled away, releasing Chiara.

"Antonio! Antonio! He's over there—be careful!" She grabbed Frank's leg. "I got him, Antonio, you shoot—here, *rapido!*"

Frank saw Allio getting to his feet. He had to shut her up, get her off him. He reached down, gave her a karate chop behind the ear, felt her collapse. Allio was on his feet now, weaving as he came forward, holding the revolver in both hands straight out in front of him.

"Ma! Where *is* he?"

Frank crawled forward, keeping close to the wall until he was past Allio.

"Ma! Answer me! Where—"

"I'm here," Frank said, his left arm snaking around

313

Allio's neck, pulling him up tight against him, the knife slicing down on his gun hand. Allio screamed, and the gun fell to the floor.

"You cut me!" he cried. "Oh, God, I'm bleeding . . . you motherfucker, I'll kill—"

"You're all done killing," Frank said. He plunged the knife into Allio's chest. "And so am I," he said as Allio's body slumped to the floor.

35

Joyce sat on Tom's old Palermo sofa. The only light in the room came from the television. She watched transfixed as body bags were loaded into ambulances. In hushed tones, the announcer tried to call the plays.

". . . what has happened here tonight defies description. There were bodies everywhere when police arrived, called to the scene by Rocco Iezzi, Tony Allio's uncle, the first to enter the compound's main house after the killers had left. Mr. Iezzi lives in one of the other houses in the compound—which, I'm told, is the one closest to the main house where the bloodbath took place. He was awakened by shots, but so far as police have been able to determine, only one of the six persons killed died of gunshot wounds. All the others were killed with what police suspect were large hunting knives. The killers cut telephone and power lines before entering the compound.

"Tony Allio's mother, Mrs. Chiara Allio—who, police believe, is the only eyewitness to the massacre that took place here tonight—is described as being in shock and unable as yet to tell police what she knows. They found her kneeling beside her son and pleading with God to bring him back to life.

"Just a moment, I see Lieutenant Ferris. Jim! Over here, please. Can you enlighten us as to what happened here tonight?"

Ferris looked straight into the camera. "It looks like another bloody episode in the factional war that has been escalating here and in Philadelphia ever since the state legalized casino gambling."

"Does this look like the work of professionals?"

"Absolutely. No question about it."

"Have you spoken with Mrs. Allio?"

"Just for a moment."

"Did she give you any indication that she knows what happened here tonight?"

"No, except that she heard several men running through the house, firing guns. She even grappled with one, but it was too dark for her to make an identification."

"Have you formed any theory as to who is behind it?"

"Nothing that I can discuss as yet." Ferris cracked the faintest smile. "All I can say is that whoever planned this attack did one hell of a job here of cleaning out this compound. All the top people in the Allio crime family have been taken out."

"Sounds like a crippling blow to the Allio forces."

"I'd go further than that. The Allio family is history."

Joyce jumped up and clapped her hands. "Jesus, I'm with you, Ferris," she said to the television set. "The fuckers are dead. Long live the rest of us!"

She went to the closet and started packing the few clothes Tom had brought her from the Ocean Towers apartment. She was free again—to go wherever she pleased, whenever she pleased, without having to look over her shoulder. As for Joey, he could fend for himself. She was all done associating with punks or selling herself to the highest bidder. She had money in the bank. Ever since Tom had been killed, she'd been thinking about Texas. Dallas was a big city now.

Maybe she'd give it a shot, open a little health food store. Health food was something she knew quite a lot about. It would be fun helping people take better care of themselves.

"Why not?" she said, switching off the television. As the saying went, it was never too late for a change. By taking her own advice on health care, she could remain thirty-six for maybe another three years. Who knew what could happen in that time?

Frank drove to Colton, showered, and went straight to bed. When the front doorbell rang an hour later, he was sound asleep. He woke up to a voice calling his name near the bedroom window.

When he opened the door, Neil Andrews stepped inside. "Holy shit, Frank, have you heard?"

"Heard what?" he said, rubbing sleep from his eyes.

"What happened in Atlantic City—Allio and his goons were wiped out."

Frank just stared at him.

"Didn't you hear what I said? They were slaughtered like the pigs they are right in the compound. It's all over the TV. Turn it on."

"Want a beer?" Frank said, going to the kitchen.

When he came back, Andrews was clenching and unclenching his hands. "Are you sleepwalking, or what? Didn't you hear what I said?"

Frank handed him a beer.

"My God, Frank—you . . ."

Frank shrugged.

Andrews dropped into a chair. "Oh, Jesus. Incredible, just fucking incredible. Frank . . . I don't know what to say."

Frank sat across from Andrews.

Andrews stood up, began pacing in front of Frank.

"Jesus, Frank, I'm having a hard time digesting this."

Frank took a swig of beer.

Andrews sat down, looked over at Frank. "Jesus, Frank, you know, I envy you . . . I really do." Andrews leaned forward. "And I admire you."

Frank looked down.

"Frank, believe me, my lips are sealed. You've got my word on that."

"Thanks."

"What are your plans?"

"I plan to bury Nancy. Then I'm going to take my name back."

"You mean you're staying here?"

"I'm done running."

"Going back to the bank?"

Frank stared at his beer a long time before answering.

"No. I want to do something else with my life," he said, glancing at Andrews. "Who knows? Maybe I'll become a cop, if they'll have me. I think Pop would have liked that."

PINNACLE'S FINEST IN SUSPENSE
AND ESPIONAGE

OPIUM   (17-077, $4.50)
by Tony Cohan

Opium! The most alluring and dangerous substance
known to man. The ultimate addiction, ensnaring all in its
lethal web. A nerve-shattering odyssey into the perilous
heart of the international narcotics trade, racing from the
beaches of Miami to the treacherous twisting alleyways of
the Casbah, from the slums of Paris to the teeming Hong
Kong streets to the war-torn jungles of Vietnam.

LAST JUDGMENT   (17-114, $4.50)
by Richard Hugo

Seeking vengeance for the senseless murders of his brother,
sister-in-law, and their three children, former S.A.S. agent
James Ross plunges into the perilous world of fanatical ter-
rorism to prevent a centuries-old vision of the Apocalypse
from becoming reality, as the approaching New Year
threatens to usher in mankind's dreaded Last Judgment.

THE JASMINE SLOOP   (17-113, $3.95)
by Frank J. Kenmore

A man of rare and lethal talents, Colin Smallpiece has
crammed ten lifetimes into his twenty-seven years. Now,
drawn from his peaceful academic life into a perilous web
of intrigue and assassination, the ex-intelligence operative
has set off to locate a U.S. senator who has vanished mys-
teriously from the face of the Earth.

*Available wherever paperbacks are sold, or order direct from the
Publisher. Send cover price plus 50¢ per copy for mailing and
handling to Pinnacle Books, Dept. 17-373, 475 Park Avenue
South, New York, N.Y. 10016. Residents of New York, New Jer-
sey and Pennsylvania must include sales tax. DO NOT SEND
CASH.*

ESPIONAGE FICTION BY LEWIS PERDUE

THE LINZ TESTAMENT   (17-117, $4.50)
Throughout World War Two the Nazis used awesome power to silence the Catholic Church to the atrocities of Hitler's regime. Now, four decades later, its existence has brought about the most devastating covert war in history — as a secret battle rages for possession of an ancient relic that could shatter the foundations of Western religion: The Shroud of Veronica, irrefutable evidence of a second Messiah. For Derek Steele it is a time of incomprehensible horror, as the ex-cop's relentless search for his missing wife ensnares him in a deadly international web of KGB assassins, Libyan terrorists, and bloodthirsty religious zealots.

THE DA VINCI LEGACY   (17-118, $4.50)
A fanatical sect of heretical monks fired by an ancient religious hatred. A page from an ancient manuscript which could tip the balance of world power towards whoever possesses it. And one man, caught in a swirling vortex of death and betrayal, who alone can prevent the enslavement of the world by the unholy alliance of the Select Brothers and the Bremen Legation. The chase is on — and the world faces the horror of The Da Vinci Legacy.

QUEENS GATE RECKONING   (17-164, $3.95)
Qaddafi's hit-man is the deadly emissary of a massive and cynical conspiracy with origins far beyond the Libyan desert, in the labyrinthine bowels of the Politburo . . . and the marble chambers of a seditious U.S. Government official. And rushing headlong against this vast consortium of treason is an improbable couple — a wounded CIA operative and defecting Soviet ballerina. Together they hurtle toward the hour of ultimate international reckoning.

Available wherever paperbacks are sold, or order direct from the Publisher. Send cover price plus 50¢ per copy for mailing and handling to Pinnacle Books, Dept.17-373, 475 Park Avenue South, New York, N.Y. 10016. Residents of New York, New Jersey and Pennsylvania must include sales tax. DO NOT SEND CASH.